EVERLY HOLLOW, BOOK 1

THE
AUTUMN LEAF BOOKSHOP

KAY MICHAELS

Copyright

Copyright ©Kay Michaels 2025

All rights reserved. No Part of this book may be reproduced in any form or by any electronic or mechanical means, including information storage and retrieval systems, without permission in writing from the publisher, except for the use of brief quotations in a book review or scholarly journal.

The characters and events portrayed in this book are fictitious or are used fictitiously. Any similarity to real persons, living or dead, is purely coincidental and not intended by the author.

Printed and bound in the United States of America.

Cover Artist: Sara Murtas (Instagram: @drawnbymoonchild)

Editor: Marissa Parker (Instagram: @themarissaparker)

ISBN (ebook) : 978-1-969395-01-7

ISBN (paperback) : 978-1-969395-00-0

To my love. I'm grateful for you. Thank you for embracing my love of fall by getting married in October.

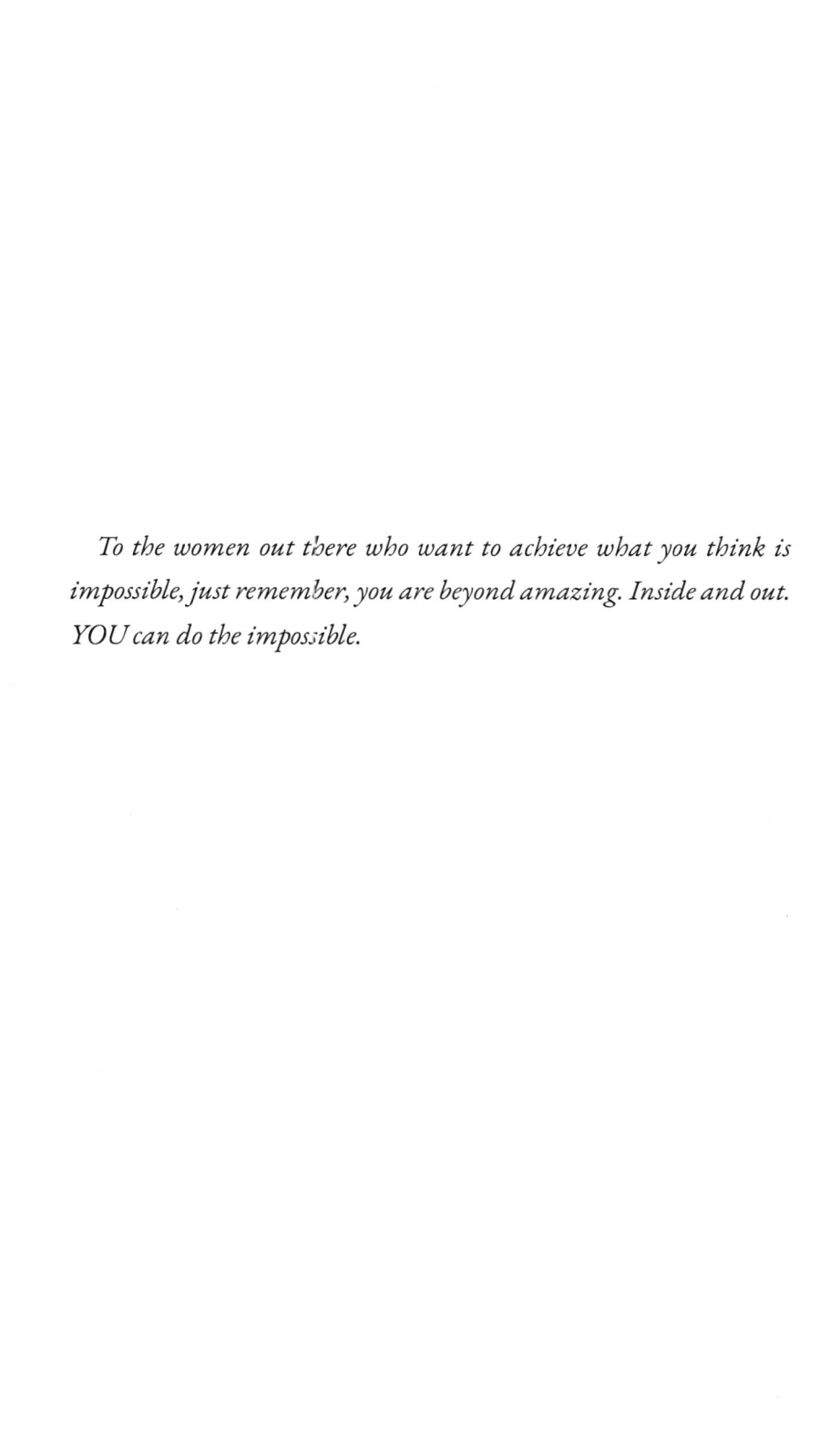

To the women out there who want to achieve what you think is impossible, just remember, you are beyond amazing. Inside and out. YOU can do the impossible.

"Every leaf speaks bliss to me,
fluttering from the Autumn tree."
- Emily Brontë

Content Warning

This book includes themes that may be sensitive to readers, such as parental death, widowhood, and cancer. Please read with care.

Prologue

Long before Everly Hollow was carved into the world, there were Seven Sisters, divine Goddesses born from the breath and light of the stars. Each one rules a season, or part of it.

Ruskaya - Goddess of Autumn - of harvest & abundance, comfort & change - *The Autumn Festival is held in her honor*

Talvithea - Goddess of Winter - silence and protection
Lumithea - Goddess of Snow - uniqueness and beauty
Jathea - Goddess of Ice - clarity, endurance, solitude

Kerathea - Goddess of Spring - fertility, new beginnings, growth
Sateathea - Goddess of Rain - cleansing, awakening, release

Aurinkothea - Goddess of Summer - vitality, hope, joy & happiness

1
Welcome to Everly Hollow
RAENE

My ass is numb, or maybe I have a blood clot starting to form. I gently sway side to side in the black leather driver's seat to alleviate some of the pressure and breathe life into either cheek.

The sun is low, casting a golden glow through the surrounding trees and over the snow-kissed mountains in the distance.

The air carries a cool breeze, flowing through the cracked windows of my silver BMW M5 alongside the music on my playlist.

I should be heading to my beach condo. Sipping a mojito. Wearing a super sexy, but adorable, bikini with an oversized sun hat so big it won't allow people to see me or my business. I would be glistening in sunscreen like a dolphin in the sun, surrounded by a salty breeze and large palm fronds.

But no, I'm on my way to Everly Hollow. A sleepy, enchanted town of real magic, where humans, monsters, and mythical creatures coexist. A maple-scented town where fall probably throws up on every storefront from August to October.

I'm excited to see my Grandma Vera. Unfortunately, she has to have hip replacement surgery, but at least I can be there for her. It's a few months earlier than planned, and luckily, she has a community of people who are willing to lend a hand.

She's an amazing, beautiful spirit, and my total opposite. She loves fall, and at seventy-one, she feels this is the place to plant roots, enjoy a beautiful garden, make friends, and gossip.

Fall doesn't arrive for another five weeks. That's plenty of time to help grandma, be back in my flip-flops, and write my next summer beach read.

But to be surrounded by crisp fall leaves, pumpkins, and apple cider donuts? It gives me the ick. People can have their fall sweaters, pumpkin spice, and everything nice, but not me. I'm not your basic PSL bitch. Miss me with the pumpkin galore.

Give me summer. I *live* for it. I breathe in coconut body spray and exhale sunshine. My entire brand as an author is built on spicy, summer-themed beach romances that leave readers sweating and panting, wishing their orgasm curled toes could be in the sand with a pool boy named Enrique.

Oceans. Popsicles. Thunderstorms that shake the sky and bare feet in the grass when it rains. I want heat. I want late-night bonfires with a book in hand and sticky fingers from ice cream that melts too fast. Instead, I'm heading into the heart of fall. Into Everly Hollow.

It's a four-hour drive from the city, and my first time visiting since Grandma moved here a year ago. Giving up my last month of summer, I'm going to spend a season I loathe the most, trapped in a town of magic.

There's about an hour left of this drive. I should have stretched when I got gas and a snack.

Will opening all the windows further and blasting Tyla help cure deep vein thrombosis? My ass is dissociating with my body.

The closer I get to Everly Hollow, the more the world around me seems to shift, like slipping through into the veil of another, softer reality.

The trees lining the road appear to lean in closer, the last bit of the sun dappling through the forest canopy.

There's a touch of warmth on my skin. It's humming around me. My fingertips tingle on the coolness of the steering wheel. There's faint gold dust floating in the air. Making my melanated skin glow.

Magic.

The scent hits me next. It smells earthy, like fresh rain and moss. Comforting. Relaxing.

A large stone comes into view. *Welcome to Everly Hollow,* is carved in swirling letters on the moss-speckled granite. A seven-pointed star is etched beneath the name.

Cobblestone roads pave the winding way and a town square. Neighborhoods full of adorable cottages and a treehouse village that peaks through the canopy with tiny balconies, rope bridges with wood planks, and rope ladders. The town square has a few stops and stores.

The one that stands out the most, as I slowly creep by with the focus of a predator is, The Autumn Leaf Bookshop.

The shop is beautiful, like an enchanted bedtime story for book lovers, even though it's decorated in pumpkins. The large trees in front are already head over heels falling for fall—leaves vibrant burnt orange, golden ochre, and deep crimson. My face is melting into a frown.

It's still summer. Wasn't it too early?

"That's freaking weird..." I mumble to myself, continuing the drive through the town to the wooded area that the map on my phone directed me to.

The gravel driveway curves to reveal my grandmother's cottage, nestled within the trees like it had just grown here.

Her garden is bursting with a variety of flowers. Hydrangeas, roses, and lavender. A few I don't recognize, but it looks like this type of lily is enchanted by the glow it illuminates and the way it moves in the light breeze.

I put the car in park and kill the engine, needing to sit. Just for a moment.

The soft ticking and clicking of my car cooling off is the only whisper until the breeze carries in a woodsy cinnamon scent. It curls around me, tightening its grip like it knows I'm resisting and won't give in. It doesn't care. It's going to seduce me into liking fall whether I want to or not.

I take a long exhale, unbuckling my seatbelt.

Finally.

An afternoon of driving and a whole year of burnout, book tours, and deadlines are behind me.

This break couldn't have come soon enough, and at least I can visit Grandma in a town where hardly anyone should know me.

My agent nearly had an aneurysm when I told her I'd be unreachable for a bit. That my grandmother needed me.

That I needed a break.

"But what about the sequel?"

I've written a series of novels, standalone works, novellas...everything. I've had bestsellers before. But this one is different. It exploded.

Barefoot & Reckless. A close-proximity spicy romance that's perfect for summer. Tropes like a stranded couple, enemies to lovers, and one hammock.

It blew up overnight, and my frontal lobe cortex hasn't known peace since. I needed out. From the pressure and demands. From all of it.

I love what I do. But at twenty-eight, with thirty coming at me like a freight train, I've realized something. If I don't start protecting my mental health now, I'll burn out before I ever finish the damn series.

But it doesn't compare to this moment, sitting at the edge of a magical town, surrounded by trees, glowing flowers, and enough peace to hear myself think again.

I want to enjoy this time without three whole months of dancing with scarecrows, jumping in leaf piles, and drinking pumpkin spice-tainted beverages by the gallons.

Ugh. I should be on a beach with a book in one hand and a Mai Tai in the other—not wandering through a leaf-crunching small town where the fall vibes are coming in hot.

But here I am. Maybe this won't be such a bad thing.

My body relaxes against the seat, as I pull my braids over my shoulder. It's quiet. No buzzing phone because I blocked anyone and everyone important for twenty-four hours. No readers at signings asking me if I really based the hot police officer in *Tangled in Blue* on my ex.

Just me, the trees, a new town full of magical beings, and the woman who raised me after my parents died when I was just ten years old.

My mouth tugs into a smile.

Let the vacation begin.

Of course, the door is unlocked.

I told her many times when planning this trip, I don't care how cozy, sweet, and polite this damn town is, lock your doors! Always. I can knock and then get a key later, but no, she left it unlocked.

Turning the knob fully, I push the door open as I juggle my laptop bag, purse, and roll my olive green suitcase behind me.

"Heeeelllo! Is anyone home?"

I shut the door and *lock* it.

"I'm the masked, big bad werewolf who's come to take your soul! Thanks for leaving the door open!" I say.

"Raene! Baby, you're here!" Grandma shouts excitedly as she makes her way over to me with the use of her cane. She's wearing her favorite jeans and a blush-colored sweater, soft and cozy like everything in this cottage. Looks like the physical therapy before her surgery is paying off.

Even with the deep laugh lines on her rich brown skin and her thick silver curls that frame her face, she's more beautiful than ever.

"Hi Granny!" I smile ear to ear. I drop my things and make my way over to her, our arms wrapping around one another in a tight, warm embrace. She smells like roses. Like home.

"Why didn't you lock your door?" I ask when she releases me, bending to take off my sneakers.

She waves her hand in the air as if my suggestion was just that. A silly piece of advice, she will choose to continue to ignore. She makes her way back to the couch, where she was enjoying a movie. The wood in the fire crackles in the hearth, spreading warmth in the living room.

"I told you it was safe here. Oh, and a werewolf does live here."

My eyes widened. "No shit?"

"Yes, Dominik. He owns the flower shop. He knows everything there is to know about flowers, even those that are enchanted. Like the moon-lilies I have in my garden. They begin to glow as the sun sets."

A werewolf who is a florist. I shake my head and laugh. Everly Hollow really is magical.

She pats the seat beside her. "I have your room all ready."

I plop down on the couch and groan in relief. Stretching my limbs, back, and neck until I hear a satisfying pop.

Comfy clothes were the right call for the drive. This cute mustard yellow crop top with a sunflower on the front and butter-soft gray joggers feels like a warm hug.

"Grandma, your surgery is in two days." I shift my body towards her. "You know I could have handled all of that."

"It's okay." She pats my hand. "I had help. Flora has been helping me. She's a Goddess sent."

I remember Grandma telling me about Flora during our phone calls. They're besties, and she seems very sweet. She's a troll and not the under-the-bridge-dwelling kind. She lives in the hills, Grandma says. She's earthy, loves to garden, and especially loves tending to her herbs.

She raves about Flora every time we talk and says her plant apothecary is a must-see before I return home.

"We also have enough food frozen to last us a good few weeks to start."

"Yay! Casserole and soup season are my favorite." I laugh and roll my eyes. But food is food, and at least neither of us will have to stress about cooking while she's healing.

She leans over to the side table, slipping on her glasses before reaching for her notebook.

"I made a list of some things I'd like for you to take care of tomorrow, if possible." Her voice is soft, but she means business.

She turns a page and hands me the notebook with a smile. Always the planner. She always has multiple things scheduled all at once and makes notes of everything so she can get it done.

Planning can help prevent stress, and if something comes up, push it away till tomorrow. That's her motto.

"So tomorrow," she begins, settling back into her seat, "I'll start packing for my overnight hospital stay on Friday after the surgery. But I'd like you to run to the market first thing. I need fresh produce, eggs, cheese, and bread. Maybe grab some snacks for us, whatever you think looks good."

I nod, mentally making a note. "Got it. No problem."

"Oh, and one more thing," she adds, lifting a brow. "Can you please make a stop at the bookshop? I placed an order last week. I want a good stack of books to read while I'm healing."

"Of course," I say. "Easy."

She grins, smug and just a little wicked. "I haven't read your newest book yet, but it's included in the pickup."

My latest book. The one with the stranded lovers, the *one hammock*, the sex scene that basically melted BookTok. *That book?*

I laugh and give her a tight smile. "Seriously, Grandma, that one?"

She winks at me like this is our little inside joke. I internally shudder. She's always been supportive, never once complained, and I love her for that, but the idea of Grandma Vera reading my sun-drenched, hammock-tangled summer smut? *I just can't.*

"Whatever you want to read, Grandma, is *not* my business," I say, holding back a wince. "But I do hope you love it. And I seriously appreciate the support. Always."

I scoot closer and rest my head on her shoulder, the scent of her rose perfume grounding me as we go over the to-do list and prep for her surgery. She already has the shower chair set up in the bathroom and a new plush cozy robe hanging by the door like she's prepping for a weekend at the spa instead of going to the hospital for a joint replacement.

When I mention ice packs, she waves a hand. "No need, baby. Flora already took care of that."

Of course she did.

"She dropped off a jar of her *Frost Leaf Serum* earlier this week," Grandma says, shuffling over to a side cabinet and pulling out a squat, hand-labeled glass jar with a shimmering swirl of silver-blue inside. "Said she made this batch special: infused it with starlight and winter mint."

"Starlight?" The word catches me off guard, my brows lifting in surprise.

Grandma shrugs. "It works. I've been using it after my physical therapy treatments. She said the more severe the pain, the more effective it gets."

Curious, I reach for the bottle. It's supposed to cool the skin and can help dull pain and inflammation.

The jar itself is cool to the touch. I dip a finger in and rub it against another fingertip. The texture is dreamy—like whipped shea butter. As soon as I apply a little to the back of my hand, my skin takes on a silver glow. A tingling sensation spreads throughout my arm. It's not like an icy shock; it's soothing waves. Coolness sweeps over my skin, followed by a slight numbing effect.

"Damn," I whisper, tilting my arm this way and that. "This knocks ibuprofen out of the park."

"Flora doesn't mess around," she says proudly, chuckling, and tucking the jar back into its home. As Grandma makes her way to the kitchen to pop a casserole into the oven, I decide it's time to go to my bedroom. Get settled and unpack a little.

"Get cozy, baby," she says. "You'll catch the scent of chicken and dumplings in the air when it's almost time."

The small staircase creaks under my feet as I climb, chest warming and hands full of luggage. I've missed her so much. I'm also excited to see what my bedroom looks like.

The door creaks open with a soft groan, and I step inside, blinking at the amazement that greets me.

The bedroom is...beautiful. The walls are painted a soft lavender that immediately soothes my senses. The sunset glides through the window, casting a warm golden glow across the space and catching on the glass vase of fresh wildflowers.

The soft scent of my grandmother's perfume of roses and lavender mingles in the air.

My bags and suitcase hit the bed with a soft thud. I step closer to the window. The wooden blinds are perched up, with billowy sheer curtains swept to each side.

A white picket fence outlines the backyard, protecting a garden that looks like it's been blessed by Mother Nature. Beyond that, a large forest and the mountains stand tall in the distance as if they are ancient sentinels. The sky is painted in soft strokes of orange and pink as the sun begins to dip into its quiet slumber.

I blink.

I blink again, just to be sure I'm not dreaming. What in the world? *What is this world?*

I wouldn't mind waking up to this view every morning. Well, maybe with a beach somewhere nearby, and remove three of the four seasons. But still. This?

A ripple of movement catches my eye. From between the trees, a creature steps into the clearing. It's slender and deer-like, but something far more...*ancient*. Its coat shimmers and shifts in a gradient of soft twilight hues to a deep lavender.

The variant shades of deep blues and silver are magnificent. Long, twisting dark grey antlers crown its head, tangled with vines and tiny blossoms that pulse faintly with a glow, in the fading light.

For a long moment, it stands still, its hooves making its mark in the thick, plush grass. Its luminous golden eyes meet mine. Like it sees *through* me.

Then, with just the blow of the wind, it turns, runs, and melts back into the shadows, leaving behind only the rustle of leaves and the crack of a stick, piercing the air.

Turning away from the view, I take in the rest of the bedroom. A queen-size bed sits against the far wall, framed by a matching walnut wood dresser and twin nightstands on either side with antique lamps. The bed is made with a deep purple, floral-printed quilt that matches the pillows.

It looks ridiculously cozy, like the kind of bed you dive into after a long day and forget the rest of the world exists. Something I desperately want to do right now.

Maybe I'll block everyone for the entirety of this trip?

Trailing my fingers atop the soft stitches on the bedding, my lungs release a deep breath.

Hopefully, I find some peace this month amongst the pumpkins.

2
Books, Dust, and Dragon Wings
SYLAS

After opening, the shop awakens and feels more alive. Sunlight spills through the many high, arched skylights above, catching in the tiny particles of dust and illuminating the vibrant canopy overhead.

The maple tree, my tree, rises right through the center of the shop, covered in fall colored leaves that never descend. The thick trunk twists up and around, branches spreading wide like an open hug towards the sun rays.

Regardless of whether it is winter, summer, or spring, this tree and the trees that surround this building will always be in fall. An enchantment I cast when I opened this shop.

Golds, rich reds, and deep copper leaves shimmer in the sunlight, rustling occasionally with a light breeze that flows through, as if whispering spells to one another.

Tiny floating lights like stars dangle from the branches, dimly lit by the impending sunshine. In the evening, they burn brighter and adjust their lighting. The tables have lamps to accompany our evening readers.

An iron-wrought staircase curls elegantly around the tree trunk to the second-floor loft, where the rarer volumes live and the air tingles with magic. Beyond the velvet curtains lies a small hall to my hidden apartment.

Well-worn, polished wood floors support towering walnut bookshelves that stretch to the vaulted ceilings, each fitted with a brass rolling ladder. Two large Prussian blue armchairs sit near the fireplace between two couches. Scattered around are more matching chairs in the same hue and tables, each with chairs, perfect for reading or computer use, are set just far enough apart for privacy.

Large windows in the front of the shop feature book displays throughout the year, along with a cozy nook for sitting and taking in the street view.

I love this place. The books, the dust, and the dragon wings. It's home.

The scent of leather and old pages lingers in the air, blending with the soft crackle of the fireplace. Lo-fi music hums through the speakers, the kind that persuades the enchanted books to move along to the rhythm.

I tug the sleeves up of my forest green quarter zip sweater so that it isn't catching on the interior of the wooden crate of new arrivals. Squatting in my comfortable but worn jeans, my boots creak quietly on the wood floor beneath me.

I brush my fingertips over the golden edges of crisp, limited-edition hardcovers. Sprayed edges. Gold foil. Embossed spines. They'll look damn good on the front display.

"One, two, three...seven, eight...twenty-two–" Pausing, a frown immediately hits my face. There are only twenty-four. I know there were twenty-five. I took one out yesterday for a photo, snapped it beside the window light with a mug of pumpkin chai tea, leaves, and real fucking cinnamon sticks. Where the hell did it go?

I scan the area behind the counter, under the table, then upward.

"Nim," I say through our bond, a mental nudge aimed at the miniature dragon. He's on the top shelf near the rolling ladder. He's the size of a large cat, but with wings, scales, and he breathes fire.

"Have you seen the book I'm missing? Fancy cover. Smells like a bestseller...one of our *shop's* best sellers, and ink."

Nim stretches. His iridescent scales in autumnal hues-molten reds, copper, and bronze cover his body, neck, and tail. His underbelly is covered in mostly gold scales. Light green eyes full of mischief. Golden spikes form a crown on his head, a neat line trailing halfway down his long tail. He glistens in the sunbeams that shine through the skylights. His wings give a lazy flutter as he pushes into a downward dog pose, spine arching, tail curling.

Nim yawns, it's long and dramatic with sharp, pointy teeth. He circles his spot like he's about to settle on a throne. *"Does it look like I'm capable of reading, Sylas?"* His voice echoes and drips in smug boredom inside my head.

Rolling my eyes, I quickly jot down a note to contact the distributor before sticking a pencil behind my pointed ear.

I begin shelving the books, spine out, labels facing the same direction, because chaos has no place in my bookshop.

"You're such an adorable, lazy beast," I grumble.

From his perch at the top of the bookshelf, Nim stretches luxuriously, cracking one eye open before letting out a self-satisfied chuff. His tail flicks, nearly knocking over a decorative leaf garland.

He cracks one eye open. *"That's why I'm the adorable pet,"* he drawls, *"And you're the owner."*

"Ass," I mutter to myself.

"Jerk," he responds.

I finish stocking the shelves and get the shop up and running before making my way to the coffee bar embellished with pumpkins and tiny gourds. There's no need for faux fall leaves, garland or pumpkins. My magic protects their lives so they can be long-term decor.

I make myself a pumpkin spice latte, adding a tall heaping of whipped cream and topping it off with a dusting of cinnamon and nutmeg, and a cinnamon stick for presentation. The cinnamon stick stirs itself lazily, sending up tiny curls of steam scented with morning routine and comfort.

Nim flies over to land on the bar, eyeing the cinnamon-dusted whipped cream with greedy intent.

"This is mine, you'll have to get your own," I tell him out loud before taking a sip, licking the cream off my lips.

He chirps once before giving me a glare, his wings expanding before fluttering close.

"*And how do you suppose I do that?*" he asks with a sharp voice down the bond. "*Do you see opposable thumbs on these paws?*"

Rolling my eyes, I give him a small smile. "Okay, okay." Already reaching for the tin of chai leaves he likes best, aged in cardamom, ginger, and cloves, and enchanted to steep quickly.

Brewing the tea with a flick of my fingers, the steam rises in sweet tendrils that twist into the shape of a falling leaf before fading away into the air.

I pour it into his favorite cup—an oversized mug—that can be equivalent to a pasta dish, heavily decorated in cottage core with vibrant red spotted mushrooms.

Two pumps of pumpkin spice syrup, a splash of soy milk, and a generous cloud of whipped cream, transforming the drink into a snow-capped mountain with specks of cinnamon and I top it with a cinnamon stick before I slide it toward him across the counter.

He sniffs it as if I've never made him this over a hundred times, purrs with pleasure, and curls his tail around the mug, like he's giving it a small hug.

"*That's better,*" he whispers, taking a slurp, licking cream off his snout. "*Thank you.*"

I curtly nod, taking another sip of my drink, smiling behind the rim.

I love moments like this. The routine. The vibes. The Autumn Leaf is more than a bookshop. It's a place of comfort to so many people.

I've loved books since I can remember. I kept a hoard of books beside my bed, begging my parents to read them all every night. Once I learned how to read, I read until I fell asleep, a book curled against my heart.

My parents are still scribes. Ink is in our blood.

I used to sit in a nook of the great library for hours as my parents worked, trying to read tomes twice the size of Nim. I would read out loud to him, and he lay beside me, his tail curled around him, his head resting on my lower legs, the book on my lap. I loved being surrounded by the scent of parchment and magic.

Books are more than stories. They are portals to another world lingering within the pages that can build you up, break you, and live in your head forever. They can change your life.

Waving to a few regulars warming by the fires, I leave Nim to his tea at the coffee bar and head toward the checkout counter.

A few of the trinkets have shifted overnight, likely from tempted, curious fingers or overly enthusiastic magic. Enchanted bookmarks that shimmer and shift with the mood of the reader, decorative potion bottles for bookshelf decor. Some labeled *Plot Twist Tonic, Pumpkin Moon Mist, Dragon Breath Brew*, and rows of fall-scented beeswax lip balms handmade by Jas down at The Honeybee Café.

Her newest flavors, *First Kiss of Fall* and *Pumpkin Toffee Chai*, already have a loyal following. There are bookish themed magnets, stickers, and wax stamps that say *Nim was here*.

A puff of crisp air trails in as the door opens again, wind chimes playing a cheerful melody.

"Sylas," growls a familiar voice.

I don't even look up from my organizing task at the counter. I know who's speaking.

"Back for more of that lip balm you pretend to hate, Viktor?"

The massive minotaur in khakis and a grey t-shirt lumbers to the checkout.

"Or maybe the garden gnome who rents a corner of your greenhouse in exchange for dewberries and emotional advice," I finish. "Sure. You're just really invested in their lip moisturization."

He scowls, grabs a tin of *Pumpkin Toffee Chai*, and drops a coin pouch on the counter. "It's a good scent," he mutters before heading toward the door.

A soft, flitting chirp echoes from the coffee bar.

"*See you next week,*" Nim teases, his words dripping with honey inside my head, his tone threaded with mischief.

To Viktor, it's just another sarcastic chirp from Nim.

The minotaur pauses at the door just long enough to lift a middle finger in Nim's general direction, then stomps out into the sunlight. I chuckle, flipping open the pouch and adding the coins to the register. Another customer walks in, someone I've never noticed here before.

Did someone new move to town?

Nim turns his head to look at me. Then to the door.

Deep brown skin glowing warm in the sunlight, braided hair flowing down to her waist. Showing her curves in a crop top that flaunts *Beach Vibes*, jean shorts that cut off mid-thigh, and sneakers.

She glances around, curious, maybe a little skeptical. Her vibrant honey brown eyes take in the bookshop like she's trying to decide if it's real. Her mouth opens slightly, taking in the tree. She quickly closes it.

Holy shit.

"*I heard that,*" Nim says as he launches upward in a smooth, elegant swoop of his autumnal hues.

His wings gently rustle the air, barely making a sound as he glides toward the tree at the heart of the shop and disappears into the golden canopy, vanishing between leaves and winding branches like a shadow slipping through light. A few leaves shimmer slightly in his wake. I swallow. My voice barely makes it out.

"Holy shit." That's not some newcomer.

That's Raene Hart.

And she's standing in my bookshop.

3
Honey Lavender Lattes & Honey Buns
RAENE

*B*efore the bookshop...

A light breeze blows over the sidewalk, my feet carrying me in the direction of the café. The coziness in the air of this town suffocates me regardless of whether I want it or not.

Every shop is adorable, quaint, and sprinkled with its own touch of magic. I was too distracted by the sage green sweater on the mannequin in the storefront window of a boutique named The Velvet Petal.

Ivy creeped lazily up the brick storefront, weaving its tendrils toward the carved wooden sign above the front door. The glossy leaves shimmered with dew. Rose bushes near the window spill over in fragrant, blush pink blooms. The ivy, emphasizing the sign and the flowers, framed the boutique like a whimsical invitation, promising shoppers of charming trinkets and clothing within.

And the vibes? Absolutely spot on. I couldn't resist grabbing that beautiful, soft sweater, a cute pair of jeans, and the most darling pair of brown suede ankle boots—each with a little bow on the side. After a sweet chat with the store's owner, who gave me a first-time shopper discount, I completed my purchase and tucked the bags safely into the trunk.

My eyes lift from the view of my feet on the sidewalk to the café, the white and yellow striped awning catches slightly in the wind. Providing shade to the wrought iron bistro tables and chairs below, each table adorned with an amber, honeycomb-shaped lantern, it also provides ample sunshine and stability to the planters above.

Lush greens and vibrant colored petals—yellows, oranges, reds, and pinks—bloom from above. Trailing blooms angle together beautifully, spilling their vines and beauty in every direction.

The little brass bell above the door jingles softly as I step into The Honeybee Café. The scent of honey, cinnamon, butter, and coffee with floral undertones hit me immediately. This place is adorable.

Cute buttery yellow booths line the far wall, each one lit by a delicate beehive-shaped wooden lantern hanging above the center of the table. It's filled with a floating orb that casts a soft, golden glow like afternoon sunshine.

The walls are dotted with vintage-style honeybee décor—painted tin signs, and framed embroidery hoops of: honeybees pollinating flowers with soft pink and purple blooms beneath them, a jar of honey with a honey dip stick, and cute quotes that say *Thanks for buzzing by, Bee Kind,* and *Sweet as Honey.*

One of the largest walls features a honeycomb cutout, its hexagonal pattern filled with everything from small bee-themed paintings to hanging plants, tea tins, and candles for sale.

Wooden tables fill the center of the café, their tops etched in a subtle honeycomb pattern that catches the light just so, surrounded by matching chairs.

The front display window near the counter is packed with rows of treats that look divine. Flaky croissants, muffins bursting with berries, honey buns dripping with glaze. Behind it, the back counter hums with energy, clinking mugs and the quiet hiss of the espresso machine and a tea kettle.

Yeah, this place is freaking adorable.

"Hi there, and welcome!" Says the cheerful voice of the woman behind the counter.

She's wearing a soft black apron over a crisp white blouse and well-fitted blue jeans, the word *Queen* stitched in gold thread across the chest with a large, regal-looking bee below it. Tiny crowns, embroidered flowers, and mini bees dance across the rest of the fabric like they were made just for her.

Her hands rest comfortably on the counter, bangles in teals and golds, jingling softly with each movement of her wrist. Her skin is a smooth, deep olive tone, giving off a beautiful glow in the soft café. A messy and curly bun sits atop her head, brown curls framing her face. Her eyes are warm and bright green.

"Hi!" I wave, approaching the counter. My voice seems too cheerful, but honestly, I feel a bit overwhelmed.

A few people are sitting in the booths. People? Magical beings? Monsters?

Two trolls are in a booth with their mugs and crossword puzzles. In the next booth, a gorgon lounges in the sun, her sunglasses perched on her head among her loosely coiled snakes. A few appear to be napping as she continues to scroll through a crystal tablet, sipping a latte and nibbling on a berry muffin.

"I'm Jasmira, but everyone calls me Jas." She smiles, then her eyes narrow, her mouth. "Wait a second." She holds up her finger before running through the swinging back door.

Okay. That was...odd.

"I know you!" She exclaims, coming back through the door, a book in hand—my latest book—shaking it gently in the air.

"I mean, I don't *know* you," she sets the book down on the counter, "but we're reading your book, for book club! I can't believe you're here! Why are you here?" She quickly covers her mouth. "I'm sorry..."

I laugh because she seems like a sweet person with energetic vibes. "You're okay. No worries. This is my first time in Everly Hollow. I'm visiting my grandmother."

"Hold up, your grandmother is Vera! Raene Hart is Vera's granddaughter? She told us you were visiting, but she didn't tell us who you were! Just that you love to write!" She laughs, lightly slapping the counter.

"She's my maternal grandmother, hence the different last name, but she raised me. I'm happy to be here with her, and this place is...it's pretty neat."

She nods her head. "I love it here, it's home. Do you have time to chat? I don't want to be a bother, but..."

"Sure! I have some time. Just running some errands before her surgery tomorrow, so I have some time." I shrug.

"Great!" She sighs in relief. "What would you like to try? It's on the house, my treat!"

"Oh, you don't have to do that!" I say quickly.

"I want to! I love your books, and this is your first time here. I would love to do this for you."

"Well...thank you. I really appreciate it," I say, smiling back, genuinely this time.

I scan the chalkboard menu above the counter, the loopy handwritten script surrounded by tiny doodles of bees and flowers. "I think I'll try the honey lavender latte and a honey bun, please. The biggest one you've got."

Like I need the calories, but it'll be my late morning snack. It could be worse.

"Perfect!" Jas claps her hands. "Find yourself a seat and I'll bring it right over."

"Will do! Thanks, Jas!"

I think I made my first friend here.

Jas approaches the cozy booth with a tray of two steaming lattes and two small plates, each cradling a large iced honey bun.

The moment the tray hits the table, the warm scent of sugar, honey, and coffee fills my senses. My stomach lets out a rude growl that's loud enough to make me glance around and pray no one noticed.

"I guess that answers whether you're hungry," Jas says with a wink, setting one of the plates in front of me.

I let out a small laugh, lifting the mug to my lips. It feels so comfortable here and cozy. "You're amazing."

The first sip is smooth, a hit of lavender, and the sweet taste of honey hits my tongue. My eyes widen as it slides down my throat. It might as well be brewed by magic.

"Okay, this is delicious," I sigh, already clutching the mug like it was a gift to solve all my problems. "and I'm pretty sure I'm about to inhale this honey bun. Did you make this?"

She laughs, lifting her mug to take a small sip, her lips curling up.

"The pastries are from our two local bakeries in town." She tears off a piece and pops it in her mouth. "They're to *die* for," she groans, licking the sugar from her fingers shamelessly. I get the feeling she's a carefree spirit.

"It was a dream of my husband and me to open this place." Jas's voice is soft, tinged with her memories as she picks up her bun.

I follow suit, chewing slowly and letting the warmth of the cinnamon and honey dance in my mouth. It's perfect.

"He was a beekeeper, and I love coffee, I mean, I was always drinking copious amounts of it in college." She laughs, the sound light and melodic.

I pause mid-sip. "I'm sorry, *was*? If you don't mind me asking, why did he stop the beekeeping business?"

"He passed away three years ago," she says gently, her fingertips slowly stroking the handle of her mug.

My chest tightens. I don't even know her, but grief recognizes grief. I remember watching my grandmother grieve my mother when I was too young to lose my parents.

I can't imagine losing someone you thought you'd spend the rest of your life with.

Still, having just met, we're connected in grief. Having to lose someone so close to you. I reach my hand out to give hers a light squeeze. "I'm sorry, Jas."

"Thank you, Raene." She gives me a small smile. The kind of smile that you give when people say those words, yet somehow they still matter. "He was pretty amazing."

"We met in college. Well, *I* was in college in the city," Jas begins, cradling her mug in the palms of her hand. "My roommate, Celeste, is a witch, and she still lives in the city. We stay in touch as often as we can."

She leans into the table, crossing her forearms as the people around us continue to chat. "She wanted to take a road trip here to Everly Hollow, which is her hometown, during spring break. She invited me to the Spring Festival." Her eyes glisten with memory as she reminisces.

"Girl," she says with a half laugh. "I had never seen anything like it before. It was beautiful and just...magical. A week-long celebration of magical flower crowns, delicious foods and treats, like fluffy-buttery honey biscuits that float off your plate if you're not quick enough to eat them."

Her grin widens. "Glowing enchanted brews, dancing in the rain, and petal parades. You never forget an experience like that, you know?"

Nodding my head, I smile. I definitely wouldn't forget it.

"Dancing in the rain?" I ask. "To honor…Mother Nature?"

She catches the slight tilt of my head and shakes hers, grinning. "Close, but no. The goddesses, Kerathea and Sateathea."

She taps her fingers gently against her mug, speaking in rhythm to the low music playing in the background. "Kerathea is the Goddess of Spring. Sateathea, her sister, is the Goddess of Rain. There are seven sisters, four that represent the seasons, and three that represent certain elements."

I give a wide-eyed gape. *That's new.* I guess that's where the seven-pointed star on the stone stands for.

"It's old magic," Jas says, as if she can read my expression, which probably screams *utter and complete confusion*.

"Every festival here is for one of the sisters, but spring…" She pauses, her smile fading into something much softer. "Spring is when everything begins anew." She tucks loose curl behind her ear, continuing. "So, the festival was beautiful and magical, but little did I know that stumbling across a honey stand would change my life. Aaryn was a beekeeper; it was his family business. He was tall, gorgeous, with dirty blonde hair, and the most beautiful green eyes. I loved his ears."

She smiles. "They came to a point. He even had one of them pierced, and I was young and thought that was so damn sexy," she laughs, and it's so damn infectious it makes me join in.

"I'm sorry if I'm oversharing," she says, wincing a little.

"Are you kidding? I love this meet-cute story. Please continue." I lift my enchanted latte, still steaming, and take a slow sip, savoring both the drink and the story.

"Well, we talked and he asked me on a date. We spent the entire next day together, talking about nothing and everything, and he showed me his favorite spots around town. That evening, he kissed me in the rain."

She sighs. "We dated long-distance after that. I finished my degree in business, and when I graduated, I moved here. I knew I wanted to open a café, and he wanted to infuse his honey into everything. So we built this place together."

She gestures at the other booths, the honeycomb wall, and the decor. "We married the following spring. Our daughter Seren was born the following June. We were so happy."

"She was one when Aaryn started getting sick. When he was diagnosed...we didn't have that much time. He tried to stay as long as he could. He fought like hell, but cancer took him from us."

A heavy silence surrounds us. I reach across and squeeze her hand again.

The café door pushes open, and a warm, scented breeze of flowers and soil flows through the door.

"Mama!" A little voice calls out.

I turn to see a beautiful little freckled-faced girl, a miniature version of Jas, with adorable Elven ears, described like her father. She's wearing a cute powder blue summer dress, and her ponytail bounces as she runs toward her mother, clutching the stems of wildflowers in her small hand.

Jas stands, swiping a hand under her eyes, both of them beaming at one another. She reaches out to pick up her daughter, enveloping her in a warm embrace.

"Hello, my little star!" She announces, burying her face in her daughter's hair. Her little face turns to me, and she gives me a toothy grin. She's a beautiful little version of Jas.

The door opens again, wider, letting in a tall, broad-shouldered man with rich brown skin and roped locs that hit his shoulder. His beard is well-manicured and trimmed to frame his sharp jaw.

The way Jas described her husband, I wonder if every man, creature, or beast that lives here is just as stunning.

He's dressed in a long sleeve shirt, the sleeves pushed back to reveal thick, muscular arms coated with dark hair and work-worn jeans smudged with dirt. He's holding a potted moon lily in one arm like it's something sacred. I recognize the flower from seeing it in Grandma's garden.

Flower pot.

Thick hair.

This must be the werewolf who owns the flower shop.

His bright, deep brown eyes scan the café in an instinctive sweep, protective, and then calm before his gaze softens the moment it lands on Jas and Seren.

Jas puts Seren down on her feet.

"Look what we made, Mama! Dominik let me pick flowers for you, and he let me water the baby roses. He told me I'm the best flowerist in the world!" She hands the wildflower bouquet to Jas.

He laughs heartily. "Florist."

She looks up at his tall stature, her nose crinkling. "That's what I said."

Jas and I laugh, sharing a glance, and when Dominik's eyes meet mine, I stand to introduce myself.

"Hi, I'm Raene, Vera's granddaughter."

He takes his hand in mine, giving it a firm shake with a smile on his face. "I'm Dominik, a friend to Jas and Godfather to Seren. Vera told us you were visiting. I'm glad you arrived safely and hope you enjoy your stay here in Everly Hollow."

"Thank you." I smile warmly.

"I'm sorry to interrupt." He turns towards Jas. "She insisted on delivering her creation in person."

"You're not interrupting," she says, looking up at him. Compared to his size, she looks tiny; there has to be a foot difference between the two of them. "I just made a new friend." She turns to me and winks.

"And this is for you, too, Mama! We planted it for you. He said by the next full moon, when school starts, there will be more blooms! It's beautiful, huh? Like you!" She does a little dance with a proud grin, showing her missing teeth, and it's adorable.

Then, without missing a beat, Seren turns and plants her small feet on top of Dominik's boots, reaching up to hold onto his hands as they walk together across the floor in tandem.

"I said the thing!" She announces, throwing herself into a fit of giggles.

His eyes crinkle at the corners as he grins widely and lifts her easily into his arms. "You nailed it," he says, spinning her once before resting her against his chest like she belongs there, and honestly, she does.

I don't even know these people, but the fact that she has a father figure in her life is amazing. This small town must be one hell of a loving community, with everyone knowing everyone.

Gathering my purse, I give Jas a grateful smile.

"Thank you for the honey bun, the latte, and the company. Seriously."

She waves me off with another wink and a promise to catch up again soon.

Time to check off the next stop on my to-do list: the bookshop.

4
An Enchanted Bookshop
RAENE

There is a tree in the bookshop.

I repeat. There is a real, live tree bursting with fall leaves in the middle of the bookshop.

I'm not sure if I need to rub the sleep from my eyes to wake myself up from this dream or pick my jaw up off the floor. Maybe I'll slap myself?

Maybe the first two. Maybe I should circle all three.

I know Grandma said the town is enchanted, but *this*? First, honeybuns that felt like a mouth orgasm, then a latte that somehow stayed warm through an entire heart-to-heart, and now *this*.

Towering shelves stretch to the vaulted ceilings, packed with a variety of books. There are rolling ladders inviting anyone brave enough to climb to reach a hidden gem. Smaller bookshelves and display tables are scattered about, forming cozy bookish labyrinths.

A gorgeous wrought iron staircase spirals around the trunk of the tree, branches extending towards the dozens of skylights.

Sunlight pours through and dances on the shimmering leaves that tremble slightly in a breeze that...shouldn't exist indoors.

Where does it come from? No clue. But the leaves respond as if the tree itself is breathing.

An enchanted bookshop.

The shop is fairly busy. Townsfolk are cozy in nooks, reading or browsing shelves with mugs in hand.

Making my way to the fiction section, I zero in on the romance like a smut-seeking missile.

I see my most recent release on display with a few others. It makes me proud and excited to see it in a small-town bookstore.

Why didn't Grandma Vera tell anyone who I really was? *I enjoy writing?* I let out a small laugh, tracing my hand on the cover of my book before scooping up a few other summery romance novels—promising sunshine, beaches, and love. Let me hold onto summer a little longer.

A small chirp catches my attention, something small and winged darts out of the canopy of branches above to a coffee bar next to the front counter. Is that...a dragon?

I hide behind a shelf, peeking around the edge like I'm a spy staying hidden. It's a freaking dragon! The small flame-throwing lizard looks to be a little under two feet tall and can't weigh more than twenty-five pounds.

Regardless, he or she is stunning. Sleek scales shimmer in deep autumnal hues of burnished copper, rich gold, glowing amber, and flickers of pumpkin orange. It's like someone bottled up fall, poured it into a cauldron, dipped a dragon in it, and set it loose in this fairy tale *bookstore. Is it a mascot? Employee? Tiny overlord?*

His wings stretch wide, translucent and delicate, veined in gold and soft amber at the tips. They catch the light from the skylights above like stained glass.

He lets out another soft chirp, a little puff of smoke curling from his snout, and turns his head toward the counter, and that's when I see him.

How the hell did I miss *him*?

He's tall. Deep tanned skin, with a clean-shaven face, dusted with light freckles. Red auburn hair with a light curl flows past his strong jawline and stops at the collar of the dark green sweater, rolled up just enough to showcase his strong, yet sexy forearms.

The dragon and the man are locked in an unspoken showdown. Green dragon eyes. Gold eyes. Neither one blinks. He reaches up, pulls a pencil from behind his ear, and ties his deep red hair back in a bun at the base of his neck, revealing pointed ears.

Pointed. Ears.

Oh.

He places his hands on his hips, still glaring at the dragon, who trills again, and then?

They both turn to look at me.

I jump like I've been caught doing scandalous things and completely drop all of my books.

They thud on the wood floor. My pride, hitting the ground right along with them.

That's not just a man.

That's a *male fae.*

The air shifts as he walks over here. *I may not like the fall, but he's yummy to look at.*

I crouch, mentally cursing myself for dropping books like I'm a walking disaster in front of him. I see his boots on the polished wood floors before he drops down beside me.

"You okay?" His voice is soft, a little husky but warm as it fills me like that lavender honey latte. *Damn.*

My eyes meet his. It's a dangerous mistake. His eyes are a light gold. The freckles on his cheek are as if someone dipped a pastry brush in cinnamon and flicked it towards his nose and the tops of his cheeks. And his scent?

Parchment, cedar, and…citrus?

My eyes drop down to his mouth. Kill me now. Make it a quick death.

Full lips. Soft, and way too kissable for a man I've known all of sixty seconds.

Nope. Absolutely not.

Get it together, Raene Juliette Hart.

I nod quickly and clear my throat before gathering the last book he puts onto my stack, our fingers brushing lightly.

"I'm okay, thanks." I tuck a few braids behind my ear and adjust my crossbody bag. "I was…umm…distracted by the dragon," I nod towards the dragon, who is watching us with far too much amusement for someone without eyebrows. "and that." I tilt my chin in the direction of the large tree.

He chuckles, a low, warm sound. "Nim is harmless, but he does tend to be a bit dramatic."

Nim. Cute.

"Welcome to The Autumn Leaf Bookshop," he says, clearing his throat, subtly adjusting the sleeves of his sweater. He pulls them down and pushes them up again before tucking his hands into his jeans pockets. His cheeks flush just the slightest bit, but it's there. I noticed.

"I'm Sylas Ashvale, the owner."

He tilts his head to the side in the direction of the counter, and I follow his graceful steps.

"You're Raene Hart," he says before I can introduce myself. As if he's been holding it in his back pocket for a while.

I blink. "I am. Nice to meet you."

He flashes a wide smile with perfect white teeth and just the hint of fangs before shaking his head sheepishly. "Sorry. I just wasn't expecting *you* today. Or...ever actually. But it's great you're here. Helping Vera. She's a town treasure."

"You know my grandma?"

"Of course, we all do. She's a friend of everyone, small-town vibes you know, everyone knows everyone. She mentioned her granddaughter was coming to help after her surgery, and I put two and two together. Plus...you look like her."

I place my stack of books on the counter, unsure of what to say next.

"I just didn't realize you were that granddaughter and I..." He pauses, rubbing the back of his neck, his eyes darting down before meeting mine again. "I've read all of your books. Twice."

Oh.

Wait...what?

My eyes widen in disbelief because I wasn't expecting that. At all. He's read all of my books. My books. *Twice?* This gorgeous male fae with golden eyes and arms that look as if he can lift bookcases for fun...enjoys my summer romances?

He doesn't look like the type of guy who would read spicy romance books, especially books that are suffocating you in summer love. Everything about Sylas screams fall. His clothes, this place, his dragon, and just *him*.

I smile shyly, my stomach fluttering in ways I can't explain under his gaze. My brain is trying to reboot.

The small dragon, Nim, chuffs. A soft puff of steam curls into the air. I can feel the small bit of warmth on my skin before it dissipates in the air.

"Is it okay if I...?" I raise my hand on instinct, drawn to the shimmer of his autumn-colored scales, but then I hesitate and let it fall to my side. I want to pet him, but now I'm questioning it. He's not your average pet. I don't even know if it's normal to go around and *pet* dragons.

Sylas sets a tote bag on the counter. "This is your grandmother's book order."

He looks over at Nim, who looks at the tea kettle before looking back at Sylas.

"If you're nice," Sylas says dryly, giving him a look, "which I *know* you can be, then I'll make you another tea."

I blink between them. My head is on a swivel, trying to track this entire conversation between a male fae and a miniature fire-breathing dragon.

"Yes, double whipped cream," Sylas mutters, his voice tinged with mirth as a chuckle escapes him.

Of course, he has dimples.

Also, *can he talk to him?*

"Can you talk to him?" I ask, eyebrows raised.

Sylas looks at me, his golden eyes glistening when they catch the light. "Sorry, yes, I can. We are bonded, so I can hear him in my mind. He can also hear my thoughts, which isn't nice because it's not reciprocal, but yes. We talk often."

"Nim, can she?"

I wait patiently, chewing on my inner cheek, my heart fluttering. *A dragon. An actual dragon.*

Sylas groans. "If you do that, I will never give you treats or tea again. I swear."

"Do...do what?" I whisper nervously.

Is he going to roast me like a marshmallow at a fire pit? Bite me? Eat me? Can small dragons widen their mouths like a snake to eat their prey? I take a half-step back, eyeing Nim with caution.

"He's bluffing," Sylas says with a soft laugh. "Go ahead. He won't hurt you."

"Are you sure?" I ask again, looking at Sylas. His expression softens as he gently nods his head.

"I promise. You will be fine. He's just a mischievous brat with wings."

Well, that's only slightly terrifying.

I take a few slow steps towards Nim. I don't want to scare him, and I don't think I will. Nim tilts his head, eyes bright and curious, as if *I'm* the peculiar creature here. Not him.

Approaching the coffee bar, I slowly reach out, my hands trembling slightly. It's going to be okay. I won't get burned, bitten, or eaten.

I gently rub the back of my pointer finger against the golden scales of his underbelly. I'm not sure what to expect, but it feels smooth like silk, yet firm and warm. He's beautiful.

"You're so beautiful." I whisper without thinking. Sylas clears his throat behind me, causing me to jump. "He said, uhhh...he said thank you."

I whip my head around, my eyes wide. "He said that?" Sylas nods, lips twitching with amusement. "Yes. He said he's very proud of his colors," I give a slight nod, "and that they shimmer best in natural light."

"Well, he's not wrong."

Sliding my hand up further under his chin, I gently stroke with my fingertips. Nim surprisingly leans into the touch, his eyes fluttering close. He releases a sigh and a soft purr like a cat basking in the sun on a bay window. I give Nim one last affectionate scratch under the chin, his little purr still rumbling in the air, before reluctantly turning back toward the counter.

As much as I'd like to spend the rest of the day petting a magical tea-loving dragon, I do still need to buy my books, get Grandma's order, and run a few more errands.

Sylas is already sliding the novels I picked into the tote bag beside her order. "Can I ask you something?"

Honestly, he could ask anything, and I'm not sure how anyone would say no with those golden eyes and that voice. It's kind, low, and just shy of nervous right now.

"Sure," I say casually, waving my hand through the air as I lean into the counter. "Ask away."

He hesitates, "I'd love it if you could sign a few of your books while you're here. If you don't mind, I mean."

My mouth quirks into a surprised smile. "I'd be honored," I say. I'm off duty, but I don't mind signing a few books for fans. "Do you have a pen?"

He grabs one from a wooden holder on the counter next to all the other trinkets. Of course, it's fall-themed with leaves and the wording *"I love fall most of all"* printed in calligraphy, screaming at me.

"You can keep it." He gives me a wink.

I let out an awkward laugh. "Ahh ha ha ha hmm…thanks."

I quickly tap my card on the e-reader, tucking it back into my wallet before heading back toward the romance section, the scent of pumpkin spice wrapping around me in a hug I can't quite shake.

I grab a stack of books and make my way to a comfy, deep blue armchair tucked in the corner with a burnt orange blanket resting across the back. Settling in, I open the first book, beginning to sign my name on the title pages, adding a heart at the end.

From here, I catch sight of Nim at Sylas' feet, his tail swishing back and forth in impatient little flicks as he waits for his tea. A heaping pile of whipped cream is finally added to his bowl, then set aside so other patrons can still reach the counter for their warm drinks. The rustling of papers and low conversation blend in with the low hum of music playing softly in the background.

After signing the last book, I tucked them back onto the shelves, a small smile lingering on my face. I wish I could sign them all, but errands are calling, and Grandma's surgery is tomorrow.

I catch myself watching Sylas at the counter, checking out customers, and addressing them by name. His voice is warm, and he's patient with everyone, grinning in his natural element.

He doesn't miss a beat when Nim chirps or lets out a low growl from his perch on top of one of the high bookshelves. They communicate with a glance, like it's second nature. I can't hear their conversation, but to mentally talk with a dragon would be amazing. I'm not sure about him hearing my thoughts, though.

But when Sylas' golden eyes lift and find me across the room, something shifts. His gaze softens, turns warmer, like I'm the only person in the shop worth noticing.

Once the counter is clear, I make my way over. I love the pink that flushes to his cheeks as he sees me make my way closer, and damn it's adorable.

"Thanks again for signing those books. I really appreciate it. I have signed edition stickers I can put on the ones you signed."

"Great, and no problem. I signed fifteen of them." I place the pen back in the wooden holder.

He nods his head, removing the elastic band from his hair, and runs his hands through it. I'm struck with the ridiculous urge to run my hands through the silk strands.

I need to get the hell out of here.

"I should head out," I say, clearing my throat. "I need to go to the grocery store for my grandmother, but it was nice meeting you."

"It was great to meet you, Raene." His voice is deep and drops to a soft tone. "I hope to see you around."

There's a pause. Just a breath too long.

His golden eyes linger on mine, something quiet but undeniable passing between us.

I smile, slow and reckless. "I'm sure you will."

As I lift the tote off the counter and turn away, I feel his gaze follow me all the way to the door. And I don't dare look back.

I take a bite of the strawberry licorice from the open package sitting by my purse in the front of the cart, the sweet, chewy bite making the grocery run feel just a little less tedious.

Pushing my way down the chip aisle, I scan the shelves, already mentally tallying what's in my cart so far: some meat, chicken stock, noodles, eggs, bread, fresh fruit—apples, blueberries, strawberries, and grapefruit and plenty of veggies for salads—spring salad mix, tomatoes, cucumbers, celery, carrots. The responsible stuff.

Now for the good stuff.

I toss a couple of bags of chips into the cart, grab some trail mix, ice cream, and wine, and add a few more snacks for good measure.

I roll my cart up to one of the two open registers and begin loading up the conveyor belt. The tall, willowy elf working the lane greets me with a warm, slightly nervous smile. He wears a light blue shirt with jeans, has creamy ivory skin, chestnut brown curls, and softly pointed ears.

"Afternoon," he says, his voice calm and cool like a breeze. His name tag reads *Thale*.

"Stocking up for the weekend?" He asks, scanning the items.

I glance at the mountain of food moving down the belt, being scanned and bagged. "Something like that," I respond with a faint smile.

He gently lifts the fruit to scan, careful not to bruise the fruit before placing it in bags. "The churro ice cream is my favorite," he says, nodding at the half-gallon. "Especially after a long day."

"Grocery runs aren't exactly my favorite thing, but this seemed like the perfect reward." I place the open bag of licorice on the belt with a shrug, pushing the cart forward. " I wasn't feeling all the fall flavors, so this sounded like something worth a try."

Thale smiles, a sparkle lighting his pale blue eyes. "I get that…autumn's a bit much around here."

He gestures vaguely at the hay bales and pumpkin displays overtaking every end cap. "It has its quiet moments too. Like warm apple pie on a late afternoon or reading by the fire."

He scans a bottle of wine, slipping it carefully into a paper sleeve. "Or enjoying a glass of wine on the porch while the leaves fall."

I huff a laugh, holding my hands up in mock surrender. "Whoa now, don't start selling me on fall."

He chuckles, telling me my total, rounds the register, and places the bags side by side in my cart.

I tap my card, and once the receipt prints, he tears it off and hands it to me with a small smile.

"Take care, and may this weekend be kind to you."

I pause at that, noting the sincerity in his voice. "Thank you. I really appreciate that," I say softly.

I make my way to my car, loading the trunk with groceries before pushing the cart to the small cart return area. I am blown away by everyone I met today. Maybe being in this small town won't be so bad after all.

5
Four Lanterns
SYLAS

I'm missing another book. Again.

What the hell is happening in this shop?

Raene said she signed fifteen books. I counted fifteen when I pulled them off the shelves, lined them up neatly on the table beside me.

I even grabbed exactly fifteen 'Signed Exclusive' stickers from the roll, because apparently, I'm the kind of guy who double-checks his math before placing stickers on romance novels. But when I came back with the stickers and got to work, I only tagged fourteen books. And somehow, I had one sticker left staring back at me like a smug little reminder that something's off.

I don't have cameras here, and maybe I should, but I haven't had this problem. Ever. Especially living in a small town. Sure, we get passersby and tourists now and then, but theft? Never. How the hell are my books going missing? I'm going to have to keep an eye on things. Actually...

"*Nim*," I call through the bond. My thoughts reach out like a quiet knock on his sleepy consciousness. There's rustling in the leaves above me as he slinks down a lower branch, stretching his body. His scales blend in with the hues of the fall leaves.

"Yes, master," he drawls, voice dripping with dramatic obedience.

I roll my eyes. He can't see it. My back's turned while I reshelve the books, but knowing Nim, he can feel the sarcasm anyway.

"I'm missing another book. Seems to be a trend lately," I say, voice tight.

The last book is finally shelved, a little harder than I expected, but I'm frustrated.

"Calm down, there, tiger." I hear his chuff echoing through my mind, lazy and amused. *"Don't you have somewhere to be? People to meet, drinks, and a certain author to continue...what do you call it again? Crushing on?"*

Huffing out a breath, I move through the shop to tidy the chairs and straighten the books. *"I have time. It's not that far of a walk."* I flick off one of the lamps, casting the corners into shadows. *"And I don't have a crush."*

Did he just snort? By the seven..

"Sure, Sylas. Whatever helps you sleep tonight. You were so flustered earlier, you couldn't tell if your sleeves were up or down."

A scowl crosses my face as he flutters up to his favorite perch atop the bookshelf, heat creeping up the back of my neck. *"You know, there are rules against workplace harassment."*

"And yet you keep me around." His arrogance radiates through the bond.

He glances up toward the skylight, wings stretching in a lazy ripple. *"Maybe I'll grab some dinner for myself as well. You know, before it gets too late."*

Grabbing my jacket, I shoot him a look. *"Just make sure you shut the skylight when you return."*

"Relax," Nim says, tail flicking with attitude. *"I'll shut the window. Wouldn't want your precious books catching a chill."*

Shaking my head, the last switch flips off, plunging the shop into darkness, save for the front porch light and the sunset peeping through the glass. "For the love of the goddesses, you're exhausting."

"But charming, yet I'm still underpaid and underappreciated," he says.

Locking the door, I can't help the low chuckle that slips out. The night air greets me, crisp and cool. Lantern light spills across the cobbled street, guiding my journey.

Yeah. I can definitely use a drink.

The bar sits tucked between two buildings, The Sugar Plum Bakery and The Stone Hearth Bakery, on the cobblestone street. Its exterior is a blend of weathered dark wood and stone. Ivy grows from the corner. Above the arched doorway, four lanterns hung in a staggered row, each glowing a golden hue. Above the lanterns, the large wooden sign, etched, Four Lanterns, swings gently in the breeze, creaking softly as if to say '*Hello*'.

A worn welcome mat lies at the door with a cheeky message embroidered in faded gold thread: *Please come in!*
Vampires.

Opening the door, warmth hits me in the face. The sound of laughter and conversation blends with the clinking of glasses, classic rock on the speakers, and the comforting scent of ale and rich, savory food fills the air.

The windows are shuttered tight to keep the daylight out, but the bar is softly illuminated by lanterns hanging from wrought-iron brackets, casting pools of light across the dark wooden floors.

Patrons fill the tables and surround the two pool tables off to the side. Behind the bar are two flat-screen TVs and a large mirror, reflecting everything within view, including the bottles of liquor and beer taps, but Malik's reflection is nowhere to be seen.

He stands with a quiet, commanding presence as he dries each glass, one by one. His skin is cool, ivory, with thick, chestnut-brown hair slicked back, just a hint of pomade, sleeves casually pushed to his elbows, revealing toned forearms. A gold watch chain gleams against his tailored vest, and a well-manicured beard frames sharp features. His piercing grey eyes hold countless stories. He's centuries old, but will forever look thirty-three years old.

As his gaze finds me, a slow, knowing smile tugs at his lips, and he raises a hand in greeting. Weaving in between the tables, I make my way to the bar.

"Your usual?" Malik asks, tossing the towel on the counter.

I nod while he grabs a hammered glass and begins making an Old Fashioned, topping it off with an orange peel.

"How was your day?" He asks, sliding the drink across the bar top as I toss a few bills on the counter in exchange.

"Not bad," I answer, but my mind drifts before the words even settle.

Raene.

I can't believe she's Vera's granddaughter, and it took her coming here for me to figure it out. Otherwise, it would have remained a well-kept secret. And now, those honey-brown eyes won't leave my head. Neither will the scent of her: coconut, sunlight, and salt-kissed skin.

And why the fuck did I tell her I read her books? Twice.

"See..." Nim's voice hums through my head with teasing delight. *"I told you. Crushing."*

I take a long sip of my drink, letting the burn anchor me back in the moment. If I'm smart, I'll keep my distance. She's here visiting. Which means temporary, and that equates to trouble.

Before I can respond, Malik tips his chin toward the front door just as it swings open.

Viktor steps through first, filling the doorway with his broad, minotaur frame. Tawny, coarse fur stretched over powerful shoulders. He runs a hand through the thick chestnut hair between his curved horns, a lazy grin stretching across his face. A well-worn flannel shirt, sleeves rolled to his elbows, clings to his massive chest, faded jeans flowing down to the side of his hooves.

Garruk follows, his black tousled hair falling across his brow, the orc's sharp gaze sweeping the bar. And last, Dominik strolls in. He's tall with dark skin, warm in the lantern light, long locs pulled back loosely. He seems calm and peaceful beneath his easy smile.

"Look who finally crawled out of his crypt," Viktor calls toward the bar, his voice booming.

"The sunshine treating you well today, Malik?" Garruk adds, lips twitching as he leans into the bar.

Smirking, Dominik slides onto a barstool. "You missed a hell of a blue sky, my friend."

Malik snorts, grabbing another glass without missing a beat. "I'll take shadows and whiskey over sunburn and sweat any day, but thanks for your concern."

"Aw, he missed us," Garruk says, nudging Viktor with his elbow.

"Like a stake to the heart," Malik deadpans.

A smile tugs at my mouth as I lift my drink. Yeah, this...this is exactly what I needed tonight.

"Bullshit!" Viktor bellows, gripping his pool cue like he's two seconds from snapping it clean in half. He cuts a sharp side-eye toward the bar.

The rest of us glance over our shoulders to find Malik already shooting daggers this way. Beside him, a tall, curvy woman named Oriana, with ocean blue hair, leans against the bar, twirling a lock around her finger. She bites her lower lip, watching Malik with open interest.

With a huff that shakes his shoulders, Viktor lays the pool cue down in defeat, glaring at Dominik, who spreads his arms wide like his smile.

"Come at me, bro."

No one really beats Dominik, but the guy's always up for giving a lesson or two when he's not busy at his flower shop. Yeah, a werewolf and a flower shop. Stop and smell the moon lily, folks.

Chuckling, I reach over to the fry basket on the table I'm standing next to. Dipping it in ketchup before popping it in my mouth.

Best Fries Ever.

These are not your average fast-food fries. These fries are *magic.* They're always hot, crispy, and perfectly salted.

"*Enough,*" he hisses, the word slithers down the edges of my mind.

"*ENOUGH about the potato,*" Nim chuffs. "*We get it. Everyone gets it. It's not your basic French fry. I'm looking for real food now. Not a root vegetable. I'm blocking you temporarily.*"

"Average French fry," I retort. Throwing a pinch of ketchup-dipped French fries into my mouth for good measure.

"Who's next?" Dominik asks, holding the pool stick out like a sword, about who is getting killed next.

His words bring me out of my mind, from where I now feel a solid wall of Nim building. I put my hands up in mock surrender, my fingers curved around the neck of my beer.

"I'm not getting my ass beat again tonight, maybe next week?" I chuckle before taking a swig of my drink.

Garruk takes a large bite of his spicy chicken sandwich before pushing his chair back and standing up, sauntering towards the pool table. "It's time to lose, once and for all," he gruffs, racking the pool balls.

"Is Ambrose coming?" Viktor asks, while eating a buffalo wing.

I shrug my shoulders. "If he hasn't come already, he isn't coming."

Ambrose. Identical twin brother to Malik, but the resemblance stops at their faces. He's not cold, just...distant. Kind, in his own quiet way. Not sociable like his brother, and yes, he's a vampire too. That's a tale Malik only shares on his darkest nights, and I've only heard it once. I'm not sure if Ambrose has ever told a soul.

Dominik lines up his shot and sinks the three ball in the corner pocket with a satisfying crack. "Maybe next time," he says, straightening with a grin.

"Any new ideas for the fall festival, Sylas?" He asks, lining up his next shot.

"Yeah, Sylas, any fresh ideas?" Dominik echoes, mouthing at me behind Garruk's back, *"Keep talking, distract him."*

"I'll let you know when the time is right."

Truth is, I love planning the Fall Festival. But right now? I'm fresh out of ideas. And with the committee down to basically me and Nim, let's just say brainstorming with a snarky miniature dragon isn't exactly a think tank.

I pause, waiting for Nim to chime in. Silence. Great. The little menace still has his mental walls up.

"How's business?" I ask, turning towards Viktor. "Finally, time to get a partner, you know…with you getting older and all?"

"You wanna talk about old?" Viktor shoots back, wiping buffalo sauce off his fingers with a napkin. "Not all of us get to walk around looking like the damn Pumpkin King."

I chuckle, taking a bite of my cheesesteak sandwich.

Viktor grins, tossing his napkin aside. "Yeah, I'm thinking by spring I'll finally take on a co-manager. Business is booming. Hard to keep up when the surrounding towns have numerous tasks along with this one."

Viktor was a contractor. It was amazing what he could fix, repair, and build. His business is growing, and I'm not sure how he does it. Sure, he hires a crew when needed, but handling the business of it all, the help is long overdue.

Propping his pool cue against the table, Dominik eyes the double bacon cheeseburger that was just delivered. He drops into his seat and unwraps the paper surrounding it like it's one of the best things he's seen all day. He takes a massive bite. "So, I met Vera's granddaughter this morning. Looks like she and Jas are on their way to being best friends after some coffee and pastries."

I nod, already waiting for someone to bring up our newest visitor. Figures it'd be him. "Yeah, she stopped by the shop. She's an author."

Dominik's eyebrows shoot up. "Any good?"

I grab a fry, chewing slowly before clearing my throat. "I've got every one of her books on my shelves. She even signed a few today. Her books sell really well."

No way in the blessed realms am I telling them I've actually read them. I'd never hear the end of it.

Garruk turns a chair backward before straddling it, resting his broad arms along the top rail like he's settling in for a good story. A slow grin creeps across his tusked face. "So...is she cute?"

Sharp pangs of jealousy tighten in my chest before I can stop it. Damn it. This is ridiculous.

Viktor lets out a booming laugh, pointing his beer bottle at me. "Look at his face. That's a yes if I've ever seen one."

I scowl, but the corner of my mouth twitches despite myself. "Relax. She's here for her grandmother, not for dating."

Garruk holds up a hand. "No one said anything about dating. Yet," he says, winking. "Just curious if she'd like to stop by the best bakery in town, say hi sometime."

Dominik points a fry at Garruk, a wicked grin spreading. "Remember the time your cinnamon rolls had the consistency of a tire?" He pops the fry in his mouth.

Laughter ripples around the table, blending with the lively atmosphere of the bar. I shake my head, wiping my hands on a napkin before I finish off my sandwich.

Garruk groans, dragging a hand down his face. "One bad batch, Dominik. One. It was right when I was opening for the first time, and I kneaded the dough for too long. A Rookie mistake."

Viktor leans back in his chair, arms crossed. "Pretty sure the townsfolk used those rolls to patch the potholes on Maple Street."

Garruk flips him off before grabbing his beer. "Laugh it up. I'll remember this when you're begging for my shop's pumpkin loaf and chocolate croissants come fall."

6
Siren Song
RAENE

Home again. *Finally.* After a long day of surgery waiting rooms, doctor updates, and far too much hospital coffee, Grandma and I are back in her little cottage, tucked away from the chaos of the outside world.

There's a bigger hospital a couple of towns over, thank the Goddesses, because the idea of driving four hours back from the city with Grandma shifting uncomfortably in the passenger seat? Hard pass.

Her post-surgery rules and discharge papers read like a scroll in need of a binder: no bending past ninety degrees, no soaking in the tub—which is her favorite, no driving, plenty of naps, and, of course, mandatory physical therapy.

I may or may not have bribed her to follow the rules by gifting her a hot pink grabber device, topped with a ridiculous silver bow. She rolled her eyes, but she smiled. I call that a win.

Now we're tucked at the kitchen table like it's our tiny fortress, wine glasses in hand, Funyuns in a shared bowl, and a puzzle stretched between us. Not just any puzzle, either. This one is a cozy farmhouse, all golden fields and distant mountains, the porch so overloaded with hay bales, gourds, and pumpkins, and seasonal flair. It looks like a craft store and a scarecrow had a baby and named him September. Honestly, it's excessive, even for fall.

Grandma clicks an orange piece into place with a sigh loud enough to echo through the cottage. I freeze mid-sip, glass hovering near my lips. Immediate panic response. Is she in pain? Do I grab the magic cream? Call the doctor? Wrap her midsection in bubble wrap?

She waves me down with a dramatic flap of her hand, settling me in my seat. "I'm fine, sweetheart. This puzzle just makes me realize I probably won't be able to decorate for fall. You know, with my moving all slow. I can't bend. I can't even try out for Little League if I wanted to." She crosses her hands and mumbles a word under her breath. If you listen closely enough, it sounds similar to *'damn healing'*.

She props her chin in her hands, sighing like some damsel in distress. "I won't be able to decorate for fall this year. Not properly. Not like last year, my first year here."

"Oh!" She says excitedly, and another puzzle piece slips into place while I'm still struggling to find a corner piece. How is she this good at puzzles when she's recovering from hip surgery?

And of course, here it comes, the need for help I wouldn't want to poke with a four-foot stick. It's wrapped in pumpkin spice and tied with a cinnamon-scented ribbon. A ribbon that is probably edible. I'm all for helping my grandma with anything. Truly anything else. Bury a body in the backyard garden under enchanted lilies? No questions asked? I'm down.

I'm your alibi. Body comes back to life because who knows what the fuck is in this magic soil...well...but seriously, fall decorating?

My soul is drawing the line here, but my shoulders sag. I already know what I'm about to do. I can practically hear the universe laughing at me because it knows my heart.

With a groan, I set my glass down and pinch the bridge of my nose. "Fine. I'll help. Even if it means battling the forces of pumpkin...everything. You know you can ask me for anything. No matter how much I hate fall, I'll do this for you."

Her face lights up as she claps her hands, delight practically glowing from her like the sun.

I'm doomed.

And this...this is only the beginning. I feel it in my bones. I lean back in my chair and take a long sip of wine, already regretting my life choices and the next question.

"When were you thinking of decorating, Grandma?"

She pops another puzzle piece in place without missing a beat, smiling sweetly like this was all part of her scheme. "Oh, right after we finish this puzzle. The day's still young."

I stare at her, Funyun halfway to my mouth. The day's still young, huh? So much for a relaxing night in. I toss back the rest of my wine.

Fall: 1. Raene: 0.

"That's the last tote," I say, pulling it out of the crawl space and setting it beside the other five.

And this is just fall. Easter, Christmas, and who knows what else are still lurking back there like holiday hoarders waiting to pounce and conquer their special day.

Unscrewing my water bottle, I take a long drink, then glance at the sea of scarecrows peeking from the tote lids. "Grandma, honest question?"

She looks up from the TV.

"How many scarecrows does one woman need? Is this a cute cottage in the woods by day and haunted scarecrow manor by night?"

Do they come awake at night? "Should I be worried?"

She just shrugs, waving me off like I'm the crazy one.

Of course. Taking a lid off the nearest tote, I begin my work.

I weave the autumn garland across the mantel, golden leaves and tiny pumpkins tucked between eucalyptus and twinkling lights. It looks…cozy. I adjust a ceramic squirrel that's a little *too* happy about holding an acorn and a prickly hedgehog with blooms growing from a few quills, then step back to assess my work.

Oh, I know! I'm forgetting something. Her *'It's Fall Y'all'* pennant banner. Gotta throw some sarcasm in while I still can.

The dining room table is next. It gets the *full luxurious experience* of the *only day in my life* special. I lay down her ivory tablecloth, then add a fall-themed table runner decorated with pumpkins in two shades of pale blue and a perfect white Cinderella pumpkin.

A few faux pumpkins and sprigs of greenery complete the centerpiece. From the cabinet, I set out her fall dishes, pairing them with deep sage cloth napkins and gold pumpkin napkin rings. I move to the kitchen adding fall trinkets to the little window inlets and scatter autumn décor around the counter tops.

Out on the porch, I string a thicker garland along the railing, hang up a fall wreath, change the rug under the welcome mat to orange and white buffalo plaid, and prop a couple of scarecrows near the steps. Just not the whole scarecrow tribe. I promised her porch pumpkins and a new welcome mat. I mentally pencil that onto my to-do list.

Lastly, I swap out the living room pillows for ones stitched with leaves and a couple of woodland animals and one shaped like a pumpkin.

Draping a chunky knit blanket over Grandma's favorite chair, I take a look around. I hate to admit it but, just like that...the cozy little cottage somehow got cozier.

And for a moment, my thoughts drift.

Sylas. The man is practically autumn personified. Does his home look like this year-round? Like him. Cozy sweaters, warm, relaxing smiles with that dimple, and perfect white teeth with fangs. I wish he would drag the pulse on my neck. A shiver runs down my spine just thinking about it.

He is beyond gorgeous and has a sexy, yet book nerd vibe, and I love that. But that bookshop...that tree in the middle of the shop. How it shimmered like sunlight with its fall leaves. The magic in that place seems to bring everything there to life.

My thoughts scatter away, hearing my phone chirp as I walk through the door. I click the notification and see an email from my publisher. She knows I'm on vacation, but she tells me any news about my newest book release.

I click the screen off and shuffle to the couch, sinking into the cushions beside Grandma. One hand automatically reaches around to massage my lower back. Okay, seriously, does Everly Hollow have a chiropractor? And if so, is it one of those giant, coiled snake shifters that may be half man who just wraps around you until your spine sings the song of its ancestors? Because honestly, I'd really consider it.

Grandma pats my leg gently. "I truly appreciate the help, thank you."

I nod my head. "You're welcome Granny."

"Take yourself a hot bubble bath," she continues. "I've got the perfect salts. They'll take the ache right out of you."

"Let me guess...they're enchanted?"

"Yes!" She says, eyes twinkling as she winks.

Hell, I'd try anything at this point. "How about you relax here. Don't move. If you need me, holler. I'm going to soak for an hour, and for dinner...I'm cooking. We need a break from all these casseroles before I turn into one," I say.

"You don't have to tell me twice," she says, adjusting herself against her pillows.

Whatever is in these bath salts, it smells amazing. It has a floral scent wrapped in cashmere and vanilla. I added them per grandma's instructions, one heaping scoop, sprinkle it over the water, and let it dissolve sore muscles away.

I twist the cork off the bottle of bubble bath elixir and tip it into the steaming water. The label reads *Siren Song Tonic: For soothing aches, stubborn stress, and your spirit. May induce musical hallucinations and provide clarity.*

Figures.

The second the shimmering lavender liquid hits the water, soft notes begin to float around the bathroom. There are no speakers. No instruments. Just a slow, hauntingly beautiful melody that wraps around my body and settles in my chest. A whimsical, enchanting voice sings along, low and achingly beautiful, like moonlight being threaded into the stars.

I pull my braids up to a high pile at the top of my head, and sink into the tub, my limbs going loose and my muscles sighing in pleasure. Warmth creeps into every inch of me, and suddenly there is a... vision?

Sylas. I see him. He's here. While I'm in...here?

The note reaches a crescendo.

I immediately sit up, the water still high enough to cover my nipples, but it doesn't hide the swell of them. He's walking toward the tub, barefoot, with golden eyes filled with lust and hunger.

Have mercy...

With every step he takes, I hear the rustling of leaves and the faint scent of fall spices and citrus around him. I audibly gulp, because vision or not, my brain's doing a damn fine job with the details.

Fuck.

The cable knit sweater? Gone, dropped on the tiled floor. Good. That's where it belongs. *Fuck you, sweater. No one likes you anyway.* His shirt follows. *Oh my fae...*

Then, his belt falls to the floor with a soft *clink*, and my breath hitches.

The music in the air shifts. It's deeper, more sultry now, like it's taken a reading of my throbbing core and racing heartbeat. The bath itself is tuned into the horny fuckery that's curling through my limbs and flowing through my veins.

Sylas stands at the edge of the tub, running his hands through those loose, rich red curls, looking as good as a wet dream if I ever had one. The steam curls around him, and I keep my eyes wide because I'm afraid that if I blink, he'll disappear.

His eyes, those autumn-gold eyes, lock on mine. My gaze trails down his sculpted chest, his arms. His fingers slowly unzip his pants. And then...those, too, fall.

Oh, my...

This has to be a dream. A very vivid, enchanted, goddess-blessed dream here in this town.

Maybe I'll start praying to them.

He steps into the tub slowly, water shifting with his weight. It rolls over the edge in soft waves. I can't even hear it hit the ground. All I hear is the music and see him. A shiver ripples through me that has nothing to do with the water. He's coming to me, and my legs part. *Yes...crawl to me.*

Did this tub get bigger?

"Raene, are you blushing?" He asks in a husky growl, voice like velvet. "Is it the water, or is it me?"

He's right there. My hands are digging into the sides of the tub for purchase.

"Both," I whisper breathlessly without thinking.

He leans in, his mouth nips on my earlobe, and I release a whimper. "You should know," he rumbles, pressing a kiss to my collarbone. *I sigh.*

"In dreams like this, I can do anything..." His hand slides up my thigh, just beneath the surface. I can feel the pressure of it as his fangs gently graze my neck, making me shudder.

He meets my eyes, and right before his mouth meets my lips...

"Raene, baby?" Grandma's voice cuts in like a record scratch.

NO.

"After your bath, can you give me my grabber device?"

I bolt upright, nearly sending another wave over the edge of the tub. I'm alone. Just bubbles and heat. No more music. No more wet, and very sexy Sylas. A very loud *what the hell* is echoing through my brain.

Head tipping back with a groan against the tub, I sigh into the steamy air. "Everly Hollow, save me."

The vision of dreamy Sylas vanishes like mist. But the heat he left behind? That's still very real.

⁂

The soup is simmering on the stove. It smells comforting and nostalgic. With Grandma fresh out of surgery, I wanted something light, and chicken noodle felt like the safest bet. The savory aroma of slow-simmered broth, tender carrots, celery, onions, and shredded chicken fills the kitchen.

Before we eat, I help Grandma with her compression stockings and escort her to the bathroom with her walker, even though she insists she's perfectly capable on her own. I gently ignore her and help her anyway. I'm grateful she decided to take the bedroom on the bottom floor and make the guest room up the small flight of stairs when she bought this cottage.

Taking our seats, we help ourselves to the hearty soup and bread.

"The soup is delicious, Raene." She smiles, after helping herself to another spoonful.

"I learned from the best," I say, adding softened
butter to the bread and taking a well-deserved bite.

"So I have just one." She holds up her hand, holding two fingers close together to show how little she's indicating, "one small favor to ask you."

I'm curious as to what she needs now and if that something is fall-oriented. Do we have to decorate the backyard? I'm not sure how much more fall I can take. I mean, I just had some sort of tonic-drug-induced fever dream in the bathroom.

"This upcoming Wednesday is the town hall meeting," she says, her voice all sweet and innocent. "I'm supposed to attend. Would you be a dear and go for me?"

I set my spoon down. "Can't someone record it? What about ZOOM? Is that a thing here?"

"I just need you to take notes and take my place."

I thought about it. Tore off a piece of bread and popped it in my mouth, chewing slowly.

"Just notes, right? Will it be enough notes that make it worth my being there, or just enough notes where it could have been an email or posted on the town hall bulletin in a drafty hallway?"

She tilts her head to the side, chewing on the thought, slowly takes a spoonful of her soup into her mouth. "Just the right amount of notes that I need you to take."

"And?" I ask, stirring my spoon into lazy circles in the broth. "Is the whole town going to be there?"

"Only the important ones." Her head nods matter-of-factly.

I sigh.

Okay, that's good then. Sylas shouldn't be there.

He's not important. He can't be the mayor or anything, right? He just owns the bookstore. A beautiful, enchanted bookstore with a tiny dragon and a magical tree inside it. I highly doubt he'll be there, which is good. Really good. Because seeing him again, *in public*, knowing what I saw in that tub?

Yeah, that would be just a little awkward.

Let's just hope he's got better things to do than show up at a boring old town hall meeting.

7
A Fall Scented Trap
RAENE

The small town auditorium smells like cinnamon and eucalyptus, which feels on-brand for Everly Hollow. They even pulled out the fall decorations. Grandma beat them to it.

The walls are strung with twinkle lights and garlands of dried autumn leaves, and there is a pumpkin patch-worth of pumpkins and other gourds at the front entrance.

I'm sitting in a slightly creaky folding chair with a piping hot coffee in my hand, the to-go cup wrapped in the cutest honeycomb-textured brown cardboard sleeve. The steam rising from the lid is the only thing saving me right now. I have my phone on my lap, notepad ready.

Jasmira is sitting to my right, bringer of this blessed beverage. She brought me my new favorite, her honey lavender latte, like a magical caffeine fairy.

I love that she is thoughtful and sweet to bring her group of girls a drink from her cafe. To think I'm one of the *girls*. I think she also knows I don't like PSLs or anything even remotely acorn-spiced because the last time she offered me one, I smiled politely and made a weird face as I said, "No thanks."

She didn't push. Just gently passed me the Honey Lavender Latte, like it held the key to all the world's problems.

I'll venture out to newer flavors eventually, I swear. But this drink? It has a hold over me.

She also gave me the lowdown on who I'd be meeting tonight. And by lowdown, I mean species list. I'm pretty excited because it is pretty fucking cool to live in a place where humans and other beings can coexist.

There aren't that many mythical beings and creatures in the city. Some may live there, but I haven't seen anyone like I have here. Everyone just seems happy.

On the other side of me is Elora, she's a dryad, a tree spirit, and she is beautiful, ethereal. Like makes you question your entire aesthetic, kind of beautiful. Her deep chestnut brown hair is tied into the most perfect braid I've ever seen—hanging over her shoulder to her waist, with flowers and vines woven in.

Wisps escape around her face, softening her already flawless features. Freckles dot her nose and cheeks on tawny brown skin, and her big, round green eyes peer over the rim of her PSL as she crosses her legs. She's wearing a burnt orange cardigan, a white tank top, a baggy olive-green maxi skirt, and long brown boots with a flat heel. If I went on Pinterest and looked up *dryad in fall,* she would come up. She's shy but seems very sweet.

Jas told me Elora owns a farm, The Sunflower Farm & Market, to be exact, and she's the only child of Lady Sylva and Mayor Eldon

Caraway. Lady Sylva doesn't appear to be on stage, but apparently, she's human, which makes Elora half-human, half magical dryad, and fully gorgeous.

In front of me sits a goddess carved from the dreams of the sea. Smooth ivory skin glows under long, deep blue hair tumbling in loose waves down her back. Her turquoise eyes gleam, bright and hypnotic, as if she can lure the soul of anyone with a look. She's not really a goddess, but she looks like one. She's a siren. Think Jessica Rabbit, but with different hair and eyes, that'd be Oriana. Flitting around her head and shoulders is Corra.

Corra is a Tide Sprite. She's absolutely adorable, and I'm not sure if she'll approve, but she is. She's no bigger than a teacup. She told me herself that she is made of seafoam and moonlight. A beautiful coloring of blues, greens, and silver. She darts around like a hummingbird to talk to different people in the crowd.

Sitting on her right is Penelope, her ash blonde ponytail swings side to side as she shakes her head slowly, her amber eyes glaring at someone who appears to be an orc. Penelope is a kitchen witch and owner of The Sugarplum Bakery.

Garruk, the orc receiving the death glare, is the owner of The Stone Hearth Bakery. When they came into the room earlier, they immediately started making snide comments to one another. *Her cinnamon rolls are fluffier than his. His bread rises perfectly every time...*they're a love story waiting to happen.

In front of him, Dominik, the florist, is sitting with arms crossed and head thrown back in laughter as he talks to a troll sitting next to him.

Taking a sip of my latte, I look in the direction of where Poppy is glaring at Garruk. I lean back slightly to see who is next to him. The place is packed. There are trolls, minotaurs, pixies, witches, elves, centaurs, and more.

Even Nim is here, resting in an alcove, like it was built just for him.

Wait a minute.

If Nim is here, then...

Golden eyes meet mine, and my stomach flips.

Sylas.

Garruk is sitting next to Sylas. I was dreading this entire meeting after Grandma asked me to step in tonight and take her place, ever since that bathroom musical seance that conjured the sex demon that looked like Sylas with tousled hair and a wicked smile.

Feeling his warm breath on my neck as his fangs scraped against my skin...bathwater rippling around muscles I had no business imagining. I haven't been able to get him out of my head.

This is my first time seeing him since, and every time his eyes flick in my direction, I quickly avert my eyes. I pretend to be *very* interested in the contents of my latte. He can't possibly know what I saw in that fever-dream vision.

Right?

And stars help me, *he's smiling.*

"Simmer down, simmer down!" The voice booms across the auditorium. The Mayor's voice is loud, powerful, and strong-willed.

A quiet hush fell over us. He stands tall, his hands on the podium as he controls the room. With large white grey antlers growing from the top of his head. "We have a lot to discuss, so let's begin."

First up on the list of town concerns: expired potions. Apparently, we are *not* supposed to dispose of them in the community recycling bins. Why? Because the last time someone did, a magical mishap caused a sentient gelatinous being to form, and now it lives peacefully in the mountains. No one really knows what it eats or what it even does out there. The assumption is that it's living its best life.

A new solution is presented: a potion recycling company that will drop a box off on your porch. You fill it up, call the number on the tag, and they'll come collect.

Next, a pixie light ordinance. Due to the glow-moth season approaching, *I have no idea what a glow-moth is and will have to ask someone knowledgeable later.* The streetlights must be turned down a notch because the brightness may be confusing to them this season. Just as Mayor Caraway clears his throat to move to the next item, there's a sound. Knock. Knock. Two sharp raps echo at the double door entrance. A few whispers ripple through the auditorium. "You'd think after all this time, he'd remember," someone giggles. "Oh, that's right." The mayor runs a hand through his salt and peppered hair, giving a shy smile. "Malik, come on in," he calls out, voice loud and warm.

The door creaks open, and in walks Malik. He has a cold aura, but kind, if that makes sense. He's timeless and extremely handsome, wearing black slacks, black shoes, and a black vest with a matching tie. He doesn't just walk in, he glides. Oriana turns around in her seat, a smile beaming on her face as she pats the empty seat beside her.

It was also shared with me that Malik is a vampire and newly engaged to Oriana. They're a striking couple. He grabs her gently by the chin before sitting and kisses her so softly, she practically melts against him.

Corra is darting around them happily as he takes his seat. She perches herself on the back of Oriana's chair, her form in shades of blues and greens with an iridescent pearl sheen that glimmers in the light.

I take another sip of my latte, still at the perfect temperature, letting the honey lavender lull me into my thoughts. I love how my brain begins to drift. Maybe I should write a vampire-siren romance next. Title it *Sin & Salt*. Or maybe *Wicked Tide*. I am still blissfully tuned out when the mayor clears his throat and taps his mic.

Tap. Tap. Followed by a loud, piercing *screeeech* of feedback in the auditorium, causing a few people, myself included, to wince.

"Now then," the Mayor says, straightening his suit jacket proudly. "Before we wrap up, let's talk about the upcoming Fall Festival."

I take another sip, letting my mind drift again as I hold my latte with one hand and type in the notes in my phone with the other.

Something about hayrides, booth signups, and pie donations for the pie-throwing booth. Whatever. I'm only here to take notes, then debrief back at the cottage like the good granddaughter I am.

"This year," he continues, with way too much cheer, "we have our wonderful coordinator spearheading the event, Sylas Ashvale."

Hearing his name makes my hand tighten around my latte, and my other hand fumbles with the phone. No one saw that. I quickly glance at Jas, and her eyes are focused on the mayor.

"...and with Vera Whitmore being out due to an unexpected surgery after signing up to volunteer, her granddaughter Raene Hart has graciously taken her place."

My stomach drops.

The words hit me like someone threw a pie in *my* face. Graciously?! I graciously did no such thing. This has Grandma written all over it. She knew. Of course, she knew.

She told me I was coming here to *take notes* at the meeting. "*Just notes*," she said, spooning soup and nodding her head innocently.

Lies.

Everyone's heads turn to get a good look at me. I stand out, I'm new. No one's seen me before, and according to Sylas, I look like my grandmother. Which, at this moment, feels like an unfortunate curse.

I sneak a glance across the auditorium at Sylas. He's talking with the minotaur, Viktor, I think, and Dominik and Garruk. His head shifts, like he senses me looking. There's a small smile tugging at his lips. One of those soft, grateful ones. Like he's genuinely relieved I'm helping him. But I didn't sign up for this.

The room breaks into polite applause, while I'm internally screaming.

Next to me, Jas leans in and whispers, "Do you need another latte? Or want me to find a sedative?"

I take a long, long sip of my drink and place my phone face down on my lap.

The Fall Festival. With *Sylas Ashvale*, when he looks like *that*? I'm going to need both.

The meeting ends, and a few people stand to leave. Others turn in their seats to talk to their friends and neighbors, while others flock to the tables of food in the back of the room.

I follow the drift of the crowd that is more food-motivated, eventually finding myself near the refreshment table. Someone hands me a plate of what they proudly call *Iced Cinderberry Cake,* topped with fresh berries of dark reds and purples. I fork a small piece and take a bite, and nearly melt on the spot.

"Raene?" I turn to the hearty voice of a short, broad-shouldered troll. Her skin is pale gray with a light lilac undertone, her tusks shimmering in a bronze polish, and her thick silver-streaked hair is tied in a low bun.

"Flora," she says in a soothing voice, offering me a warm, calloused hand. "I'm a friend of your grandmother's and the owner of Oak & Moss Apothecary."

"Oh! Yes, hi! She always talks about you, so I feel like I've known you for a while." I laugh gently, shaking her hand. "The cream you made is *amazing*. She says she's feeling way better already. She'll be heading back to physical therapy soon."

Flora beams. "Glad to hear it. I'm popping by to see her tomorrow in person. You should stop by sometime, too. We've got a calming tonic that helps when you're surrounded by chaos...or men." She lets out a hearty laugh.

My eyes flick across the room to Sylas. Surrounded by his friends, hands tucked into pockets. Speak of the fae himself.

"Definitely," I say quickly, before Flora gives me a cheeky wave and turns to claim a thick slice of what can only be described as chocolate decadence.

It's got layers of rich cake, creamy frosting, a pile of fresh berries on top, and it's dusted with powdered sugar. I look down at my own plate, wondering if it would look too odd to top the half-eaten slice with another slice of another dessert.

Before I can spiral deeper into my dessert-topped thoughts, Sylas steps into my peripheral.

"Raene," he says.

My name on his lips, in that voice of his, is both grounding and...dangerous. I turn slowly.

"I just wanted to say thank you for stepping in for your grandmother. That was incredibly kind."

I stare at him, blinking. *Don't think of the bathroom.* "There's no need to thank me."

I lean on my left leg, popping my hip out. "It was a setup. A fall scented trap—*very* Scooby-Doo—also, I'm not sure I'm doing it." I fork another bite and pop it into my mouth, his eyes watching the movement as it slides between my lips.

His lips part, showing his fangs. He quickly licks his lips, and his brows raise in amusement. "You sound so sure."

Shaking my head, my eyes hit the ground before they met his. "I don't do autumn, Sylas." The corner of his mouth curled up just the faintest.

"Besides, I'm going to talk with my grandmother," I say matter-of-factly, like a child needing to ask for permission.

He steps closer. *Too close.*

My God, he smells good. All the notes of his scent mixed with something deeply male that I want to bottle it up and name it *Terrible Decisions, No Regrets*. I wrap both hands tighter around my plate, so I don't do something impulsive like tuck his hair behind his pointed ear.

What is wrong with me?

He smiles, the kind that makes his eyes crinkle slightly. "I'm sure if Vera didn't want you to do this, she wouldn't have told Eldon you graciously volunteered."

I roll my eyes at him. "There's that word, *graciously*."

He shrugs, rocking back on his heels. "I'm just saying, if you don't want to let the town down...or your grandmother...maybe sleep on it."

His fingers rake through his thick, loose red hair, letting them fall over his shoulders in waves. Then he holds out his hand. "Your phone?"

I cock my head, looking him over. "Why?"

"So you can text me. Just in case. If you do decide to help, you'll need my number. You know, for planning purposes."

Right. *Planning.* I pull my phone from my back pocket, placing it into his waiting hand. My fingers brush the palm of his hand, and it's totally fine. I'm fine. It wasn't distracting at all.

He taps quickly, then looks back up. His golden eyes sparkle as if they cast a glow. "If you do this, I'd really appreciate it. I'd love to hear new ideas."

Across the room, Nim's tail sways lazily like an annoyed cat from his shadowed alcove.

Sylas glances up, nose wrinkling slightly as he glares at the dragon. I have *no idea* what just passed between them, but I cover my mouth to hide the grin that tries to break free.

"Anyway, text me, either way," he says, handing the phone back, and I slide it in my back pocket, "and we'll schedule our first meeting if you're up for it."

Then, with absolutely zero shame, he reaches out and takes a piece of *my* cake, pops it into his mouth, and sucks the frosting off the tip of his thumb.

My breath hitches. *Did that just happen?*

He gives me a small smile, turning to leave, but not before saying, "See you later, Raene."

I stand there, needing a moment as my racing heart files a noise complaint.

Yeah, I'm going to need Flora's calming tonic.

8
Sooner rather than later
SYLAS

She definitely fills out those jeans. Those hips, thighs...and that ass. I stopped to stare. I went to make us drinks as soon as she arrived after closing. When I asked what she wanted to drink, she told me anything, as long as it wasn't conceived in the fall. I made her a white chocolate mocha, and I think that was a safe choice.

By doing this for hundreds of years, I don't even need the recipe book anymore. But I leave it there for decoration. She chose the large armchairs near the fireplace for sitting with end tables beside them.

Standing in front of me, dark hair flowing down her back, an oversized blue sweater that slips off her left shoulder, revealing radiant, deep brown skin. Her back is turned as she pulls a book off the wall to read.

I knew she would text me back, but I didn't know what her response would be. I'm grateful for the help. I like being around her, but I'm not sure how spending all this time together is going to feel.

After all, she doesn't seem enthusiastic about the change of the season. I place a mug on her end table and my pumpkin caramel latte on mine. The ceramic hitting the wooden tabletop startles her. She immediately shuts the book.

"Those aren't for sale." I smile.

"Sorry." She quickly tries to reshelve it.

Fuck. I'm off to a bad start.

"Raene, I'm kidding! Well," my hand passes through my hair and settles on the back of my neck, "they aren't for sale. They can't leave the building, but you're more than welcome to read it."

She brings the book back towards her, holding it to her chest as if it's precious and it is. These beautiful leather books, where she is standing, talk of our history here at Everly Hollow.

"Come on over here and bring it with you," I wave her over. "I wanted to show them to you tonight anyway."

It's a good thing she picked the first volume. She hands me the book and sits down in her chair, grabbing a small notebook and pen from her bag. Her body relaxes in the seat, getting comfortable before grabbing her mug, taking a sip, and licking the whipped cream from the top of her lip. Of course, my eyes track the movement. Every time I'm around her, my senses are in overdrive, especially the scent of her.

"You make a great mocha." She smiles, lifting the mug as a toast. "Is there anything you can't do?"

"Juggle," I say.

She laughs, shaking her head slightly as she sits her mug down.

"I'm joking, I'm a great juggler." I wink.

"Before we start," she says, eyes darting to the fire. "I'm sorry about the town hall. For how I acted?"

Her eyes meet mine again. "I really don't want to let my grandmother down, and the whole town hates her because I said no. She's also healing, and I don't want her to stress. Her body doesn't need that when recovering."

I nod my head.

"But when I say I don't do fall, I really mean it. I don't do fall."

"Noted." I give her a stern nod to show her I mean it.

"So there are seven goddesses?" She leans forward into the arm of the chair, her hands holding her second drink of the evening, this one a caramel macchiato.

I nod my head. I briefly went over the town, some history, and now I've named all the goddesses.

"Ruskaya is our Goddess of Autumn. She represents harvest, abundance, comfort, hearth & change."

Leaning back, my fingers wrap loosely around the warm mug, my eyes watching the movement of the crackling fire. "Most people outside of Everly Hollow have never heard of her, but she is woven into everything here. The trees, our fall traditions and even the shift of the wind and change of the leaves when September comes."

Raene listens, only pausing to sip from her mug. The steam wafting above the liquid.

"It is said that the seven divine Goddesses were born from the breath and light of the stars. Ruskaya was known as the Goddess of endings that also felt like beginnings. She helped people change and grow, reminding them that there is beauty in all things, even after they end."

"I like that, but if I didn't participate," she says with a sly smile. "Will we need to spread pumpkin spice fig jam above every doorway, before locusts come for the pumpkin patch and everyone starts running around saying, 'Oh my Gourd?'"

A laugh escapes me before I can stop it.

She sits up straight in her seat and on her chest. "Oh shit, am I going to be smited?"

"No, you're not going to get punished if you change your mind about not helping with the festival."

I close the book, looking at her. She just sits there watching me, the tension leaving her shoulders and relaxing. "I really could use the help. I need fresh ideas, I want to make it something more memorable and fun."

Pen tapping her notepad, her eyes dart upward as she thinks. Her eyes catch on to Nim on a low branch of the tree. He's sprawled on his back, his paws bent over the golden scales of his underbelly. He is adorable when he isn't talking.

She asked me earlier how old he was, and I told her I wasn't sure of how old his egg was when I was gifted him on my third birthday. But Nim and I have been pretty inseparable ever since.

"So what do you already do, and let's work with that. Build up on some ideas?" she asks, clicking her pen.

I grab my notebook and pen from the side table and open it up. "Well, typically we start with a fall feast on day one."

She begins to write it down, but then strikes through it. "How about we make the feast last?"

Starting to chime in, she holds up her hand. I gesture to her. She has the floor.

"I think a feast at the beginning is too much. It seems too final. Plus a lot of good eating. Then there is still food, I'm assuming at the booths that are held right?"

I nod my head and smile. Her voice is tinged with a dash of excitement, and it's fucking cute.

"Let's move it to the last day of the festival. You said it lasts seven days, so we will have a big feast on the last day. We can have music, lights, and a lot of tables and seating, maybe potluck style. We can ask the bakeries for desserts that we can purchase, and maybe a few that they would like to donate?" She writes all this down and then glances up at me.

"What do you think?" She shrugs, her eyes giving me a deadpan stare, because truly she doesn't care. Does she?

"I think that you're enjoying this." I give her a wicked grin, and she shifts her hips in her seat.

"No, I'm not," she says, wrenching her eyes from me until they land on her mug.

"The drinks here are fabulous. Perfectly hot." She takes a long sip, and hums, licking those lips again.

"And the company is fine, I guess," she sighs, but a sly smile dances on her lips. "This reminds me of writing. When you're brainstorming new ideas. It's fun. Fall, not so much fun."

"Okay, so let's say we move the feast to the last day." I edge closer in my seat, notebook in hand. "What do we do on day one?"

She rests her chin on her hand, fingers tapping a slow rhythm on her cheeks. She looks around the shop as if inspiration will spread its wings and fly right for her. She eyes Nim again.

"I like kites," she says out loud, her eyes never losing focus on him.

Was this an inner thought that somehow escaped? That was random.

"I like kites, too?" I chuckle, curious to see where she is going with this.

She rolls her eyes playfully. "What I meant was, I like kites. Of course, they're only reserved for the best season ever." Her wink catches me off guard, but I still can't pull my eyes away from that pretty mouth of hers. "But this is *the* Fall Festival," she finishes. A playful glint dances in her eyes. "How do you feel about opening with a lantern parade?"

A lantern parade? That's not a bad idea. It would be magical. Those attending would have something new and different. We can supply the lanterns, decorations, and tables with benches so everyone can participate. I can enchant the paper so that once a flame is added, they will float until the flame extinguishes, then the lantern will fade away like a dusting of gold sugar.

"It could be a night event," she continues, scribbling it all down. "So we don't have to rush into anything during the day. Just let people arrive, decorate a lantern individually or as a family, enjoy the booths of food and trinkets for sale. Then, as the sun sets, we kick things off."

"I like it. See what you did there?" I lift my mug toward her in a mock-toast. "You're bringing your love of summer into fall."

"What else am I supposed to do, Ash?" She shrugs, lifting her mug and taking a long, satisfying drink. Her lids flutter closed for a moment.

Ash? Did she just nickname me? No one has shortened my last name and called me by it.

A flicker of something stirs in my chest. Warm and unexpected. It sounds intimate coming from her lips. Like, I'm deeply familiar with her when I shouldn't be. Yet.

My mug hovers near my mouth, but I don't drink. I watch her over the rim, trying to decide what the hell that nickname just did to me.

I hope she says it again.

We're both looking over our notes after another two hours of discussion. I'm four deep into another festive pumpkin drink.

Raene snorted when she eyed the third mug as she sipped from her bottle of water. She said too much sugar would keep her awake at night.

"So." She clears her throat. "The festival is for seven days starting on the first day of fall."

I nod my head.

"Which this year, it is September twenty-second."

"Yes, and planning typically starts now."

"Of course you do," she barely mumbles under her breath, not realizing I can hear her.

"What was that?" I ask, my head tilting slightly to the side.

She ignores me but her lips curve into a small smile. "So we start with the Autumn Lights and Lantern Parade on the first day," she says, circling it on her paper before glancing up, looking for my approval.

"Yes."

"Then the second day, we're doing the Golden Twilight Market. From the golden rays of the sun to the twilight of the day, we'll have more booths for shopping, food booths, and the adults will also see drink stands with a Sip Passport as they go from booth to booth."

The Sip Passport is actually a brilliant idea and another fun thing to throw in, especially for adults wanting to try new drinks or even just tea or coffee.

"Days three and four are the carnival..."

"Nope." I say, shaking my head, cutting her off.

Not this again. This is what caused us to only be this far in the planning. She wants to do two days of a carnival.

No.

And fuck clowns.

I shouldn't have told her the budget is limitless.

"Ash." She looks at me, her big, round, bright honey eyes.

"No. No carnival." I stand up to go wash out my mug. "No clowns…I mean, no circus acts either. We don't allow carnies in our town."

She giggles but stands to follow me to the coffee bar. "You know a carnival would be fucking awesome. The families would love it, and not just the kids, the adults too. We could even do a pie throwing contest too. You wanted fresh ideas? I'm giving them." She holds her hands out wide before tucking them back into her back pockets.

Great. Now I'm thinking about her ass again. I turn back to finish scrubbing the mug, giving it a quick rinse before drying and shelving.

"Okay, you have me there," I say, turning around and leaning against the bar.

"But really, Ash, clowns?" Her nose wrinkles a bit before she laughs, and it's the cutest fucking thing ever.

"We can do a carnival but no circus or clowns, but I will settle for a petting zoo. The baby animals at Elora's farm would be a hit for the kids," I say.

She holds out her hand. "Deal."

I reach out, taking her hand in mine. It's small, soft, but feels perfect in mine. I give it a quick shake before releasing her. Holding it for a second too long. Maybe two.

"How about I order us a pizza?" I ask, voice a little rougher than intended. "Then we can power through the rest of this list."

She purses her lips. "Nice change in subject. Is the food magical, too?"

I smirk. "Well, it's pretty damn good, stays piping hot in the box, and won't get ruined in delivery. So maybe."

"You didn't have to persuade me this hard," she says, turning away with a shrug. "You had me at *stays hot.*"

There's a notebook in front of each of us and the pizza within reach. I stretch my legs under the table. This might be my favorite part of festival planning so far.

She licks a bit of red sauce off her thumb before grabbing another napkin, and I swear I almost groan. The little noises she makes when she takes that first bite?

Damn.

She has one leg curled under her as she takes notes, proudly eating her pizza. I tear my gaze away and tap my pen against my notebook. Focus.

"So, day five," I say, drawing her attention back from whatever pizza trance she was floating in. I lean back in my chair and give her a look. "How about a ball?"

Her eyes go wide and blink like she misheard me. I watch the wheels turn, and realization dawns as her lips curl into a slow smile.

"That is *your* idea?" she asks, setting down her crust and wiping her hands before pulling her notebook closer. "Look at you, Ash, throwing in fresh ideas of your own."

I shrug, but the grin I'm wearing is cheesy as hell while she sprinkles me with pride. "I figured the ladies would love it. Evening in the town square, twinkle lights, nice music, refreshments, gowns and suits…what's not to love?"

Her pen is already scribbling. "Everyone can dress up as extravagantly as they want. We can have a dance floor, oh, and definitely live music!"

My brows raise. "See? I plant the seed, and you water it. Together we bloom."

She laughs. "Oh, you wish, pumpkin."

She taps the pen to her lips, thinking, then points it at me. "We need a signature cocktail, something moody and dramatic for the sixth night! Catered just for adults. Low lights, live music…we make it an experience."

I nod, jotting it down. "Drinks. Velvet. Deep blues and purples."

"Then on day seven, we end on a feast."

I write it down, tap my pen to the paper, but my eyes are still on her. "Remind me why you don't think you're good at this?"

She smirks. "Oh, I know I'm good at planning, Ash. But for all of this," her finger twirls slowly in the air, "I was tricked. Hoodwinked"

I lean closer, elbow on the table, chin in my hand. "If this is you tricked, I am itching to see what you do on purpose."

The cool air greets us as I lean against the door frame of the shop's entrance. I feel pretty good about the Fall Festival right now. I went in not knowing what to add or change. I knew I needed to freshen it up, and when Vera volunteered, I was excited, but with Raene being a writer, she's a natural. She's creative and sees the little details in things.

She pulls the edges of her sweater sleeves down, catching the fabric in the palm of her hand.

"I had fun," she says, voice light. "The planning, getting to know you, and...the town."

I nod, and it's harder than it should be to keep my voice even. "I'm grateful for your help, Raene." I mean it more than I expected to. The streetlamps catch in the shine of her hair and the softness of her face. She's beautiful.

Fingers dancing in the air, she gives me a small wave. "I'll text you."

Then she smiles while tossing over her shoulder, "Bye, Ash." She hops into her car, readies herself to leave, and drives away.

And fuck it if I don't hope she texts me sooner rather than later.

9
Sweet Potato Hand Pies
Raene

*S*unday evening texts...

Me: *So, where are we plotting autumn world domination from?*

Ash: *That depends. Do you prefer coffee, pastries, or people watching?*

Me: *All three. But if I had to choose, coffee wins. You host at the bookshop, I'll surprise you with food and drinks?*

Ash: *If you're bringing those indecent little noises you made over pizza last time. Then yes, definitely, bring food.*

Me: *First of all, rude, but I won't kink shame. Second of all... they were delicious noises. The pizza was indeed magical.*

Ash: *Told you. Magic pizza. Okay, bookshop tomorrow, late morning. Monday's are pretty slow.*

Me: *Okay, see you.*

I hit the button on the blender, sending it to a roaring echo around the kitchen. Grandma is being picked up by Flora for physical therapy. I'm heading to get coffee and treats, which will be the main highlight of my day. At least, before meeting Ash, who is at his bookshop for more Fall Festival planning.

It's not that I didn't like spending time with Ash. I did enjoy being around him. He's too beautiful not to look at. And as for the new nickname I gave him? *Ash* just felt right. Sy just sounded too weird.

I love planning. It's a fun project to do while I'm not writing and trying to enjoy a five-week break, but I didn't envision myself doing this.

Grandma was so excited when I came home after the town hall meeting, and I told her, with gritted teeth and a too-bright smile, that I would help with the festival planning.

"You sure you don't want me to take you to your appointment?" I ask as she shuffles into the kitchen with her walker.

I pour us each a glass of the strawberry mango smoothie, insert a straw, and set her glass on the table. Taking a careful seat, she waves me off, reaching for the glass and takes a slow sip.

"I'll be okay. You have your plans. I appreciate what you're doing."

"Did I really have a choice?" I lift my glass, stirring it lazily with the straw before taking a sip. The sweet-tart flavor is delicious and refreshing. There's no bite in my tone, just an edge of honest curiosity.

She chuckles. "You had choices. You just made the one that made your grandma happy."

Her eyes sparkle in delight, and I know from the look on her face, she's proud. There is pride in her voice. Ash was right. I didn't want to let the town down. I didn't want to let my grandmother down. I wanted my presence here not to bring stress, and if this is what she needs help with during her recovery, then so be it. I am here to help. No matter how much I dislike the season. She needs me, and along with a few of her friends here, she's counting on me.

Grandma takes another sip of her smoothie, then sets the glass down with a soft *clink* on the table top. Her eyes flick to the chair across from her. "Sit with me for a minute, baby. We have time."

I make my way to the table, take a seat, and hold the glass in my hands as her hands stay folded on the table in front of her.

"I know this Fall Festival wasn't what you had planned," she says, her voice gentle. "But you're helping the town, you're helping someone in need, making new friends…"

She gives me a look, and I arch an eyebrow at her. "And most importantly, you're helping me. That means more than I can say. I didn't want to tell them I couldn't do it when this sprung up on me." She gestures toward her hip.

I look down at my drink. "I said yes because I love you. I didn't want you disappointed in me, or stressed."

"I know, sweetie, but I wouldn't be disappointed, mad, or stressed." She reaches across the table and lays her hand over mine. Her skin is soft and warm as she gives my hand a tight squeeze. "I know fall's not your favorite. Hasn't been for a long time."

My heart tightens. I don't say anything. The silence in the air is thick, heavy.

"I don't mean to push," she says. "But maybe...maybe helping bring a little joy to this season could help you take some of it back as well." Her head tilts in anticipation of my response.

I nod slowly, giving her hand a soft squeeze in return. Her smile returns, small and sweet. "Besides, no one can rock a flannel like a boss and carry a clipboard with a checklist like a Hart girl."

That gets a laugh out of me, even past the lump in my throat. "I'll see you later," I say before gulping down the rest of my smoothie, rinsing out the glass in the sink. "I need to make a few stops before I go to the bookshop."

"Well, have fun. Flora will be here in a minute." She relaxes into her seat. "I'm excited to see what you two come up with."

I smile back. My nerves are buzzing. Let the day begin.

"Do you want any pastries to go with your drinks?" Jas asks, sliding a cinnamon-roll latte into the sturdy cardboard carrier beside the PSL she's already labeled for Ash.

"Actually..." I tap my card on the reader, watching the screen flash green. "I'm going to hit up one of the bakeries. Try something new."

Jas cocks her head. "Which one?"

I hesitate. "Umm...I'm not sure yet."

She grins, leaning in like she's about to share a town secret. "Choose wisely. And try not to get caught."

My brows pinch together. What does she mean? *Caught.*

"Caught?"

"Oh yeah." She laughs. "Poppy and Garruk? Those two are in a never-ending battle of baked goods."

She begins to count off her fingers. "Cinnamon rolls vs. cookies, croissants vs. pies, it's a serious feud. I carry both in the café to keep the peace. But if you go to one and skip the other," she says, crossing her arms and smiling, "it's like picking a side in a cake-battered war."

I chew on my lip. "So what do I do?"

"Play it safe. Stop by both. They each run a daily special, and it's totally worth it. Just...avoid eye contact if they ask whose you liked better. Trust me. It's safer that way." She nods her head.

"Thanks for the warning and the coffee." I grin, grab the carrier, and head to the door. Mentally preparing myself for my next mission, or the battle of the pastries.

I step inside The Stone Hearth Bakery, the soft thrum of low rock music buzzing gently through the speakers. The smell of freshly baked bread dances in the air along with a sugary scent. Together, the two are a tantalizing concoction.

A few tables hold guests. Some read a newspaper, a book, or scroll through their phones. A small coven of older women giggle and laugh at some shared secret, as they nibble on their pastries.

I make my way to the long glass display case, my eyes hooked on the delectable, baked treats in the display. Garruk walks out of the back in his apron, barely able to cover the large expanse of his chest.

"Welcome, Raene!" he beams, holding a tray of muffins with a streusel topping that looks delicious. His smile stretches wide, tusk to tusk, all pride and warmth.

News travels fast.

"Hello, Garruk," I say, giving him a small wave with my free hand. "I just wanted to pop in and see what your special is for today."

"Well, I've got two today," he says, holding up one of the muffins before gently nestling it into the display case. "Spiced carrot with golden raisins and a spiced streusel topping, or apple cider crullers, fresh from the fryer with a dusting of cinnamon sugar glaze on them."

Decisions. Decisions. Since Ash is a total slut for anything fall-flavored, he can have the donut.

"I'll take one of each."

"Good choice." He grabs his tongs, picks up a donut, and slides the donut into a small, crisp white paper sleeve before placing it gently into a small brown box. He carefully sets the muffin in parchment, before placing that into the box. He ties it off with twine and adds a circular sticker of the bakery name with a logo of a cartoon orc gleefully devouring a pastry.

"Thanks so much, they look amazing," I say, tapping my card to pay.

"Best baked goods in town." He winks. "Don't be a stranger!"

I walk out, turn about ten paces to the right, and I'm at my next stop.

The little bell above the door jingles as I step inside The Sugarplum Bakery. The warm scent of vanilla, sugar, and something sweet, tinged with something else I can't put my finger on, smells amazing. Someone could probably catch a sugar high just *breathing* between here and Stone Hearth without a single granule on your tongue.

The walls are painted a soft blush pink, with one accent wall behind the counter in lavender. Rows of pastel cake stands in robin's egg blue, lemon yellow, powder pink, and lilac line the counters, each one showing off frosted treats too pretty to eat.

Behind the counter, Penelope finishes checking out a customer. They thank her and walk out with two large pink boxes stacked in their arms.

"Well, if it isn't our newest little Autumn conspirator," she says, grinning as she wipes her hands on a pink and white tea towel. "I'm so excited to see you again, Raene!"

"You too, Penelope." I smile warmly.

"Please, call me *Poppy*." She dusts a bit of flour off her deep blue apron before she eyes the box tucked under my arm.

"Judging by that suspiciously familiar brown box wrapped with twine," she teases, "you've already been by Stone Hearth."

I press my lips together, not quite guilty but definitely caught. "I couldn't help myself." I shrug. "The spiced carrot muffins looked like an experience."

"Well," she says, with a wink, flipping open the curved glass display, "you're about to meet *my* special of the day." She plucks one from the tray, breaks it in half with her hands, and offers me a piece.

I graciously accept.

"Sweet Potato Hand Pies. Fresh from the oven with a flaky, golden crust. A cinnamon, nutmeg, and brown sugar sweet potato filling. I even added decorative sugar on top because I believe dessert should sparkle. Oh, and a dash of magic." She takes a bite and closes her eyes, savoring the taste of the creation she made by hand and baked.

It tastes like perfection and sin, because these may be my new weaknesses. I eat the half she has given me in a few more bites. They taste like...*home*. Like my Mom's sweet potato...I shake myself loose from the memory.

"I'll take four," I say. "I think my grandmother would love to have these as a dessert later."

Poppy clutches her chest, her amber eyes shining brightly, like I just handed her a James Beard award. "A girl after my own heart."

She places a sheet of light blue parchment into a lavender box and gently nestles the four hand pies inside, then closes the lid with a routine flick.

With a small wave of her fingers and a few soft words, a deep purple satin ribbon shimmers into existence and ties itself into a perfect bow around the box. A large square sticker blooms beneath it, proudly stamped with The Sugarplum Bakery in swirly script.

"That's incredible!" I say, reaching into my purse to pay. "Thank you so much."

Her cheeks bloom a soft pink at the compliment. "You're most welcome."

She gently tucks both bakery boxes into a large brown paper bag. "Easier carrying and hey, let's plan a girl's night soon, yeah? I think we'd have a blast."

"I'd actually love that." I shake my head in agreement, returning her broad smile.

As I turn to leave, she grabs her chalk and follows me out, the bakery door swinging open behind us. She kneels on the sidewalk and adds *Sweet Potato Hand Pies—TODAY'S SPECIAL* in a curly script to her pastel pink chalkboard. She even draws a cute little hand pie below it. Her ponytail sways with each stroke.

"Ohhh?" A deep voice carries across the sidewalk.

I look over, standing next to Poppy as she finishes her drawing. Garruk strolls out of his shop, wiping his hands on a towel before tossing it over his shoulder. His tusks glint in the sunlight.

"Didn't know you had time to visit *both* bakeries today," he says loudly, arms folding over his broad chest. "Thought you already made your pick."

Before I can even speak, Poppy doesn't miss a beat. She stands up slowly and turns around, arms folded. "She saved the best for last, *Garbear*."

She gives him a saccharine-sweet smile, tucking wisps of hair behind her ear. The way she said that nickname sarcastically makes it sound like a hex.

"You wish you were the best," he fires back, lips twitching with amusement. "If those hand pies were any flakier, they'd ghost you after a first date."

"Ha!" She places her hands on her hips. "That's rich coming from someone whose cookies once had the consistency of a hockey puck," she says, flipping her ponytail over her shoulder. "I'm sure the children with a loose tooth or two would *love* to nibble on them. Maybe strike a deal with the Tooth Fairy? Maybe a few dogs?"

Garruk just grunts. His mouth turns into a frown, as he walks back inside, shaking his head and mumbling something incoherent under his breath.

Poppy beams, brushing chalk dust from her fingers. "Ignore him," she says sweetly. "He knows I win every time."

Shaking my head, I try not to laugh while holding the bag of baked goods in one hand and the coffee carrier in the other. I make my way toward the bookshop. This town is sweet with some spice, and I'm here for it.

10
Where the lanterns float
SYLAS

"*Lose the suspenders...*" Nim says down the bond.

"No," I say out loud.

I look down at my brown dress shoes, deep brown slacks, white shirt, a few buttons undone at the top, and sleeves stopping mid-forearm. To top it off, suspenders in a deep, burnt orange. I wanted something I feel good in. Being around Raene...also makes me feel good.

I reach for the band around my wrist, ready to tie my hair up, but think better of it and let it fall loose instead.

"*Your nervousness is showing*," Nim growls.

"Hush, you're not helping the situation. She's going to be here any minute."

The bell jingles and she walks in, wearing white sneakers, black leggings, and an oversized gray tee with three little flowers and their names scrawled beneath them. The shirt slides off one shoulder like it's trying to tease me on purpose. Her hair is in a half-up, half-down style. I love that she's curvy and tall, but she still has to look up to me.

I don't know where the fuck that came from.

"I come bearing treats!" she sings-songs, making her way towards me.

"Tell her she's the treat," he chuffs. "I know you're thinking about it."

"Sounds great!" I say, already smiling.

Sending a mental *shut the fuck up* to Nim. I motion to the quiet table near the window, just a few feet from the register. She sets the drink carrier and bag down on the table, placing her purse beside it.

"Pumpkin tears for you." She hands me the coffee cup. She takes the stopper out of her drink, gives it a good inhale, and hugs it to her chest. "Cinnamon roll."

Taking a seat and making herself comfortable, she puts the stopper in her mouth and sucks the coffee remnants off the stick.

Fuck.

I take the stopper from my cup and toss it in the drink carrier. I take a slow sip, trying to shift my focus anywhere else, anywhere but her mouth.

She takes a small pie out of the bag and hands it to me. "You have to try this."

I hear Nim chirp, and I know he's hoping there is something in this bag for him. Every fall season, his diet consists of small rodents and sweets. A lot of tea. He's not too fond of coffee.

"What flavor did she make this time?" I ask, looking it over in my hand, eyeing the sugar crystal coating. I take a small bite, savoring the flavor.

"Sweet potato," we both say at the same time, her mouth curves up into a small smile.

She peels the muffin from the bag next, her fingers delicate as she rotates it slowly, peeling off the paper wrapping the stem. She slowly lifts the edges of the muffin top, bit by bit. "Do you always eat your muffins like that?" I ask, taking another bite of the pie.

"Muffin tops are the best part. You save the best for last." She pops a piece of the base into her mouth like this is her favorite ritual.

"So what's the plan today?" She crosses her legs, continuing to eat her muffin.

I stay standing and polish off my pie.

"My part-time help, Cian, is coming in about twenty minutes. When he gets here, we're going to take a drive."

"A drive?" She asks, chewing on her muffin.

"Yes, I thought of a great spot for the lantern festival. It's not a long drive, a good walk from the town square, but after that, I want to take you to Brookeridge. It's about a forty-five minute drive, and they have some carnival equipment we can talk to them about."

"Okay. What about the next time we meet up? When, where, and what's on the list? That way, we can have at least this week planned."

Pulling out a chair, I take a seat. "If we have time tonight, I can take you to the farm. We have storage in one of the barns on Elora's property, that's where we store the majority of the decor for all the festivals and some supplies."

She nods her head. "Okay, let's go."

"There are homes in these hills?" she asks, peering out the window of my 4Runner. Her voice is caught between disbelief and curiosity.

The hills stretch out in gentle, rolling swells, blanketed in lush, thick green grass that gently ripples under the breeze. As we get closer, the details start to appear.

Rounded wooden doors tucked into the hill bases, some in deep shades of walnut, others painted in bright, joyful colors. Tiny chimneys protrude up through the grassy earth like tree trunks, smoke, lazily drifting skyward. Small round windows peek from the slopes, edged with climbing ivy or outlined by flowering vines, some with decorative shutters. There are even wooden steps to easily move about from one home to the next on the rolling hills.

When we passed the treehouse village, I thought I would have to pick her jaw off the ground. She loved the houses and how big they looked, built around the trees and branches, rope ladders leading to the bridges, and even an elevator pulley system.

"Yes. Flora has her home and apothecary there. Jas lives in the treehouse village. That's where Aaryn grew up, so she stayed."

"Did you know him?" she asks. I catch her looking at me from the corner of my eye.

"Yeah, I did. We were all good friends. He and Dominik were like brothers. They were childhood best friends."

She nods and lets it settle for a second before her tone shifts to a lighter, teasing note. "So…" She turns a little in her seat to glance into the back. "Why isn't he flying to meet us there? Does he just enjoy a car ride now and then?"

I glance in the rear view mirror. Nim sits in the middle of the seat with his wings tucked in tight, looking straight ahead like a regular passenger. He looks at Raene, crawls in a circle, and kneads the seat before resting on his belly in a dragon sploot.

"Pretty much," I say, easing around a bend in the road, approaching our destination.

She watches him a second longer, her eyes narrowing in on him. "Does he need a…like a car seat or something?"

I bite down the laugh that tries to escape. My mouth curves into a smile before I can help it, and I glance at the mirror again, just to see Nim's stoic face.

Nim sighs in my head. *"She can't be serious."*

After opening the rear window for Nim, Raene and I step out onto the dirt. We are parked off to the side, under a willow tree. She begins to twirl slowly in a circle, taking it all in.

We're deep in the Emerald Wood. A large clearing is ahead, and just beyond it is our beautiful, blue lake, Sapphire Lake, fed by a roaring waterfall cascading down stone cliffs. This location will be perfect for the lanterns to take off on day one for the opening ceremony. I enjoy coming here to think at times.

Nim launches from the backseat in a silent burst of movement, wings stretching wide as he lifts into the trees above. He vanishes into the canopy while the sun's rays filter through the leaves. The colors are soft and shimmer in golden light, spraying across the forest floor, not yet touched by Ruskaya's blessing.

I follow Raene with my eyes. She walks toward the clearing like she's being pulled by something magnetic. Her steps are slow, fingers brushing the low branches of trees like a gentle touch asking permission to enter.

She loves it here. I can hear it in her heartbeat, the calmness, the steadiness of taking it all in. I'm glad the fall festival planning is going well. If she agrees on this location, and I really feel she will, it'll be an item we can check off the list.

A cool breeze comes through, and it feels just right, like a sign from the Goddess of Autumn's imminent arrival.

Raene doesn't like fall. It was her most recent confession. I guess I just wonder why she doesn't. It's not that I need to know. We just met. We don't know each other on that personal level. I don't know her past or her deepest secrets. I just know she was raised by her grandmother.

I know she writes those breezy, sunny, and sexy love stories. Maybe that's where she feels safest, so she stays in that realm. It's her happy bubble of warm beaches, cold drinks, guaranteed happy endings in the sand and under the sun.

But I can't help wondering what made her turn her back on the fall. Something about the way she says it, *that she doesn't do fall*, like autumn once let her down, and she never wants to go back.

It's not my business. She doesn't know me, nor does she trust me. Still, I'd like to change that. I could be her friend. I *want* to be her friend. *Even if that means just for a month?*

She then stops, standing at the edge where the trees part into the open sky. Her gaze lifts to the blue skies above. "It's magical," she says softly, breath catching. "I love the feeling here. It just makes me feel...calm. What is this place?"

I swallow. She's not wrong. There's something about this place that settles everything in your chest and smooths it out. Like the air knows what stirs inside you and wants you to sit down, ease it off of you.

"Sateathea, the Goddess of Rain, it is said that her tears for her and her sisters creating Everly Hollow, were tears of happiness. Rain spilled and filled the lakes and waterfalls, a celebration of new beginnings.

She glances back at me, smiling, and calls me by the nickname she uses. Taking a deep breath, her eyes turn to the sky. "This is where the lanterns float. It's perfect, Ash. I think everybody's going to love it."

I look up toward the sky, already imagining it. "Yeah, tables will go up in the town square that morning. We can get supplies set up—glue, ribbon, and paint. We'll look for lanterns in bulk, pre-made, because that will save us a lot of time. I can enchant them once they're ready. Make sure they float and that the flame lasts at least thirty minutes or so before fading."

Her smile widens. "Do you think Nim would light them? Be the official lantern lighter?"

I glance up to where Nim circles above the falls. His scales make him a kaleidoscope of fall colors shimmering in the sunlight.

"What do you think of that job title, oh great mini-dragon?" I ask him mentally.

He dives down low in answer, wings folding at the last moment before he lands on the sun-warmed grass with a dramatic *flop*. Then, like a corgi with its legs spread wide and paws bent awkwardly, he rolls onto his back and rubs against the moss, twisting in different directions. His wings flare out like he's making grass angels, his tongue sticking out for a moment.

I grin. "That's a yes."

Raene laughs, the sound soft and surprised. I can't stop watching her. The way her eyes get gold flecks when the sun hits them. The ease in her shoulders. Like this place has finally given her space to breathe, and for once, she isn't thinking of fall.

11
Within Reason
RAENE

"So how old are you?" I ask, turning my body towards Ash. Nim is out cold in the backseat, his entire body stretched dramatically across the three seats.

Ash chuckles, eyes still on the road. "By the Seven. Do you really want to know? He gives me a lopsided smile.

By the Seven? Oh, I get it now.

He's pretty relaxed in the driver's seat, like this endless string of questions is a welcome distraction instead of an annoyance. I've lost track of how many questions we've asked now as we drive to Brookeridge. His birthday is in October. *Shocker.*

Nim is a breed of dragon created by the Goddess of Fall, hence his coloring. Glow-moths are like fireflies, a little bigger. They come in the late summer, stay during the fall, then leave again until next year. We're definitely past twenty-one. We're just...talking. And it's oddly easy.

His hand rests on the gear shift, the other loosely at the top of the wheel.

My eyes catch the hand gripping the wheel, his thumb at the side tapping lightly on the leather to the soft and steady beat of the music that hums low in the background. I love how big his hands are.

Someone give me strength.

The hair tie around his wrist catches my eye. His sleeves are pushed up to show his forearms. It's the sexiest thing about his outfit. His suspenders are a nice touch. His ass looks good, too.

"Guess." His voice lulls me from the fantasy of the bathroom scene, moving to the bedroom.

"It's not nice to guess one's age," I say, opening my water bottle and taking a few sips. Stopping by that little convenience store just out of Everly Hollow was a great idea.

"How old do I look, in your puny human terms?"

"Puny human?" I narrow my eyes on him.

"I'm a fae male. Emphasis on the male. We're not created like human men. We're very different."

My eyes glance to the tips of his ears, to his forearms, and to the lap of his pants.

"Did you hear yourself, *like human men*?" I giggle after trying to lower my voice in a mocking tone to his.

He smirks and shoots me a side eye.

"Alright, alright," I say. "Well, to me, you look like you'd be maybe a little bit older than me. I'd guess thirty-five."

"A long time ago I once was," he says.

"Three-hundred and twelve."

"No, lower, but you're not that far off."

My water bottle halts mid-air, and I lower it slowly. "Wait. You're seriously in the hundreds?"

"Yeah."

"How old?"

"You'll have to keep guessing," he says, turning us into a parking lot. We're the only car here, along with a truck. He puts the car into park, turns off the engine, and smiles at me. My eyes glare at him for turning his age into a guessing game.

"Two-hundred and seven," I say.

"Nope."

"Thanks for meeting with us," Ash says, shaking the hand of Gabriel, the owner of World of Whimsy. We're in an office, a small building on the property beside a few large warehouses.

He's a little bit taller than me, though not as tall as Ash. Mid-fifties, maybe, with thick black hair streaked through with silver. At the top of his head, horns curl like a ram's and rounded glasses frame light grey eyes. He smiles brightly, extending his hand. We shake, and his warm, calloused hand engulfs mine.

"Feel free to walk around, look, and see what games and rides you want us to haul out and set up for the two days we discussed on the phone." Gabriel hands me a tablet. "Whatever catches your eye, select it on this tablet, and it will be added to your list."

We say our thanks and part ways, Gabriel turning to head in the other direction. I look up ahead at one of the large warehouses in front of us.

He steps beside me as we head to the doors. "So, any idea of what you think would be good for two carnival days?" he asks, pulling the door open.

Why does it smell like cotton candy in here, and how?

"Well, definitely a cotton candy machine, game booths with fabulous prizes, and a Ferris wheel," I say, mentally checking off my list. "Maybe spinning acorns and oh!"

I stop, turn to him, a grin spreading on my face. "Bumper cars, but what if they were pumpkins and we could call them *Smashing Pumpkins*."

"See, I told you that you were enjoying this," he says, chuckling.

"Nope," I say, popping the 'p' for emphasis. "But you know it would be fun."

I turn back to walk ahead of me, gently bumping my shoulder against him, because my shoulder can't reach his, unless my legs are wrapped around his...

"How about two hundred and two?" I ask, walking up to a game booth.

I feel like I'm going to be guessing his age for a while. In the hundreds? I need whatever he is having.

"Close," he says with a smile, accepting the tablet I hand out to him. "But no."

That smile of his makes my knees weak, the kind of weak that is going to cause my collapse into embarrassment by face planting on this floor. And he knows it. I know he knows it. That's why he looks and smells the way he does, why he's standing there with that wicked, cocky grin.

"What about this game?" I ask over my shoulder, as I stand in front of it.

He steps closer, and I catch his shadow stretching over mine. His gaze flicks to the name of the game before he glances down at the tablet in his hand.

The screen's glow lights his face in a soft glow, making the freckles across his nose look like constellations in a night sky. His hair brushes the sides of his face. He scrolls with a quick swipe of his thumb. "A-ha! Here it is, Pumpkin Pitch."

"This will be fun for kids and adults," I say, tapping the corner of the booth.

I point at the pumpkin-shaped beanbags stacked neatly beside numbered cutouts. "Nothing like a little competition to win a lot of tickets."

"Sounds like you're already planning to beat everyone," he teases, clicking the option on the tablet. The name shifts to our master list.

"Okay." He glances up at me with that slow, deliberate smile that makes my stomach feel like I've stepped off a ride. "Where to next?"

We've been here for a little over an hour now. So far, we have added eight rides, including a Ferris wheel, spinning apples, and a carousel with woodland creatures instead of horses. We have a good amount of games on our list, too.

"What are we doing with game prizes?" I ask as we approach a game called *Luna Glow Hoops*.

He leans against the game, crossing his ankles and arms, his muscles tightening a bit in his shirt.

I glance back at the game because he's a whole distraction. Our eyes meet when we hear a low humming noise. The ring toss game I'm standing in front of, Ash is leaning against, starts to shimmer in iridescent colors of blue, pink, and lavender. Suddenly, silver rings begin to hover in front of us to grab and toss.

"This is pretty bad ass," Ash says, smirking and giving me a look. "These games are powered with faerie magic. So we don't have to worry about prizes at all."

"You think it still works?" I ask, giving him a puzzled look, about to ask him what he means.

He just grabs a ring and hands it to me. "Only one way to find out."

Did his eyes just get darker?

"You ready, Raene?" He sets the tablet down on the game edge.

I gently take the ring and toss it. The ring bounces off a pearl colored glass bottle, landing between the bottles in a *plink*.

Ash takes a ring and loops it perfectly over the neck of a glowing bottle. A little jingle plays, and the bottle gives off a cheery chime.

I roll my shoulders, my crossbody bag shifting lightly against my hip as I adjust my stance. I grab a ring and toss it. Once again, it wobbles through the air, clips the side of the bottle, and slips into the darkness in between. But on the rebound, it bends, curves upwards, and locks into a bottle with quiet precision. A pulsing glow flickers as the jingle plays, followed by another excited chime.

I blink, eyes wide. "That...should not have counted."

Ash steps closer. "I think it likes you," he whispers. I laugh. That's not possible. It would be adorable and pretty cool.

We toss more rings for a couple more minutes, and a floating scoreboard appears. It has glowing glyphs that change from our names—*how the fuck did it know that*—to the score.

Ash tosses his final ring. It swings perfectly around the final glowing bottle. The whole game lights up in its colors, and the scoreboard reads *SYLAS*. He throws his hands in the air, slowly spinning in a circle.

Laughing, I say, "Let's not let it all go to your head, there, big guy."

He laughs and grabs the tablet.

"So, how will the prizes work?" I ask, looking at the fading glow of the game.

"Oh yeah." He hands me the tablet, and I take it. He closes his eyes, holds his hands out in front of him, and a plush appears.

When he holds it up and turns it side to side, I burst out laughing. "Is that...a pumpkin spice latte?"

A literal PSL plush that's about fifteen inches tall, orange, and wrapped in a brown fabric band. On the band are cartoonish eyeballs, rosy cheeks, and a mouth. The top is finished with a swirl of white plush fur, a tiny sewn-on pumpkin, and two miniature cinnamon sticks.

"It's perfect," I say, unable to stop the curve of my lips. "So it grants your deepest, darkest desires...within reason?"

His golden eyes catch mine, and he smirks.

"You couldn't handle my deepest desires, Raene...so I settled within reason."

Well, that went to level one-hundred real quick.

My pulse stumbles. That was a line. A *very* good line.

"But yes," his voice pulls me from my thoughts. "To answer your question, human or magical being, you can conjure up your ideal carnival dream prize when you win."

I clear my throat. "Let's add this one to the list, and then I think we're done here."

He nods, and we trade. I hand him the tablet, taking the plush, and clutching it tighter than necessary.

What does he even mean by that? Is he teasing, or...nope, we're not going to overthink this, Raene. Absolutely not. I'll find myself down a rabbit hole. Still, I can't stop myself from wondering. Who even says something like that and makes it sound more like a promise, instead of a joke?

We finished our selection of games and rides, and Ash put down the deposit. Saying our goodbyes, we begin our walk back to the car, Nim swooping in from the back window, making himself comfortable for the ride back home.

"Are you hungry?" he asks, quickly reaching the door handle before me, opening the door for me.

"Sure, I could eat."

He rounds the front of the 4Runner and slides into the driver's seat. "I know the perfect place."

Settling ourselves into the booth at a cute diner named The Sugar Maple Bistro, we're pretty lucky we were able to snag one of the last booths available. Vintage photographs hang on the walls, and a jukebox sits in the corner, singing a tune.

The counter is full of magical patrons and humans, with glass domes covering pies and cakes. A teen walks over with a bubblegum pink pixie cut, light shimmery blue skin, and grey antlers. She's in light blue, high-waisted, baggy jeans, and a long-sleeved purple bodysuit with an apron. Her deep yellow-green eyes go bright as she smiles with her braces.

"Hi, I'm Sage! I'm your server here today! First timers?"

We both smile and nod our heads to her.

"Well, welcome! Here are our menus," she sits one in front of us, "my favorite is the club sandwich with fries and our homemade ranch."

She winks. "What would you like to drink?"

I ask for sweet tea, and Ash asks for lemonade.

"Let me get your drinks, and when I come back, I'll take your order."

We both eye our menu, sitting a table's width away from one another. I shift to cross my legs, and my foot brushes his leg.

"Sorry," I murmur, barely peeking above the menu.

"It's okay," he says, making direct eye contact over the menu.

"Have you made your decision?" Sage asks with enthusiasm as she approaches our table, setting straws and our cold drinks in front of us, breaking the tension of whatever the hell this is.

Sitting my menu down, I order a club sandwich with fries and the ranch with a side of ketchup as well. Ash orders the same. We hand her our menus and begin to sip our drinks.

Why is it so fucking awkward right now?

"So," I say, crossing my arms in front of me. "How are you feeling about the planning so far?"

He takes a drink, taking a quick sip from the straw. "I think we're off to a good start. I'm glad about that. I'm happy for the help."

A hand reaches back to rub his neck. "I really think these changes are going to bring even more people from all over to celebrate. It was a great idea."

I do a mock bow in the limited space of the booth, and he lets out a laugh that rumbles through his chest.

"So will we still have prizes at the game booths—the kind that the winner can conjure?"

"Sure, it's easy to do and we can have prizes for them to choose," he replies. I think back to the smiley PSL sitting on my seat in the car.

I nod my head as Sage walks over with our plates in hand. She sits them down and gives us another beaming smile, "Enjoy!"

Ash doesn't hesitate to pick up half of his sandwich, stacked high with toasted bread, bacon, lettuce, sliced avocado, turkey, and tomato, and lifts it in the air like a glass. I can't hold back the laugh that escapes my lips. This male is something else. I raise half of my club sandwich in return, meeting him with a mock toast.

12
What the fuck was that?
SYLAS

"What the fuck...was that?" Raene sits up from the ground, her knees are bent, her hands braced out behind her, keeping her steady. She's surrounded by leaves, a few in her hair.

I hold out my hand as she grabs it and quickly scrambles off the leaf pile. Her hair partially covers her face until she runs her hands through it, and the leaves fall out, fluttering to the ground.

"Seriously, Ash! What is that?" Her voice cracks into a high-pitched squeal, jabbing a finger at the pile of leaves as if it were alive. She takes a step away from it.

"I'm sorry." I hold my hands up like that'll make this better. "I tried to catch you! You're the one who said leaf piles aren't portals."

My hand rakes through my hair as I try not to laugh at the pure horror on her face. "The kids love it. I was going to set up a few of these throughout the fall festival."

"Those are death traps! What kind of child would love this? I thought I was going through a fucking wormhole, and next thing I know I'm falling *out* of the air, and back into that cursed leaf pile."

She leans over, places her hands on her knees, and takes a few deep breaths.

I bend over to pick up her purse as she steadies herself. She groans. As sexy and cute as she can be, I feel bad for her because she actually was afraid and probably thought she was having a near-death experience. "I think I'm about to vomit out of my ass right now."

Elora hears the commotion and runs over, her braid bouncing behind her as she jogs in her worn boots, knee-length skirt swaying, and an oversized knitted sweater. She slows when she sees Raene hunched over, her chocolate lab, Oakley, trots along following her. Elora glances at the leaf pile I'm standing next to.

One hand flies to her face, and she groans, shaking her head. "Not the leaf pile, Sylas," she says, pinching the bridge of her nose with her thumb and index finger, her other hand on her hip.

"Hey, Raene," Elora crouches down beside her, reaching out to rub light circles on her back. "Are you okay?" Her voice is gentle and soothing.

Raene slowly nods her head. "I love rides and even roller coasters, but I didn't expect *that*..."

She squints at me and Elora, the sun in her face. "Kids actually enjoy that? The feeling of their stomach falling out of their ass?"

"I'm sorry, Raene, really." Nim was rolling around near the leaves when he suddenly burst into the tree, knocking Raene off balance as he tumbled into the leaf loop-hole. I couldn't reach out in time.

"Tell her to just be steadier on her feet next time," Nim says nonchalantly.

"Nim says he's sorry," I say. Holding her purse out to her.

"Ugh, fine. Sorry," he purrs.

I feel like he's using a corner of my mind like a fucking scratching post right now. He stretches on a low branch in front of us.

Raene nods her head, accepting her purse, draping it over her chest, slowly coming to a stand. "Tell him, apology accepted." She fixes her hair and sends a warm smile to Elora, mouthing a quiet *thank you.*

"Well, let me know when you both are done with the barn." She gives us a small smile, patting her thigh to get Oakley's attention, pausing from her sniffing. She trots to Elora's side, tail wagging as they continue their journey back to the main house.

"Are you doing okay?" I ask, my voice filled with worry.

"I'm fine," she says, quickly glancing at my face, then looks away, "and thanks for trying to catch me, but we may need to get hazard signs for whatever leaf piles you want to set up, okay?"

I lightly chuckle. I'm glad she's able to joke, but I can still see the sheer look of panic when she fell, went through the loop, and gravity pulled her back to Earth.

I shove my hands into my pockets as we begin walking towards the barn. I stay a few steps behind her. I don't want to hover over her. She needs her space, but Goddesses, I want to keep her steady, to keep her from toppling over again.

Why is she getting underneath my skin like this?

Her smiles, her laughs, her dislike for the fall season—she's knee deep in planning this festival with me—that she says, isn't her thing.

Lightly jogging, I catch up to her. "Let me show you what we have inside. I don't think we'll have to get anything new, it's all in pretty great condition."

"Alright, but there better not be any more loopholes or hula hoops," she says, pulling open the barn door and stepping inside.

"It's like a warehouse for the holiday seasons," she whispers. She takes in the totes stacked, shelves of large decor, and the signs telling us which section is which.

I can't help but grin as I watch her take it all in. From the towering totes to the neat rows of shelving stacked high with garlands, lanterns, and enough seasonal décor to decorate our small town for every season. She's got that spark in her eye again, like she's seeing possibilities that I'd never notice. It's kind of addictive, watching her mind work.

"Pretty cool, huh? This is where the good stuff is anyway," I say, leading us to the sign that says *autumn*. I point at the sign, sending her a wink. The way she rolls her eyes, but is unable to hide the smile.

One word.

TROUBLE.

We begin our search to see what we can use for the town square and shopfronts.

She sets her purse down and begins to open totes, taking notes on her phone of her findings.

We find garland and wreaths, and lights. I can easily enhance them with my magic. Scarecrows—she lets out a laugh—faux pumpkins, porch signs, and hay bales.

When she shifts a couple of totes aside and gasps, it's soft but sharp enough to catch my attention. Immediately, I looked up.

"Oh...Ash, look at these."

She moves the lid fully off the container and pulls out a plush oversized floor pillow, in deep blues, purples with a silver design threaded in. I've never seen these before. We didn't use them last year.

"These are gorgeous! We can use these for the tent event." She looks at me, her voice excited as she runs a hand over it. Her fingers trail over the silver stitching, the same way she touched the tree branches earlier, like she's testing its worthiness.

"It will be like stepping out of fall...just for the evening. Do you have low-lying tables we could use with these?" She asks. She's so into her planning, I'm not sure if she's talking to me or making a mental note.

"I'm thinking a tent, picnic table vibes with seating on the floor cushions with the live music, maybe an appetizer spread with the drinks?" She nods her head as if to agree with her decisions, laying the pillow back in the tote.

I can picture her there with a drink in her hand, skin glowing in the low lantern light, her legs tucked under her as she sits on a pillow, swaying to the music. My heart pounds at the image.

"I'm going to go check around for the tables. Can you check and see how many floor pillows we have?" She asks, walking away but tossing the question over her shoulder.

"Sure thing," I say, beginning my work through the totes, turning to see her walk towards the ladder, hips swaying with each step as she climbs to the loft.

Focus, Sylas. Pillows. Not her ass. Pillows.

I count through the first tote, six. Another tote, eight. I go through all the totes that are in the vicinity. "There's enough here to build a pillow fort. I count twenty," I call up to her.

"I see three low picnic tables up here!" Her voice echoes from above in glee. She may not like fall, but when her ideas are coming together, there is a brightness in her eyes and her voice.

A sunbeam filters in through the loft window, dust dancing in the air. I glance up, shading my eyes with my hand, seeing her crouched over the tables.

"I'm not sure what they were used for, but they'll work for the tent event if you like them."

She starts down the ladder, one hand gripping the side, the other holding her phone. "Perfect. We can dress them up with table runners, lanterns, flowers, and I'm thinking lots of—"

Her voice cuts off abruptly.

Shit. Her foot slips on the fourth rung.

I don't think, I just move as fast as I can. I couldn't catch her last time, but I will now.

I'm there, arms ready. Catching her as she tumbles, one arm braced around her waist, the other steadying her shoulder. Her breath catches as she clings to me, our faces only inches apart. Her breasts are pressed against me. She's panting, her hands holding onto my shoulders, nails digging into my flesh, but it's a pain I gladly welcome. I shouldn't be hard right now.

"I got you," I murmur.

Her wide eyes meet mine, and for a second, everything feels too still. Too close. She's too fucking close.

I'm aware of everything: her full, glossy lips parting and the way her eyes quickly dart to my mouth before meeting my eyes again. The warmth of her body pressed to mine, the soft rasp of her breathing, her scent, her arousal. It's faint, but it's fucking there, and it's intertwining with my pulse that is roaring in my ears.

"Thanks for catching me," she whispers, her voice husky, brushing against my skin like the touch of a feather.

"You sure you're okay?" My hand instinctively lifts, cupping her cheek. My thumb glides across her cheekbone, slow and unthinking, because my body knows what it wants before I can think to stop it.

She starts to lean into my touch, just a fraction, just enough to place an ache in my chest, until she pulls herself away.

"Sorry." She winces, retracting her nails from me. And just like that, she let go.

The warmth of her body is gone, but it lingers on my skin. I'm left standing here, my muscles tight, my body turned on, watching her adjust herself like she didn't just knock the very breath out of me.

13
I should have let him kiss me
RAENE

"So how is the planning going?" Oriana asks, flips her long blue hair over her shoulder.

She's wearing a black sweater and hip-hugging blue jeans, accentuating her curves, with black boots. I really need to ask her where she got the outfit from. Her sparkly blue nails tap her mug gently as a smile tugs at the corners of her lips. "You know, with Ash?"

I sigh, already feeling heat creeping into my cheeks even if a blush will never show. I knew I would be teased. That's what new friends did, right? Teasing was a sign of acceptance. At least, that's what I'm telling myself.

I love being here with them on the days in between seeing Ash. This is starting to be our hangout, and it was perfect because new friends plus sweet treats and amazing coffee, it doesn't get better than that.

"Sylas is a sweetie," Jas chimes in, her voice warm, as he sets two plates with an iced lemon sweet roll on the table in front of each of us.

Ensuring there is frosting on the end of the soft, fluffy roll, I tear off a piece, gently placing it on my tongue. It's delicious. Tangy lemon, fluffy, and the sweet aroma is amazing.

"Mm-hmm," Oriana hums, bringing the mug to her lips with a slowness that would make anyone draw their attention to her. Her eyes flick up at me over the rim, and I can see the grin she's holding back. "and he's single."

"Oh, is he?" I ask, rolling my eyes playfully. My stomach does a traitorous little flip.

I hope he is single, especially when four days ago, he looked at me and held my face like he wanted to kiss me. I wanted to so badly.

My body pressed against his, feeling him against me, my nails digging into his shoulder, and wanting him to kiss me. I want my tongue to taste him and run along those fangs.

"Don't play coy," Jas teases, sliding into the free seat next to me and leaning forward on her elbows.

"You two have been spending a lot of time together. Planning festivals, making lists…oh, the romance of it all. I miss the dating stage." She props her chin on her hand and gazes dreamily at the ceiling.

I chew on a piece of the fluffy pastry and snort. "We are not dating."

"Nothing says romance like checklists and frolicking in leaves," Oriana says, chewing slowly, then sucking the icing off her thumb.

It's been…what, a little over a year? Probably more since I've had sex worth remembering. My fictional characters have had more sex than I've had lately. The female main character in my last book got laid twice in one chapter. *Twice.* Me? I'm over here getting flustered because Sylas smiled at me while looking at pillows.

I'm pathetic. And don't even get me started on that ladder moment. I *should* have let him kiss me. Hell, I should have grabbed him by the suspenders and kissed him like my life depended on it. He could've had me pressed against those rungs, my legs wrapped around his waist, his hands moving from my waist to my ass.

I felt him, his hardness, against my belly when he caught me and held me close, and it had my core aching in a way that made me want to throw the little bit of common sense my brain was trying to hang on to out of the window.

Oriana catches me zoning out and smirks. "You're thinking about him right now, aren't you? Those golden eyes? All that muscle? Just...everything?"

I throw a balled-up napkin at her, laughing. "You're impossible."

She responds with her melodic laugh, flicking it out of the way before it hits her square in the forehead. She smiles, taking another sip of her latte. "Anyone and everyone would notice a fae male like Sylas, your Ash."

My Ash?

"Aren't you engaged?" Jas teases, elbowing Oriana gently.

Oriana crosses her legs, leaning back. "Happily. But that doesn't mean I won't notice an attractive male and woman when they're together."

She quickly uncrosses her legs and leans forward. "Seriously, Raene, you're gorgeous and he is...so..."

I laugh, finishing the rest of my roll.

Just then, the bell above the café door jingles, and Elora strolls in with her usual mix of grace and shyness.

Jas welcomes her and walks her to the front.

Her braid sways down her back, small leaves decorating it whimsically for the season. She steps up to the counter, and in no time, she's picking up a drink carrier loaded with three cups and a bag of pastries.

"Hey, ladies," she says with a bright smile, her skirt swaying as she turns, stopping at our table. "See you next Friday?"

I blink. "Wait, what's happening next Friday?"

"Girl's night," Oriana says with a tantalizing smile, her eyebrows jumping up and down. "On her farm, the main house, around six that evening. Don't make us drag you there."

"Yeah, come hang out," Jas adds. "It'll be good for you. Wine, food, and probably embarrassing stories. My mother-in-law is going to watch Seren for me, and I could use a girl's night before the school year starts again."

"Okay," I say with a nod, my lips curving into a smile. "I'll check on my grandmother first, but I'd love to be there."

"Perfect." Elora gives us a quick wave and heads out with her items. It's a cute view through the cafe window, of her dog's head sticking out the passenger window, tongue lolled out, as she loads her things into her truck, giving the dog a quick scratch behind the ear as she eases out of the lot to leave.

Jas leans back in her chair, watching Elora leave. "She's probably meeting her parents. As an only child, they're super close-knit," she tells me.

Protective parents of a young adult. Got it.

Oriana taps her nails on her mug again. Her smile gets pretty fucking wicked when she's conspiring.

I wonder if she lured Malik in this way or with her siren song. The thought makes me hold back a laugh.

"Speaking of close-knit," she pulls her hand from the mug, examining her nails, "why, you and Ash are two patches on a quilt. When are you seeing him again?"

I chew on my lip, cross my ankles, and uncross them before admitting. "Tonight. We're meeting at the Four Lanterns to go over drink ideas for one of the festival events."

"Ohhh, I like that," Oriana drags the word out with a knowing grin. "Perfect excuse to sit across from him or side by side, you know, share body heat while *pretending* to talk about cocktails. You'll both be tipsy before the menu's even finalized."

"Stop," I say, chuckling.

My mind is beginning to question if she is right.

"Besides, my younger cousin Hannah will be there; she's part siren. She can create whatever drink you want, or just tell her the vibe you're going for, and she will concoct something magical. She's training under Malik so she can open her first bar in the city."

I laugh nervously, though a tingle of curiosity lingers. Magical drinks and a siren bartender? "As in... like singing enchantments into her drinks?"

"I do the same with my candles, and yes, you need to stop by sometime. I'll give you a free sample, but seriously, wait until you try her signature drink, *A Twilight's Kiss*," Oriana says with a knowing smile. "Sometimes she'll ask what you're feeling, and the drink will *answer*."

Jas waggles her brows. "Careful, Rae. That's the kind of drink that leads to bad decisions...or some really, *really* good ones."

I nearly choke on my coffee. First, Jas calling me *Rae* is adorable, but the way she's teasing? With all the romance books she's been reading, mine included, she's been single long enough that she's starting to daydream through my characters, and I get it.

I would miss companionship, too. Love always looks so shiny and sparkly from the outside. It sucks you in, and you gravitate towards it, unable to hold yourself back to protect and shield your heart from the full blow of it all.

I can't help but wonder if she's quietly thinking about dipping her toe back into the dating pool.

Then again, maybe I should think about that too? *Maybe.*

I sip my coffee, trying not to smile too hard. But I can't help thinking about Sylas, his warm hands, his golden eyes, and wondering what kind of trouble a siren-crafted drink might stir up between us.

I'm craving pasta. So, I do what any normal person would do when they're craving pasta: I make it. I *could* order it, but I don't even know the nearest restaurant that delivers. Besides, cooking helps quiet the conversation in my head. The one from the café that's been playing on repeat like a scratched record.

If I keep my hands busy, maybe I won't think about Ash's hands…on me—touching, kneading, or moving inside me. I shake my head, freeing my head from the sudden detour of thoughts, hoping it'll go down the other fork of the road, because nope. I will not go there. Not right now.

I grab a wicker serving tray so Grandma can rest easy and not have to move too much. She's been doing great with her continued physical therapy sessions, but she's earned a lazy afternoon.

She's been sitting on the patio, tucked under the umbrella, reading for almost an hour. Now and then, she gets up to stretch. It's such a beautiful day, so why not eat outside and enjoy the view?

I load up our plates with pasta. We had some Cajun Andouille sausage left over, so I sliced it, sautéed it with onions, garlic, and green bell pepper, and stirred it into a jar of alfredo sauce with fettuccine. Simple, easy, and *so* damn good. I add a side of oven-baked garlic bread, the cheesy store-bought kind that makes my soul happy because *butter*.

Then set two glasses of sweet tea on the tray, our forks, and a few napkins, and slide the patio door open.

"Lunch is served," I say with a grin, setting her plate in front of her and taking a seat.

"You spoil me," she says, slipping her bookmark into her mystery novel and setting it aside.

"How's your book?" I ask, stabbing a piece of sausage before twirling noodles around my fork.

"It's good. I think the gardener did it."

I laugh at her assumption, reaching for my garlic bread, because she is pretty spot on with these mystery books. We eat quietly for a few moments, light chatter, and just enjoy the warm weather.

"So," she says, glancing at me over the rim of her glass. "How is the planning going? The Fall Festival will be here before you know it, and then you'll be off to the city again, writing your next bestseller."

She's smiling, but it doesn't fully reach her eyes. I know she's sad I'll be leaving right after the festival. Maybe I can make more plans to visit more often. *Right?*

"It's going pretty good," I say, shrugging. "I like the planning aspect of it all. The season, though? Still a hard pass."

A contented hum releases from her throat as she sips her tea. "When are you meeting Sylas next? What's on the agenda?"

I finish chewing and wipe my buttery hands on a napkin. "We're meeting this evening at Four Lanterns to finalize the drink menu for the tent event. I made extra pasta, so we have more than enough for dinner tonight and leftovers for our lunch tomorrow."

"Much appreciated, my dear. But don't worry about me. I can hold my own."

She gives me that sly grandmotherly smile that knows way too much. "I want you to have fun. Enjoy yourself. Sylas is a nice fellow and very handsome."

I shoot her a deadpan look. "He's older than you, Grandma."

Maybe he's one hundred and twelve?

"Well, age is nothing but a number," she says with a grin that tells me she's enjoying this *way* too much.

14
The Blackberry Moon Lily Drop
SYLAS

Glancing at the clock on the wall is a dangerous move. I got here early to meet Raene, and I'm nervous.

I *touched* her. I felt her warmth pressed against me, the soft curves of her body fitting perfectly against mine. I wanted to kiss her. Hell, I still want to kiss her, and I swear I sensed the change in her scent. She wanted it too. Maybe even more.

But when she stepped back, I gave her space. What else could I do? I half-expected her to text me saying she wouldn't meet me tonight, that she was done helping with the festival.

Instead, she gave me that shy, awkward little smile that knocked the air out of me when we first met. And all she said was, *"See you Friday."*

Hannah and Malik are huddled over the drink menu she curated for the evening. Her warm, light brown skin practically glows under the low bar lights, perfectly complementing the soft lavender of her messy bun. Those pale gray eyes of hers sparkle with excitement, like she's already imagining the magic she's about to pour into our glasses tonight.

"Why are you so nervous?" Nim sighs, his voice dripping with impatience as it curls through my mind.

"I'm fine," I mumble.

"You literally just admitted that..."

"Nim," I mutter, before taking a swig of my beer.

Okay, well in that case...bring me home some fries, will you? It would be greatly appreciated."

Hearing the door, I turn. She's here.

"You're going to have to ask me about those fries later." My mental shield goes up.

She's looking around, scanning the room for me, wearing a jean jacket over an olive-green dress that dips just enough to show the middle of her breasts.

Fuck.

She looks *incredible* in that color, like the Goddess herself dressed her just to torment me.

She spots me. I raise a hand in a quick wave, trying to play it cool while my pulse kicks up a notch. Her smile hits me. She walks toward me, hips swaying, the skirt of her dress brushing over knee-high brown boots.

I stand to greet her, not sure if I should shake her hand or hell, what's normal here? Squeeze her shoulder?

My brain stalls, but she solves the problem with a quick hug, her head resting against my chest, her arms wrapped around my waist, and my arms do not hesitate to do the same.

Her scent hits me, she's like summer and sunshine, with a warm undercurrent of coconut.

I don't move for a second too long, afraid that if I breathe her in again, I'll say something I can't take back.

"Thanks for coming," I managed to stumble out. *What the fuck! Did I say that? Why does she make me so nervous?*

"And turn down amazing drinks? Never," she says, slipping her purse off her shoulder and strapping it to the back of the barstool before taking a seat.

She leans forward, her elbows propped on the bar as she narrows her eyes at me. "One-hundred and...ten," she guesses, her voice laced with mock confidence. "No, wait...one-hundred." I laugh, shaking my head as I sip water.

"That laugh," she mutters, staring openly at my lips like she's caught herself in the act but doesn't care.

"You're terrible at this game," I say with a sly grin. "Keep going. Maybe you'll hit the mark before we finish our drinks."

"Any hints?"

"Nope."

"One-hundred and seven?"

"Not even close," I tease, loving the way her lips purse in concentration.

Before she can fire off another number, Hannah slides in front of us with a tray balanced on her hand. "I'm Hannah, and I'm excited to make some amazing drinks for you both."

We smile, and I nod for her to continue. "I've made three different drinks for you to try.

"First up, we have *A Dawn's Kiss*," she says warmly.

The glass is delicate, with pale pink liquid shimmering faintly like sunlight. "It's vodka, rose syrup, lime juice, and a hint of pear. Sweet, romantic, but with just enough bite to keep things interesting." Raene's lips curl into a grin. "It's pretty and the name sounds dreamy." We each take a small glass and take a drink, letting the flavors hit our tongues.

"I like this," I say, stirring the two miniature black straws in the drink. "The pear is subtle, but it's refreshing."

I look over to Raene, and she is sipping hers through the straws. Her eyes crinkle as she lifts a shoulder into a lazy shrug.

"What? I'm savoring it?"

"You like it?"

"It's good," she says, tilting her head as if weighing the flavors and the appearance of the drink. "But it doesn't fit the aesthetic I'm hoping for. You know...moody, dark blues, like the pillows...twilight."

"So, a moody drink to match your moody dislike of fall?" I tease, letting a grin creep in.

Her lips press together, holding back a smile. "Precisely."

"But seriously," she says, setting her glass down, "wouldn't it be nice to have an event that isn't completely dragged down the fall clearance aisle?"

I nod. I get it. Not everyone loves fall the way I do. I've been surrounded by it my whole life. The warm hues, the earthy and spicy scents, and the bite of the crisp air.

The autumn realm is autumn, all the time, and I wouldn't trade it for anything. Yes, I enjoy the changing seasons and their celebrations, but fall? Fall is home. It's heart.

"You're looking at me like I'm supposed to apologize. Sorry, but I'll defend my pumpkin lattes and apple cider donuts to the bitter end." I say, laughing.

She smirks and takes a sip of her drink again. "Of course you would. I bet you even own one of those *Hello Pumpkin* mugs."

I look around at everyone, listen to the music a bit before leaning closer. "Guilty. But don't worry, I promise I won't make you drink out of it, unless you're into that sort of thing."

She laughs into the back of her hand. "You're a mess."

I flag down a waitress and order food: an appetizer spread of hot wings, chips, and queso, and French fries with ranch.

"Oh, and an order of fries to go," I say.

Raene tilts her head, a knowing smile on her lips. "For Nim?"

I nod my head. "I can't leave here without them."

She shakes her head, her laughter soft and easy. "You two are ridiculous."

When Malik appears to help serve the second drink, he introduces himself to Raene with a warm smile. "It's nice to finally meet you," Raene says, extending her hand. "And congratulations on the engagement. Oriana seems really special." His expression softens, his eyes light up like a man who knows he's found his person. His lips curve up into a wide smile, showing his fangs. "Yeah, she's...my forever," he says quietly, giving me a slight bow, before he steps away to help another customer.

Hannah steps in his place with the next drink, and Raene's eyes widen. Hannah calls it *The Blackberry Moon Lily Drop*. A metal skewer rests across the rim, studded with plump blackberries, and the drink itself is a swirling masterpiece of deep purple and silver shimmer, garnished with mint and a moon lily perched delicately on the edge. "This one is my favorite," she says, setting a glass in front of each of us. "Blackberry syrup, mint, soda, lemon juice, and just a whisper of moon lily nectar. It is a mocktail, but if you choose this as your drink special and some of your guests want alcohol, then we can always add white rum." Raene takes the first sip, her eyes fluttering closed for a second. "Okay...that's unfair."

She looks down at her drink, the shimmery liquid catching the light and reflecting in her eyes. "That's not just a drink. It's life-changing."

I take a sip, savoring the cool sweetness, just as our food is served, three colorful platters set between us, along with two small plates and a reminder that I'll get my order of fries when I leave.

Raene carefully plates a little bit of everything and nabs one of the small dishes of ranch, leaving me the other.

"So, what do you think?" She asks before biting into a wing, sauce glistening on her lip.

"It is delicious," I say, loading up my plate.

I refuse to make eye contact. I refuse to watch her tongue poke out and lick the sauce off her lips. "And I like that we can keep it as a mocktail and jazz it up if we want. It fits your aesthetic pretty spot on."

She nods her head in agreement, setting her wing down and wiping her fingers on the black, cloth napkin. "So," she turns to me, her knees brushing mine in a soft, deliberate graze, "you're admitting my aesthetic wins over your pumpkin-loving heart?"

I pop a few fries into my mouth. "Only this time, Raene." I wink.

She chuckles, turning to face her plate once again. We fall into an easy rhythm, sipping our drinks and sharing food with the soft hum of conversation around us fading into the background.

"How is Vera healing?" I ask, genuinely curious.

She's doing great, actually," She nibbles on a chip covered in queso. "Keeping up with her sessions and getting around pretty well. I feel like the recovery here versus the city is... better. She's more relaxed, and she has some amazing tools to help that she can't get anywhere else. Flora's products have been a *Goddess sent,* Grandma's words exactly. So for that, I'm grateful."

"I'm glad to hear it."

Before I can ask another question, Hannah appears with the last drink. *Starry Night* arrives in a deep violet hue containing vodka, blueberry purée, and lemonade, glimmering under the warm lights.

"So, this one is definitely a contender," Raene says, tracing her finger around the rim of her glass, her nail skimming the rim in a way that steals my attention. "But I love the silver of the moon lily drop drink."

"You know, this night is your idea," I say, leaning back slightly but watching her. "We can make whatever drink and food menu *you* want. We could do all three as drink specials," I offer. "Then serve other refreshments, plus an open bar. What do you think?"

Her large eyes widen, softening as they meet mine, and she gives me a smile that feels like it slips past all my defenses. "I'd love that. I think it would be amazing. Thanks, Ash."

I catch myself staring at Raene as she laughs softly at something Hannah says. It hits me then, this whole night feels like it's wrapped around her, the way the moonlight clings to dark water, its reflection glowing brightly.

I want this event to have her fingerprints all over it. I want to see that look on her face again when she tastes the drink and calls it an experience.

Goddess, she's magnetic.

The way she tilts her head when she's thinking, chewing on her inner cheek, the way she tucks her hair behind her ear without even realizing she's doing it. And those moments, like when her knees brushed against mine, where I swear the rest of the world blurs out and I can't hear a damn thing, even in a busy bar on a Friday night.

I pick up the glass beside Starry Night, take another sip of the drink, and smile to myself. Yeah, the *Blackberry Moon Lily Drop* is the winner. Not because it's the best drink, but because it's hers.

15
I want you to burn me
RAENE

I'm fully clothed, yet I swear I have hay in places hay shouldn't be. I settled on a t-shirt, leggings, and my sneakers because comfort and mobility are non-negotiable for decorating today.

The countdown to fall officially begins with September first, now blessing us with its presence. The leaves are already flirting with shades of gold, and honestly, the cool breeze feels amazing against my skin after all the work we've been putting in.

Sylas' part-time help is coming later this afternoon, but he's been popping out here and there, just enough to nod his approval, tell me exactly where decor should go, and insisting that anything involving a ladder is *his* job. I think it's because he doesn't want me to fall again…I wouldn't mind falling into his arms once more, and this time not resisting.

He looks good today, too, in that constant way he doesn't even notice. A light blue short-sleeve shirt, worn jeans, and black boots. It's a little out of his usual fall comfort zone, but damn.

It's sexy seeing his arms on full display…and it's distracting. *Really* distracting.

I'm arranging a cluster of fake and real pumpkins along the stoops of some of the shops around the town square, stepping back every so often to see if they look *just right*. The colors are blue, orange, and some of the pumpkins are white.

I'm bent over, debating the angle of a white pumpkin, when I hear a voice.

"All hail, the princess of fall who has come to greet us with her presence."

I laugh and roll my eyes before straightening and turning around. "Hello, Oriana."

"Rae." She smiles, handing me a bottle of water that I happily accept and chug half the bottle.

"Thanks," I say, replacing the cap. I can't help but think Oriana could walk around in a garbage bag and still make it look chic and runway-ready.

"It's lovely so far," she says, looking around.

"You're coming with me," she says in a tone that leaves little room for argument, so I don't say anything. "You've been out here for hours, you need a break."

I sigh, but I'm already tempted. "A break does sound good..."

She links her arm through mine, leading me toward her candle shop, The Siren's Flame. The moment we step inside, I'm hit with a wave of warmth, invigorating scents that take hold of one another, humming and dancing to the magic.

"Hi, Raene!" Corra darts quickly over to me from the other side of the shop before moving along. Her shimmery form of seafoam darts from one shelf to the next, her wings fluttering at a rapid speed, tiny pumpkins and fall leaves decorating the shelves.

"Hey, Corra!" My eyes try to catch the movement as she zips by in a blur of seafoam blues and greens, wings glittering like stardust. She moves so fast it's like she's trying to decorate every corner and shelf of the shop at once.

"Doesn't it look amazing?" Oriana says, her turquoise eyes glistening as she holds her hands to her heart in awe.

She pulls me toward a row of glowing candles, each one with a handwritten label. "I just finished pouring a new scent this morning, Pumpkin Ember. You *have* to smell it."

"I'm not a fan of pumpkin, but I have a feeling you're going to try to persuade me." The corners of my mouth tilt upward.

"Facts." She laughs, handing me a candle in an amber colored jar.

She lights it, then steps back, gently folding her arms as she whispers to me, "Listen."

I cast my eyes downward, taking in the flickering flame, the pool of wax beginning to grow around the wick. Soft music begins to rise, a melody both sweet and aching, and then a voice, beautiful and otherworldly, spills into my ears.

It's so moving, so unshakably pure, that I glance up at Oriana with a smile, a tear already sliding down my cheek.

"Do you hear it too?" I ask her softly. "It's so beautiful."

"Why, thank you," she says with gleaming eyes, pulling me into a quick hug before leaning down to gently blow out the candle.

"That is my voice. My siren song. But I can't hear it, it's my magic. It will sing to you, to your soul. Only you can hear it."

"What does it mean? The song?" I ask, my eyes fixed on the melted wax as it cools and hardens into stillness.

"Only you know."

After I finished my visit with Oriana, I set my candle, a gift from Oriana, gently in the passenger seat of my car. I lingered there for a moment, staring at it a little too long, wondering what the song truly meant. It stirred something inside me I can't even put into words.

Powerful, beautiful, yet so heavy. It made me feel...*everything* all at once. It's no wonder I found myself crying, but it wasn't sadness at all. Just this beautiful, overwhelming feeling.

Ash steps down from the ladder, the metal clinking softly under his boots, and lifts it in his arms, his biceps flexing in a way that makes a bit of drool threaten to pool in the corner of my mouth. I snap my gaze back up before he catches me staring and follows him to the next spot, festive, fall-themed wreaths clutched in my hands.

"It's looking pretty good," I say, glancing around at the town square.

People pause to admire the decor, snapping photos. A few glance my way and wave, knowingly. Parents chasing after their kids into the toy shop or stepping out of their cars to browse the storefronts. The whole place hums with that early fall energy, warm and buzzing.

Ash made us sandwiches for lunch earlier, carrying them down from his apartment with that easy grin of his. And now, with the perks of being the boss, as soon as Cian left for the day, he closed up an hour early, just for us to get this done and get it crossed off our never-ending list.

"So, you like what you see?" He says, rooting me back to the present. He gives me a cocky smirk as he holds out his hand to take the wreath from me.

I blink, caught in the act of staring at him again.

Like what I see? Oh, if you only knew.

"You wish," I say, handing him the wreath. My voice sounds too playful, like I'm covering for something, and I know this male can read me like a damn book.

"Oh, I know," he replies, that smirk growing as he steps closer to grab the wreath from my hands. His fingers brush mine, slow enough that I feel it up my arm.

I cross my arms, trying to look unaffected.

Is it working?

"You're confident for someone who just spent ten minutes arguing with me about pumpkin placement due to the various colors."

"You know I was right about the pumpkins," Ash says, flashing that wicked grin that shows all his teeth.

The fangs.

He hooks the wreath underneath the lantern on the street post. With the wave of his hand, the wreath gives off a faint luminescent glow. Then grows larger and turns more realistic.

His head tilts to the side as if one of those things weren't supposed to happen, but he shrugs it off. "Besides, I saw you staring. Don't think I didn't notice."

"I wasn't staring." I wipe my palms on my leggings because I feel like I'm beginning to overheat. "I was…supervising, I have to make sure you don't fall."

"Supervising, huh?" He looks at me, eyes glinting in the late afternoon light as he makes his way down the ladder. His eyes narrow, but there is a playful smirk on his face.

"Do you have a professional opinion on my…technique?"

I twist my lips and wriggle my nose, which is a terrible idea because his gaze drops right to my mouth. *Stop it. Right now, Raene.*

"Your technique is…adequate." My voice cracks, betraying me.

"Adequate?" He leans just a fraction closer.

"You wound me, Raene," he purrs. I'll just have to try harder to impress you then."

Once we finish the last wreath, Ash dusts his hands off and grabs the ladder, and I fall into step behind him. "Viktor will pick that up later," he says, leaning it against the wall near his shop. "No point in hauling it back just yet."

"Got it," I say, dusting my hands off.

"Can you help me carry the totes back into the bookstore?" He asks. "I'll take them to the barn tomorrow."

"Of course," I reply, lifting one of the lighter bins.

We walk side by side, and the air between us begins to feel charged, like a live wire ready to snap.

Once all the totes are in the shop, I help him stack them off to the side near the front entrance. He sets his tote down and reaches for a folded piece of paper on the counter.

"This is what's next," he says, handing it to me. "It's a list of people we need to talk to about the markets and food booths, vendors, too. I made each of us a list. That way, we can tackle it head-on, together, and get it done faster."

"Thanks," I say, taking the paper. "I'll get this handled." Tucking it carefully into my bag, as it rests on the table.

"And...thanks for lunch," I add, giving him a small smile. "You didn't have to make me a sandwich, but you did anyway. I appreciate that."

He tucks his hands into his pockets. "You're welcome. You're helping me a lot. A seven-day event like this...well, the least I can do is feed you."

I laugh, but it comes out wrong. As if my nerves have me in a chokehold. What is it about goodbyes? I turn toward the door, adjusting my bag on my shoulder. "I guess I should get going...bye, Ash."

I'm almost at the door. My hand reaches for the doorknob as he quickly stops me. My purse hits the ground, and he spins me.

My back presses against the doorframe. I wasn't expecting that. I look up at him. He towers over me, but *fuck,* it's in a good way.

"Are you going to let me leave?" I joke, my voice soft, breathless.

His gaze drops to my lips, lingering there, and suddenly my joke feels like it's dissolving in the heat between us. His hand stays braced on the frame near my head, the other brushing my hip, slow and possessive, like he's testing how far he can go. How far will I let him?

"Maybe I don't want you to," he murmurs.

My heart stutters, and I don't know if it's from the words or the way his voice dips even lower, it's smooth like silk and heat all at once. "Ash…"

"I love it when you call me that." His mouth curves faintly, but his eyes are like fire as they lock onto mine. "Raene…"

My name sounds like a confession on his tongue.

I shouldn't be turned on by hearing him say my name. I can feel heat curling in my core and wetness starting to pool in my underwear. Should I accept it or be disturbed by how he makes me feel?

He leans closer, so close I feel his breath warm against my skin as his hand slides from my hip to my cheek, his thumb grazing my jaw in the most gentle caress.

I press my palms against his chest, my brain is telling me to push him back, but the hard lines of muscle under my hands make me melt, and somehow, I keep my hand there. I'm entranced by the way he smells, like warm spices and citrus, books, and something purely *him.*

I can't resist. Not anymore.

My fingers curl around the back of his neck, pulling him closer, closer to my lips. The kiss starts gently, teasing-like, like neither of us is ready to let go of the anticipation. We pull back just enough to search each other's faces, to see if we're both ready to lose this battle, and then our mouths crash together, hungry and desperate.

I cling to him like my body has wanted it forever. He grabs my ass with a roughness that takes my breath away and lifts me as if I weigh nothing, never breaking the kiss. His tongue slides against mine, demanding and intoxicating, and I wrap my arms around his neck, my legs instinctively hooking around his waist, locking at the ankles.

A whimper escapes my lips, and he swallows it like he's starving for every damn sound. Then he gives me a low, guttural moan that vibrates against my mouth, and it's one of the sexiest sounds I've ever heard.

As much as I hate fall, he tastes like it. Like cool autumn air, strong coffee, and a hint of cinnamon. He tastes like a craving I never knew I had, especially for this season, but it's something I'd give anything to keep.

His body presses me deeper against the doorframe, and it makes my pulse thrum in my ears. His hands move to the sides of my thighs that are squeezing his waist, his fingers digging into my leggings like he's trying to ground me to him, and every damn nerve in my body is on alight.

"You have no idea what you do to me." He breathes the words like a secret against my mouth, yet they're rough and broken, like it's difficult to get them out.

I gasp when his hips shift, the friction sending a sharp, dizzying bolt through me. I can feel the wetness of the fabric rub against my clit.

I say his name, my voice shuddering, and honestly, I'm not sure if it teeters on the cusp of a warning or a plea.

He leans back just enough to look at me, his eyes luminescent, the intensity of his gaze threatening to burn right through me. He takes a deep breath, shivers slightly, and presses his forehead against mine. "Say my name like that again, and I won't want to let you go."

I *don't* want him to let me go. Not now.

I kiss him again, harder this time, and he groans low in his chest. His hand slides up my side, under my shirt, fingertips brushing bare skin. I arch into his touch without thinking, and moan when his thumb grazes my ribs, underneath one of my breasts.

He pulls back again, his lips swollen from kissing, his voice a rasp. "You taste like summer," he says, his mouth curls into a sexy smirk that makes my stomach somersault.

"Good," I whisper, my lips brushing his. "Then we're even on the seasonal front."

His hand cups the back of my neck, and he kisses me again, slower this time, like he's taking his time, wanting to memorize the shape of my mouth, the taste of it.

His other hand grips my ass tighter, pressing me closer to him, and my whole body melts into his. I can feel every hard, perfect inch of him through my leggings, and it's maddening. My fingers tangle in his hair, and it's just as soft as I hoped it would be. Tugging slightly, he moans into the kiss. It's low and raw.

"Careful, Raene," he murmurs against my lips. "You're playing with fire."

I love the way his nose brushes mine; the subtle intimacy makes me smile and sigh, as I run my hands through his hair.

"Then I want you to burn me," I tell him, my voice shaky but certain.

The look he gives me can torture a woman...as his hand starts to go lower. *Please don't stop.* I can feel myself throbbing with anticipation, wanting him inside me.

"Tell me if you want me to stop," he says, his tone low, strained, as if he is barely hanging on by a thread.

I shake my head, my hands on his shoulders. "I don't want you to stop."

Something flashes in his eyes, like all control has snapped. His hand moves lower, slipping into my leggings.

He leans forward, his fangs scraping that sensitive pulse point on my neck as I tilt my head to give him access. A violent shudder rolls through me.

"I can smell your arousal before I even touch your pussy..." His fingers dip lower, teasing the slick heat of me, just one finger stroking through my wetness before pulling back to trace slow circles over my clit.

My head immediately falls to his shoulder, my nails dig in, and I suck in a breath before letting out a moan.

"*By the Seven*, Raene..." he breathes, forehead pressing to mine as he dips a finger inside me, deep and slow, then adds another as his thumb continues its torturous rhythm.

"Oh my..." I groan, like I'm already falling apart, every pump of his fingers steals my breath. My head tips back against the doorframe, eyes fluttering shut, as he moves slowly, finding the rhythm that makes my knees go weak around his waist as I creep closer to that edge.

It feels so good.

"Look at me," he commands, and when I force my eyes open, his gaze is locked on me. "I want to see you."

Fuck.

I can feel the heat building inside of me, and it's unbearable. It's too much. My hips rock against his hand, my breath coming out in short, shaky gasps as his fingers curl upward to hit the right spot.

"Just like that," he murmurs, his lips lightly brushing my jaw, my neck.

"Just..." I moan, rocking against him with a sharper roll of my hips, "like..." the word torn from me as heat pools even lower, "that." I cry out, my voice shaking as I grind harder, desperate for more, not breaking eye contact.

"You're so beautiful like this. The Goddess herself would envy you, Raene."

The pleasure coils tighter and tighter, so sharp I dig my nails into his shoulders, nearly breaking the skin.

"Ash...I—" My lips part, but no words come out. I can't speak. I can't even think, I just feel, caught entirely by the pull of him.

"I've got you," he growls, his lips brushing my ear, the warmth of his breath sending shivers down my spine. "You're close, aren't you? So perfect for me..." He pauses, his teeth grazing my earlobe. "...but I need you to let go, Goddess."

And I do. The wave crashes through me, and I cry out, sobbing as my body trembles and clenches around his fingers. He doesn't stop; he keeps moving inside me through every pulsing aftershock.

His lips are against my temple, murmuring words I can't even hear because I don't think I can process anything coherent at the moment.

When the world finally starts to piece itself back together, and the stars have floated away from my vision, I'm limp in his arms, my forehead once again pressed to his shoulder.

He exhales a shaky breath, kissing my hair before slowly lowering my legs from around his waist, setting me on my feet. Only my feet don't quite work. My knees buckle, and I grab onto his shirt, still panting and breathless. My heart is trying to get back under control.

"Easy," he says, one arm around my waist, holding me steady. His eyes are bright, a beautiful gold that pulls me in even further, and his jaw is tight like he's fighting for control. "I've got you."

I glance down, catching the obvious strain of him through his jeans, and heat floods me all over again. I want to fix that. I want to give him the same undoing he just gave me.

I reach for his belt, but his fingers close gently but firmly around my wrist. "Another time," he says with a small, crooked smile, bending to pick my purse off the ground for me. His restraint feels almost unbearable.

"But..." I start, but the shake of his head cuts me off, handing me my purse.

"I'm okay," he says, voice rough. "I'm more of a *giver*. I hope you consider that...adequate, he teases, but his face is serious.

Whoa.

"Alright then," I say, my eyes not leaving his face.

A flutter of wings draws my gaze upward to see Nim, swooping back into the shop through an open skylight. He dives into the tree, and as he does, a single leaf drifts down and lands softly on the floor. I tilt my head.

"Is that normal?" I ask, pointing at the leaf.

Ash turns, his gaze following mine. He walks toward it, and I fall in step behind him. Crouching down, he picks up the leaf by the stem, turning it over in his hand as if it might reveal some secret as to why it has fallen. He straightens and runs a hand through his hair.

His face shifts, worry and puzzlement shadowing his features. "I've never seen a leaf fall, ever. With the enchantment, it shouldn't be possible."

"Are you okay?" I ask softly, reaching out, needing to touch him. A moment ago, it was all heat, and now he's looking at the leaf as if his world is ending.

"Yeah..." he says, though it sounds more like a reflex than the truth. His gaze drops down to the leaf again, before he sets it carefully on the counter as if it will shatter. "Yeah." He says a final time, but his eyes lift back to mine, and unease still flickers there.

"I know you have to get going, but are you sure I can't convince you to stay? Just a little bit longer?" His hands slide to my waist, tugging me closer.

I reach up, my thumb brushing over the stubble on his jaw. "I wish I could, but I have plans with my grandmother. Just know..." my lips curve. "I had a nice time with you today, decorating...and accomplishing some other...things."

His chuckle is low and warm. "Yeah?"

"Mm-hmm..."

He kisses me, soft and gentle, like that very first time, and it's enough to make me want to stay.

"I'll talk to you soon," I whisper, forcing myself to pull away before I change my mind.

Even as I leave, I can still feel him. His hands are imprinted on my skin, his mouth owns mine, and the way he made me come apart like I was something delicate and precious in his arms, it lingers like a mark on my soul that will never leave.

Where the hell do we go from here?

16
Three Days
SYLAS

Me: *I can't get you out of my mind.*

Raene: *This sounds like your problem.*

Me: *Definitely my problem, but you're not helping.*

Raene: *I offered to help with my mouth. But shouldn't you be busy with vendor phone calls, running an adorable bookstore?*

Me: *Ohhh, you're trouble. So, you think fall is adorable?*

Raene: *No. Your bookstore is adorable, and I'm winning anyway. I'm halfway through my list of vendors and others who are setting up food booths.*

Me: *Is it a challenge?*

Raene: *Of course, you made two lists...*

Me: *What's the prize?*

Raene: *Hmmm... I'll think on it.*

Me: *I have some input.*

Raene: *I'm sure you do.*

Three days.

It's been three days since I saw her. Kissed her. Felt her in my arms. Three days since I had her riding my hand. The sounds she made are tattooed on my brain. I'll never forget her whimpers. The gasp of her breath being taken away.

I wanted her to stay that night. Goddess, I wanted her. I wanted to push past the boundary of firsts, take her deeper, give her everything, but I didn't want her to regret it. I need Raene to be one hundred percent sure she wants this, wants *me*.

The way she kissed me. It was supposed to be just a kiss. That's all I'd let myself imagine. A taste. A moment. A way to finally feel what I'd been denying every time she looked at me with those wide, curious eyes.

But then her mouth touched mine, and everything I thought I could control melted away. It was hunger. It was a surrender. It was need. I had her in my arms, but she was in control the whole time. She told me what she wanted, and I gave her exactly that.

Her fingers curling into me like she was holding on, like I was the only thing tethering her to the ground. And when she pulled me back for more...when her eyes searched mine before her lips claimed me again, it undid me. That look? That silent plea, hoping we were on the same page? I'll never forget it.

And then there was her body. Soft and warm, pressing closer, moving against me. The roll of her hips when my fingers were inside her made me think of things I shouldn't, things that would keep me awake tonight. Fuck, the thought of her actually riding me...her knees braced on either side of my hips, her head tipped back as she moaned my name. It does things to my chest, to my head. I'm already too far gone.

And then there was the scent of her arousal, sweet and unmistakable. It soaked into my skin and flooded my senses. Her body made that for me. *Because of me.*

I was the reason her breath hitched, the reason she trembled, the reason she was wet and wanting. Just knowing I could make her feel like that, make her *want* like that, sent a low, deep ache straight through me.

She has no idea what she's done to me. No idea how badly I want her again. How badly I want all of her. Her mouth, her hands, her voice, her body moving against mine until neither of us can breathe.

That night, my self-control? Nonexistent. I had to take the edge off, my mind replaying her voice in my head. Thinking of how she felt, so tight and wet. Even then, it wasn't enough. It'll never be enough.

I come downstairs a few hours before opening, still in my grey sweats and a black t-shirt that's seen better days. I need coffee before I can even think about dealing with the festival flyers or whatever the hell is going on with my magic.

The wreaths were enhanced yesterday to look more realistic. For some reason, they grew too. That wasn't supposed to happen. Now I have falling leaves, and I look at the shimmering enchanted tree, my beautiful tree, and notice a few more leaves have fallen. The last thing I need is a mystery a few weeks before the fall festival.

The shop is quiet, soon filled with the familiar sounds of coffee brewing and tea steeping. The rich aroma anchors me.

"Nice outfit, boss," Nim says, swooping down from the open skylight. Here we go.

"Are you going for the 'I just rolled out of bed thinking about Raene' look?"

I grunt, grabbing my mug and pouring coffee like it's my saving grace. "It's called comfort, Nim," I say out loud, adding pumpkin caramel creamer to the mug. "Not that you'd know anything about it."

"Deflecting," he sing-songs, the words slipping into my mind like smoke, curling around each thought. He flutters in a lazy circle above my head before landing on the edge of the coffee bar with a thump.

"You're brooooooding," Nim croons down the bond. *"I know why."*

"Do you?" I grit down the bond, taking a sip, willing the coffee to hit my veins faster.

"Three guesses," Nim says, beginning to slurp from the bowl of tea I had set down for him. *"And I'll only need one. Starts with 'R,' ends with 'aene,' and she's been living rent-free in your brain since the kiss."*

I sigh, leaning against the counter. "You're really not going to let this go, are you?"

"Nope." His voice hums through the bond, smug as hell. I *think* he's smirking, hell, I can practically *feel* it. It's not just his voice in my head; it's the faint ripple of satisfaction rolling off him, like the twitch of his tiny snout is sending chills straight down my spine.

His tiny face is too expressive for his own good. *"You're walking around like a lovesick human. Are you adding hearts to the festival flyers you printed yet? Or is that next on the list?"*

"You're hilarious," I mutter, grabbing the stack of flyers I printed earlier and moving them to the counter. I catch myself staring at the top one for too long, like maybe I'm trying to distract myself with the words.

"And no, I'm not lovesick. I'm just...thinking."

"Uh-huh, whatever helps you sleep tonight."

"Enough," I growl, heat rushing to my face to the points of my ears. I set my mug down a little too hard, and Nim chuffs, his wings flickering like he's laughing with his whole body.

"Touchy," he says. *"But seriously, Ash, when's the last time you were this worked up over someone? Like, ever?"*

I stare into my coffee, the steam wafts to my nose, and settles me some. "That's none of your business. You're a dragon, Nim. You can't help me with my problems."

"It's literally all my business," Nim says, pretending to dust his wings. *"Because when you're distracted, things get weird. Like, say, your magic deciding to go haywire and make leaves fall indoors? I can feel it."*

That makes me pause. My jaw tightens. "I'll handle it."

"Sure," Nim says, unconvinced, polishing off his tea. *"But maybe, just maybe, figuring out your emotions would fix both problems. Ever think about that?"*

I glare at him, but he only flashes that smug, sharp-toothed grin before flitting into the tree, curling up on his branch like he's the king of everything. And the worst part? He's fucking right. My magic *is* tied to my emotions, something I haven't had to face in a very long time, and now I don't know what the hell to do about it because Raene is going to leave.

Dominik's place looks like the ultimate bachelor pad and smells like pizza and beer as I'm greeted by the sound of the pregame commentary blaring from the TV.

He's got a spread of snacks on the counter, too—potato chips in a bowl with various dips and tortilla chips alongside a mini crockpot of his famous spicy queso that's probably going to wreck someone's guts later, but we will regret nothing. I add my contribution to the mix, setting down the boxes of wings from the bar, garlic parm, and buffalo.

"About time you showed," Viktor says from the kitchen, popping the lid off a pizza box, the steam exhaling its scent in the air. "I was starting to think you'd hoard those wings for yourself."

"You underestimate my generosity," I shoot back, smirking as I open a container.

Dominik strolls in from down his hallway, wiping his hands on a towel. "Beer's in the fridge. Help yourself. And don't forget Garruk's cookies."

Garruk, leaning against the counter with his arms crossed, gives a sheepish shrug. "I do my best." He lifts the lid off his container of chocolate chip cookies, and the smell immediately hits me: chocolate and sugar.

I grab a cookie because sometimes dessert is best to have first. Chewy center, crisp edges, chocolate melting on my tongue. Perfect.

"Does anyone want pizza?" Viktor asks, throwing a few slices on his plate before closing the box and moving on to the wings.

"Did you bring anything other than just pepperoni, mushrooms, and black olives?" Garruk asks, grabbing a paper plate.

"I brought three boxes, including a meat lover's and a supreme."

Garruk dives into the supreme, throwing two slices on his plate. "So you brought that monstrosity because you're the only one that's going to be eating it, right?" He laughs, taking a bite of his pizza before adding some chips and queso to his plate.

I opened the box of Viktor's special to take a look. It didn't look *that* bad, but my face must scream something else.

"Looks weird, huh?" Garruk asks. "Like what kind of mushrooms are those? They have a purple-pinkish hue to them."

Viktor takes a large bite, shrugging his large shoulders. "Well, I like it."

Dominik just shakes his head, amused. "This is why I just buy the beer and host. It shuts all of you up."

We all laugh at that.

I make my way to the living room with my loaded plate to sit on the couch, resting my plate on the coffee table. Viktor sits on the other end, Dominik in his reclining chair, and Garruk at the barstool near the island.

"So," Viktor says around a mouthful of pepperoni, "the deck project is finally coming together. Though the weather would screw me over with rain in the forecast. I'm getting the railing up this week. It'll be good to go before the rain sets in."

Dominik nods, looking at the game on the TV. "You're taking on another job after that?"

"Maybe one smaller project before winter hits. Then I'll switch to indoor stuff. Elora wants the space above her second barn remodeled into a small apartment."

"Really, what for?" Garruk chimes in, licking wing sauce off his thumb. "Is she going to just rent the space out?"

Viktor nods his head, eyes on the screen. "I think so. Late fall and winter will be perfect to work on, have it ready by March."

Dominik leans back against the couch and turns to me. "I know you wanted to talk to me about a booth this year during the fall festival. I'll set up a booth for floral arrangements. Mostly bouquets, maybe a few of my dried arrangements if I can get enough stock done in time. I think people will like the mix of fresh but also seasonal."

"That sounds good," I say, eating a wing. "I'm sure it'll go great."

Dominik grins. "That's the plan. Are you good on your end? I know you were nervous about Vera not being able to help. You can't tell us you weren't. How's everything shaping up with Raene?"

"Going well, she has a lot of great ideas," I say easily, because it's true. Mostly. I even got a bulk order placed for the lanterns. "Flyers are printed and posted. I dropped some off around town already.

I'll hit the rest of the businesses, your businesses as well, and the town hall tomorrow, make sure everyone knows the itinerary."

They all nod, satisfied with my report. I leave it at that. I don't want to mention more about Raene. Not in detail, anyway. Not the way she looked at me like I was the only thing that existed when I had her pinned against a wall, or the way her lips felt when they brushed mine. That fucking mouth. I just say, "I'm getting to know her," because anything more would probably make me give away too much, and with a small town. Everyone knows everything, and no one knows how to stay out of your business.

Yeah, I think as I sip my beer, *I'm definitely getting to know her.*

The memory of her is constantly buzzing on my skin and replaying in my head like a record on repeat.

My body remembers every single second.

"PICK-SIX!" Garruk suddenly yells, launching up from the stool so fast he nearly spills his beer.

He's pointing at the TV like the players can hear him. "Go, go, go!"

We all jump to our feet just as the defense intercepts and runs the ball down the field. The room explodes in shouts and cheers. Viktor's fist-pumping, clapping Garruk on the back like he's proud. Dominik's laughing. I can't help it, I'm yelling too, adrenaline rushing as we see one of our favorite players crossing into the end zone.

"Hell yes!" Garruk exclaims, hopping in place like one big ass kid. "That's how it's done!"

"Damn," Viktor says, sinking back onto the couch. "That is one hell of a way to start the season."

"Yeah," I agree, dropping back into my seat with a grin. "That's a good way to start his contract year."

Garruk shoves a queso-loaded chip into his mouth. "Is he in the last year of his rookie contract already?"

"Yeah, we'd better resign him at the end of the season," I chime in.

The game rolls on, but my mind drifts again. Flyers. The festival. Raene. She's everywhere in my head, like she belongs there, and soon, I'll see her again. I already know it's going to be so fucking hard to keep my hands to myself.

Everly Hollow

Fall Festival
September 22- 28th

Day 1 - Autumn Lights & Lantern Parade
Day 2 - The Golden Twilight Market
Day 3 - Carnival
Day 4 - Carnival
Day 5 - Fall Ball
Day 6 - The Blackberry Moon Lily Drop Tent
Day 7 - Feast of Falling Leaves

17
To Nights Like This
RAENE

"Faerie wine?" I mumble, lifting the teal goblet to my lips and taking a sip. The bubbles dance on my tongue, sweet and fruity, and as soon as I swallow, warmth spreads throughout my body. The girls are watching me, their goblets in hand, waiting for my reaction.

We're outside in Elora's backyard, wrapped in the warm colors of the setting sun, and the glow of twinkling lights strung across the pergola. The outdoor furniture is ridiculously comfy, the kind that makes you sink into another world and never want to leave. I can even feel the plushness of the cushions through my leggings. A small table between us is covered in a spread of food that looks divine, and then there's the wine…delicious, dangerous faerie wine.

I take another drink, peering down into my glass. "Is this going to get me drunk?" I laugh. "I feel like this can get addicting…it's so good!"

"Maybe a little bit," Jas says with a grin, tucking her legs underneath her on the sofa before leaning forward to grab a slice of cheese and a cracker. She takes a bite, then pauses, staring down at it like it suddenly spoke to her heart, and sighs.

"I love our girl nights," she admits softly. "I needed this. I've been feeling a little overwhelmed lately with Seren, the business, and...she's starting Kindergarten. Aaryn isn't here." She pops the remaining cracker in her mouth.

Next to her, Poppy reaches over, giving her shoulder a light rub. "Is she at *her* house right now?"

Jas nods, lifting her glass for a sip. "Yeah, she's having a sleepover there."

I glance between Jas and Poppy, brows raised. "Who is *her*? Are we just...not naming this mysterious person?"

Oriana snorts with laughter, and Jas cracks a smile, shaking her head.

"Sorry," Jas says, running her fingers through her curls, only to get them caught halfway. She wiggles them free with a soft groan. Even her hair is exhausted.

"My mother-in-law," she explains. "Aaryn's mom, Elowen."

Her tone shifts as she says the name, like it carries a heavy weight. "She's...quite the character. She adores Seren, but ever since Aaryn died, something's changed. I mean, I get it, he was her only son. But she doesn't warm to me the way she used to. I don't know."

She shrugs, but her shoulders stay tense, as if her confession won't fall off.

"I'm sorry to hear that," I tell her, and I am. I can't imagine losing my spouse and then his mother acting like I put a bad taste in her mouth. She needs all the love and support she can get. It's good she has help with Seren, but I don't know how I would feel if someone treated me like family and then, when the one person that brought us together is gone, they change. I'm grateful I had my grandmother when my parents died.

"We're all happy you're here, Jas, and if you need help with anything, let us know, okay?" Elora pipes up from her hammock swing.

She's curled into it, wearing shorts and a tank top, which I've honestly never seen her in. She usually wears skirts and dresses like a goddess of the woods. Her bare feet dangle lazily, an anklet bracelet made of twine and little flowers with toes painted a soft pink. Her waist-long hair is braided into a crown, an abundance of flowers blooming between the strands.

Oriana raises her glass, "I second that!"

"Same," Poppy says. "If you need a break or help, let us know."

Jas looks around, her eyes glistening, tears forming in the corners, and she wipes them gently before they fall. "I appreciate you girls."

Poppy gives Jas's thigh a quick, reassuring pat before reaching for a carrot stick and dipping it into a spread that looks like hummus but is not. They told me it's made from some other type of legume, something similar to chickpeas, though I've already forgotten the name. The color is a shade darker, and when I tried it earlier, the flavor surprised me. It's good, similar to hummus, but with this warm, nutty undertone that lingers on your tongue.

"How is the festival planning going?" Elora asks, munching on a few items from her plate. "I know we talked about my booth, but do you need a list of the produce items I will have there?"

"I think a sign of all the fruits and veggies will be great to have at your booth, and I'm excited to see it." I pop a chip in my mouth and chew slowly as I feel Oriana's gaze on me.

She swirls her glass. Her blue eyes look like shimmering pools of light as she crosses her legs, popping a grape into her mouth.

"And Sylas...or Ash, as you call him, how is he?

Once again, every pair of eyes is on me.

"We...we um...we kissed..." I pull up the shoulder of my oversized t-shirt, but it slides back down. That's the purpose of the outfit. Tease of the shoulders, which I love, but I'm nervous as hell.

Oriana stands up to dance to the music that is playing, her skirt swishing with the movement of her hips. Jas screams, a happy, giddy scream. Elora's eyes go wide, but she gives me the sweetest smile with the faintest blush on her cheeks, and Poppy just gives me a lopsided grin like she knew it would happen. It was only a matter of time.

"I knew it! I knew he wanted you! I mean, look at you, Raene!" Oriana says before sitting down to catch her breath.

Look at all of you. What's in the water here?

Oriana refills her glass before adding a few more items to her plate. "Okay, I got my snacks, now I'm ready for you to share the deets, so spill."

I laugh, sipping my wine. "I am not sharing this with you."

Oriana tsks, wagging a finger at me. "Nope, wrong answer, Rae. It's girls' night. We all share secrets and gossip."

"We do?" Elora asks.

"Oh absolutely...we do!" Jas interrupts, her lips curve into a mischievous grin. "Was the kiss tender and sweet, or was it one of those kisses that was life-altering and took your soul?

Took my soul?

"Life-altering and soul-taking? You guys are ridiculous," I say, covering my face with both hands.

"It was..."

"Tell us everything," Poppy says, her tone firm but her grin wicked. "Don't hesitate to share the details. Where were his hands? Where were you guys when this kiss happened? Did anything else happen?"

Elora was quiet, but she leaned in, balancing on the edge of the hammock.

"Do you *really* want to know what happened?" I ask, my face in my hands.

I need more wine for this.

"Yes," Oriana waves her hands in a shooing motion.

"You're a brilliant writer, so I know you'll be able to share your story. So spill. Or I'll start making things up...and trust me, I'm very creative."

"You *are* creative," Poppy chimes in. "But I think we deserve the real story."

I sigh, but it's useless. I'm grinning like an idiot, and they all know I'm going to share the details. I'm glad guys don't do this because then the majority of Everly Hollow will know what went down in the bookshop.

"Fine. It was..." My voice dips, soft, like I'm replaying it in my mind, and I am because I will never forget that day. "It was slow at first. Like we didn't know if we wanted to give in or not, like we were testing one another. It was very tender but perfect. But then it got..."

"Hot?" Poppy interrupts.

"Yes. Very hot," I admit, laughing. "He's...intense. The way he looked at me with my legs around him..." My breath hitches just thinking about it.

Poppy puts her hand up in the air. "Wait, your legs were around him?" Her head tilts. "Time to sprinkle the details on the cupcake. Where were you?"

"The bookshop."

"Where in the bookshop?"

"Against the door."

"Oh, scandalous. That anticipation building of possibly getting caught...and his hands?"

"On my ass, on my thighs..." I ponder on if I want to disclose further details, but what the hell, "Under my shirt...inside my leggings..."

My hands quickly shot up to stifle the laugh that was about to escape.

"Goddess above," Jas groans. "That's so damn sexy."

It was. Very much so. I can't get his voice out of my head, and the thought of his fingers on my skin again is torture.

"So, when are you seeing him again?" Oriana asks.

Hopefully soon.

"I don't know, maybe this weekend or next week?" I say more of a question because I'm not sure. We haven't talked about when we will meet up next, and I know we still have a few things left to do before all the heavy work starts the week of the festival, but when we do see each other, what the hell am I going to say? My gaze drifts off to the fields, and I see something flickering lightly.

"What is that?" I point, and everyone turns their heads in the direction of my finger.

"Goddess!" Elora exclaims, leaping up out of her swing and running off the patio and into the lush grass. "It's a glow-moth!"

We all follow her, and the coolness of it feels amazing on my feet.

"I've never seen one a few weeks early," Elora whispers. We stand at a distance as it flutters over some flowers. It's small, but much larger than a firefly. It's a glowing moth that has a fuzzy body and is brown, cream, and deep blue. It's adorable and beautiful. I don't touch it, but I can't take my eyes away either.

Elora, Jas, and Poppy are all huddled chatting while Oriana skips her way over to me. "I have two things to ask you."

"Okay." I stand tall, roll my shoulders back.

"First, do you want to come to the book club tomorrow evening at seven-thirty at the cafe? We're starting a new dark romance."

"I'd love to!" I beam. When spending so much time writing books, I rarely get to actually sit down and enjoy them anymore.

"Secondly, you need to go see Flora."

"Flora?" I ask. My nose wriggles a bit. "What for?"

"A tonic," she says, giving me a small smile. "Just to be safe."

A tonic. The wheels in my head are spinning. I'm thinking, but maybe too hard until it clicks. A tonic. *Just to be safe.* A contraceptive tonic.

"Okay," I say. That's something I'm going to have to look into.

We stay here for a few minutes to see if any more moths come, but this little one goes back into the forest. We go back to our seats and continue in our conversations about books, life, and occasionally Ash.

"Okay," Oriana says, getting to her feet. "Everyone, stand, grab your glass, and make sure it's full!"

With glasses refilled with the sparkling pink wine, we stand and together hold our glasses to the moon beam that shines its way through.

"To nights like this." Oriana begins. "To friendship, and a new friend." She turns her head towards me with a smile. "To blessings from the Goddesses. To our hopes, dreams, and successes. To love, good health, and happiness. To secrets, laughter, and too much wine!"

She holds her glass up higher and shimmies her hips to the light music.

We all laugh and dance along.

"May we always have nights like this," Oriana says, her face serious but radiant in just love and happiness. "May we never forget the reasons to celebrate together and celebrate who we are."

Our glasses clink and I close my eyes...smile, and drink.

18
I'd break all my rules for you
SYLAS

Me: *Good morning.*

Raene: *Morning, Ash. Miss me?*

Me: *Yes. When can I see you again? You know, for festival planning.*

Raene: *Is that what we're calling it now? I like a male who is straight to the point. LOL.*

Raene: *I'm spending time with my grandma today, then going to the cafe later. I was invited to the book club. I may get some pumpkins from the grocery market.*

Me: *Sounds like a good day. Well, if you are free later on, let me know. I hope you enjoy the book club.*

Raene: *Thanks*

Me: *And pumpkins? That's a good girl.*

"You missed one," Nim yawns and stretches on the lowest branch of the tree as I sweep up more falling leaves.

I sweep up another pile of fallen leaves, muttering under my breath. "You could help, you know."

"Leaf loop, then I'll help," he says.

"Fine," I say down the bond, but it brings a small smile to my face.

I twirl a finger at the small pile of leaves on the ground until a gold shimmering ring reveals itself, then another forms midair, before they fade away.

Nim leans down from the branch. With a quick wriggle of his bottom, tail swaying, he launches himself into the loop, diving headfirst into the leaves until the tip of his tail disappears under the surface. He bursts back out, does a quick spin, and dives again.

Nim continues to play while the bristles hit the wood floor, adding leaves into his pile that continue to flutter out with each turn he takes. All the while, I'm able to quickly ring up two customers who are loving the entertainment of a dragon in leaf piles.

What's bad is that my customers are asking me if I changed the tree enchantment.

What do I say? Sure! I'm changing up the aesthetic this year!

My emotions appear to be out of control right now, so my magic is beginning to spiral.

I've never been with a woman, human at that, that has my emotions in a chokehold. This morning, I woke up aching. Thinking of her had me grinding my teeth in the shower, needing to take the edge off before I lost my damn mind. Still, even after that, she lingers in my head. I'm completely fucked, and my magic is showing it. I like her. I *really* fucking like her. I like being around her.

A flash of movement catches my eye. Nim is now rolling in the leaf pile like some deranged cat, his tiny wings fluttering while he chuffs smoke in excitement. A laugh bubbles out of me despite everything, the sound surprising even me.

"Having fun?" I ask him, leaning on the broom.

"Best leaf pile yet. You should thank Raene for that. She's clearly...inspiring you," he says through the bond, voice cheerful.

I grit my teeth but can't fight the heat creeping up my neck to my ears. *"Shut it."*

Before he can taunt me again, a toddler from the children's book section waddles over, her mother following behind her. The tiny toddler is all chubby freckled cheeks and wide blue eyes. Her furry ears perk up on her head, and her brown tail with white fur at the end swings quickly in excitement. It has Nim pausing mid-roll, watching her approach, but then she squeals and dives into the leaves beside him, giggling.

Nim chirps back at her, flaring his wings like he's putting on a show.

Something twists in my chest. It's stupid, but the sight of them, this tiny dragon and this tiny little girl playing together, hits me right in the gut. Raene would smile at this.

Hell, I can almost *see* her in my mind, crouching down beside them, her laugh carrying through the shop like sunlight through the trees. I know she would keep her distance when it was in loop mode to not have a mishap like last time.

Damn it.

If I don't get myself under control soon, I'm going to have more than falling leaves to explain.

There's a knock on the door just after nine. It's not late, but I'm not expecting anyone. No texts or calls from anyone saying they are stopping by. I pull on a plain white tee to go with my black joggers, bare feet padding down the spiral staircase as I rake a hand through my hair.

I unlock the door and open it wide. When the hinges creak, Raene glances over her shoulder, a faint smile softening her lips. I'm not thinking at all. I just reach out, my hand sliding around her wrist as I gently pull her closer. "Why are you leaving?"

Her eyes quickly darted side to side at my question. "Sorry to just show up like this," she says.

"I should've texted after the book club. I was going to go straight home, but..." she hesitates, looking up at me, "I wanted to stop by. When you didn't answer right away, I figured you weren't home, so I was just going to leave and text you later."

"You don't have to apologize for not texting me," I murmur, my hands finding her waist. Her body presses against mine, warm and soft, and for a moment, I forget how to breathe. "I like surprises."

"Do you?" Her smile widens, her gaze holding mine like she's searching for something.

"I had to get a shirt on," I say, my voice low and teasing, "but if I'd known it was you, I could've kept it off."

She throws her head back, laughing, the sound making my stomach flip. Her hands grip my arms. They are light, warm, and leave a burn on my skin that makes me want to pull her closer. *Her touch does things to me.*

"Come inside," I say, brushing my thumb across her hip as I guide her in and close the door.

Nim is perched on a branch near the staircase, his little head cocked to the side, eyes bright as he watches her. She lights up the second she spots him.

"Hey, you," she says softly, reaching out to give him a few light pets. He tilts his head into her touch, purring, his little leg twitching as she scratches under his chin.

She laughs, glancing back at me. "He acts like a dog sometimes. He's adorable."

I shake my head, smirking. "Don't inflate his ego. He'll never let me hear the end of it."

"She speaks the truth," Nim hums. Which makes me chuckle.

We climb the last few steps together, stepping into my apartment with her for the first time. She puts her purse onto the brown leather couch, her gaze taking everything in with that curious softness I've come to love.

The place isn't huge, but it's pretty spacious. A small living room with a TV, an armchair, and a couch with an olive-green blanket draped across it. A decent-sized kitchen with a laundry nook off to the side, and a narrow pantry tucked beside it.

Two doors are down the hall, one to the bathroom, the other to my bedroom. A single candle flickers on the coffee table, filling the space with a warm, subtle scent of cedar and amber. A couple of skylights allow the natural lighting to spill across the floor, and the kitchen window looks out over part of the town behind the bookstore.

"It's cozy," she says, her eyes roaming the room before landing on me. "Like you."

I arch a brow, stepping closer. "Like me?"

"Yes. You're all tall, golden, and handsome, and with your fall vibes, you're cozy. You're like a walking knitted sweater," she says, smiling in that soft way that punches straight through my chest.

I grin, tilting my head. I only heard one thing from what she said. "You think I'm handsome?"

"Mm-hmm." She nods, not even hesitating. "Very."

I try not to let that go to my head as I ask, "Can I get you anything?"

"Just some water, please," she says, sinking into the couch.

I return a moment later with two glasses, handing her one before setting mine down on the coffee table after a sip.

"Thanks," she says, taking a drink. A quiet sigh escapes her as she sets the glass on the table.

"So," I ask, leaning back into the couch beside her, propping my head up with my hand, my elbow resting on the back of the couch, "how was book club? What's the genre this time?"

Her eyes brighten instantly. "It was a lot of fun! I downloaded the book after girls' night and couldn't put it down, so I was able to catch up to where they were. They all just started it, too." She pauses, a sly smile tugging at her lips. "It's a dark romance."

She picks up the glass and takes another sip. Clearing her throat.

I can't help but watch her mouth.

I take another sip of water, mostly to give my hands something to do other than reach for her. "So what's this one about?"

She leans forward, her voice low but serious, like she's about to disclose a secret. "It's about this morally grey anti-hero, you know...the kind of man you shouldn't root for, but you do anyway. I love the banter, and the tension..."

Her eyes meet mine for just a second, and I can hear her pulse beating rapidly.

I smirk, letting the silence stretch. "It sounds like I have competition."

Her eyes narrow playfully. "Oh, you think you're in the running?"

"Oh, I know I am," I murmur, inching closer. "The question is, do I have to be morally gray, or do I just have to keep you on the edge of your seat...waiting for more?"

Her heart is racing, but she doesn't look away. "Edge of my seat."

She reaches out and takes my glass, setting it on the coffee table.

"What are you doing?" I ask, trying my hardest to keep my voice steady.

"Something I wanted to do a few days ago..." she whispers, straddling my lap.

Shit.

My cock stirs immediately, hard and ready.

She knows it. Hell, she feels it because she shifts her hips and lines herself up perfectly, grinding against me with slow pressure that punches the air out of my lungs. My hands are on her, gripping her hips, sliding lower to cup her perfect ass because I *need* to feel her. Every inch of her feels like she's made to fucking ruin me.

A soft, broken whimper vibrates against my neck, her lips barely brushing my skin. Then she presses her mouth fully there with her hands in my hair. She's kissing and tasting, her tongue gliding over a spot just below my jaw before sucking lightly. The sensation has my hips jerk up against her, and she laughs against my skin.

"Raene…" The words escape on a moan, my soul teetering on the edge of begging.

She pulls back to look at me, her eyes are dark, heavy-lidded, and full of lust. Tucking strands of hair behind my pointed ear, her fingers lightly trace the shape of it, as if she is trying to burn it to her memory.

"I really like your ears." A small smile is on her lips as she whispers her confession to me.

"I really, *really* like your mouth," I respond, tracing her lower lip with my thumb.

Her tongue darts out, gently sucking the top of it. Her eyes flutter closed as I pull my finger out of her mouth and slide my hand to grip the back of her neck and pull her face back to mine.

The kiss is instant, desperate. She softens into me, arms around my neck, hips rocking in a rhythm that has my body screaming for more. Her tongue teases and slides against mine. I can and will succumb to her taste, her warmth…her everything.

When she breaks the kiss, I'm already on the edge of losing all control. Her breath ghosts over my lips. Slowly, seductively, she slips off my lap.

"Raene..." I rasp, but she doesn't answer.

She drops gracefully to her knees between my legs, the sight alone is enough to make my pulse hammer. Her eyes lift to mine as hands drag up my thighs, nails lightly raking the fabric. I have to bite my tongue not to whimper like I've already lost the war before it's begun.

"Fuck," I whisper as she hooks her fingers into the waistband of my joggers.

She licks her lips, tugging them down in one smooth motion, my cock springing free, aching and heavy. The cool air hits me for a second, and then it's just her. Her breath inches away from me. I hiss out a breath when her fingers wrap around me, stroking slowly, her thumb brushing over the sensitive head, rubbing the precum into my skin like she's testing to see what I do. "Raene," I grit out.

Her tongue flicks out, wet and hot, tasting me with a teasing swipe that sends a bolt of heat straight through my spine. My hand automatically drops to her hair, threading into her braids, holding but not forcing. For this ride, I need something to hold on to.

Then she takes me into her mouth.

"Goddess..." My head falls back against the couch, eyes slamming shut as I feel her lips slide down around me. Her tongue swirls, slow and deliberate, and I'm already coming undone.

She sets a pace, stroking with one hand while sucking with her mouth. Every time she hollows her cheeks, it pulls a deep, guttural sound from my chest. I can't stop it.

The nails of her other hand drag lightly over my thighs, just enough pressure to make me shudder, and then she takes me deeper, so much deeper, until the back of her throat welcomes me.

My hips buck up without permission, thrusting into the wet heat of her mouth.

"*Ahh*, fuck, you're so good at this." I'm trying to hold back, trying to make this last, but she's too good at this.

She moans around me at the praise, and the vibration nearly undoes me. One hand is gripping the blanket that tumbled beside me, but the one tangled in her hair tightens, guiding her as my hips thrust up and down, fucking her mouth.

I open my eyes just to see her looking up at me, her lashes in a low sweep, but her gaze is locked on mine, and she's enjoying every second of watching me unravel.

That mouth on me is the hottest, most dangerous thing I've ever seen.

"Raene, I'm..." The words break off into a moan as she begins sucking harder, faster.

I'm gone. My hips thrust once, twice, and then I come with a sharp moan, spilling into her mouth. She doesn't stop either. She swallows every single drop, her tongue still lapping me until I'm twitching from the overstimulation and sensitivity.

"Shit," I breathe, leaning forward slightly, my hand still tangled in her hair, my heart pounding out of my chest.

She pulls back slowly, licking her lips, and wipes the corner of her mouth with the back of her hand. The wicked smile she gives me makes my knees weak.

"You're going to be the death of me," I say hoarsely, pulling my boxers and joggers up.

She laughs softly, settling back into my lap, her warmth pressed against me. I'm still trying to catch my breath and steady my heartbeat, but now all I can think about is how badly I want her. Every bit of her.

"Raene..." I tilt her chin up with a finger so she's looking right at me. "Stay tonight."

Her lips curve as her eyes read my face. "Stay?"

"Yeah." I lean in, brushing my mouth against hers. "In my bed. With me. I want you."

She kisses me gently, her lips still tasting faintly of me, and fuck if that doesn't do something to my chest because the images of her on her knees, between my legs, are flipping through my mind.

Her fingers play with the hair at the nape of my neck. "Not tonight," she whispers against my mouth. She lets out a light sigh. "But another time."

I groan softly, resting my forehead against hers. "You're killing me."

"I don't want to rush it," she says, her hand resting on my chest, right over my heartbeat.

Can she feel how fast it's still beating for her?

"Besides," she shrugs, "it's kind of fun watching you look at me like you're about to explode."

"Fun for you, maybe," I mumble with a small grin, wrapping my arms around her waist, holding her closer. "But in reality, it's torture."

She laughs, a beautiful sound that makes me want to devour her. "You'll survive, Ash."

Taking a deep breath, my hands squeeze her hips.

"Do you have any idea how hard it is for me not to just pick you up and carry you to that bedroom?"

Her brows lift, her smile turning sly. "Is that your usual technique?"

"No." I pause, my gaze dropping to her lips. "But for you? Fuck yeah, I'd break all my rules for you."

She presses another slow kiss to my mouth.

"Next time," she repeats, her voice softer now, like a promise.

"Next time," I echo, though I don't let her go just yet. I just hold her there against me, pausing the moment because the way she looks at me, it's like this may be something worth keeping.

19
It was waiting for you
RAENE

This week, I like Mondays. It's been three weeks since Grandma's surgery and two weeks till the fall festival begins, but I'm pretty damn excited about it. Just the thought of seeing all our plans coming to fruition makes me anxious, but in a good way, and excited.

Totally *not* falling for fall.

Grandma has been healing well. She's putting more weight on her leg, and her recovery is going quickly. We have magic to thank for that. She's even starting swimming this week.

But that's not the only reason I'm smiling like the Cheshire cat as I eat my sandwich. This afternoon, Oriana, Jas, and I are going shopping for dresses at the boutique in town.

It's not just any boutique, either. The owner, Ivy, is a modiste and a witch who weaves magic into every single stitch. The reviews on her social media and website are raving five stars. Even people from the city get dresses made by her. Some are so beautiful I wouldn't even want to wear them for fear of ruining them. Some shimmer like starlight, like they've been blessed by the moon and stars themselves.

Oriana swears that Ivy can take your measurements, snap her fingers, and have a gown ready in days. It's like something straight out of a fairy tale.

While I've never been to a ball, the excitement of getting all dressed up and having a dress made with love and magic makes my heart race a little. Maybe it's because I know *he'll* be there, Ash. I wonder what he'll wear.

A suit? Tux? Will he wear those suspenders again? He and his fall-vibe charm are already deep under my skin, its claws sinking deep.

I pop a chip into my mouth, brushing crumbs off my fingers as I check emails. My publisher wants to finalize the draft deadline for the next book in my series.

I fire off a quick response, but my mind keeps wandering. It doesn't help that a scribbled note sits beside my laptop, bearing the address to Flora's apothecary in the hills.

Grandma thinks I just want to check out the shop like I promised her I would, but really, I'm going there for the tonic Oriana recommended. Because when a hot, fae male with golden eyes looks at you like *he* does, a girl has to be prepared.

Just thinking about our last encounter—tasting him, feeling him in my hands and my mouth—my God, I wanted him so badly to pick me up like he wanted and toss me on his bed, to have his way with all of me.

I was supposed to accumulate miles on this trip, not catch feelings, and I am.

The way he makes me feel when he says he misses me? When he asked me to stay, the plea in his voice was dangerous, intimate. The look he gave me, those goddamn *fuck me* eyes, like I'm the only thing he wants. It's too much and not enough all at once.

I'm leaving in three weeks. Three. Weeks.

So what the hell am I doing? I keep telling myself this is just fun, a friend with benefits situationship, whatever I want to call it to make it sound casual. However, I'm a whole ass adult and I can do what I want, and can do whomever I want.

But the way my chest tightens when I think of him seems to be constant. Yeah. I'm in trouble.

Guess I'll just enjoy it while I can. Before reality catches up and I have to leave this enchanted little bubble we're in, and him along with it.

Me: *Heading out now. Gotta run a quick errand first, then I'll meet you at Ivy's.*

Oriana: *Oh! Okay! Can't wait!!*

Jas: *I'm already here, parked outside the boutique. I call dibs on first peek at the gowns. LOL. I am getting one for Seren too! She's at the flower shop with Dominik today.*

Elora: *Ugh, I wish I could come! Next time, okay? I want one of Ivy's dresses so badly, so I'll have to see her in a few days. Too busy at the farm today.*

Me: *We'll take pictures! If you want someone to tag along with you, let me know!*

Elora: *Deal. Love you girls.*

I find Flora's home easily. I love that her shop takes up a large part of it—it seems to be that way for many people here. Convenient and close to your passion.

The apothecary smells of lavender, herbs, and something rich I can't place, maybe it's from the hills. Glass bottles of every color and size line the shelves, each labeled in neat handwriting.

Flora, with her hair pulled into a bun and eyes bright with wisdom, greets me warmly. "Oriana mentioned you might be coming by."

I offer a smile. I don't mind Oriana speaking on my behalf to give Flora a heads up, but honestly, my chest hurts at the thought of the new friends I've made here, and that in just three weeks, I'll be back to my life in the city.

She mixes the tonic right in front of me, a shimmering purple liquid that smells faintly of berries. "One spoonful, once a week," she explains. "Pick a day and stick to it. It'll take about twenty-four hours to settle into your system. This will last you thirty days. You might notice mild cramping, maybe headaches, but if you feel unwell at all or something seems alarming, contact me immediately."

I slowly nod my head in understanding at the warning, but my nerves begin to fill with worry.

"Nothing to be scared of dear. No one has had any serious side effects. It's just a precaution. The ingredients are not dangerous, but too much of something in one person's body can cause some issues. You should adjust quickly, but it is natural, safe, and very effective." She slips it into a velvet pouch before handing it to me.

"Got it," I say, clutching the small bottle like it's something precious.

"And Raene?" Her eyes soften. "This visit stays between us. My shop is a safe place. Everything here is confidential."

Relief washes through me. I'm open with my grandmother, and I know she and Flora are close, but this is something I really want to keep between Ash and me right now.

"Thank you, Flora. Truly."

I wave goodbye, tucking the pouch into my purse and pulling out my phone to send another quick message to the group chat.

Raene: *Done! Heading your way now.*

Oriana: *Hurry! Ivy just brought out a rack of gowns for some inspo, and I'm dying.*

I grin and hurry toward the boutique, my heart skipping at the thought of what's waiting. A dress spun from magic, and maybe the thought of Ash's jaw dropping seeing me in it.

"There she is!" Oriana calls, waving me over. She takes a sip of the glass of champagne and hands me one. I feel like I'm starring in an episode of *Say Yes to the Dress—Fall Ball Edition.*

"Look at this," she whispers to me, pointing to the dress on the rack beside her. It's a mermaid-style dress in a light green. It's sexy, beautiful, and the lace gives it a vintage feel.

"You will look absolutely breathtaking in this," I murmur, my fingers running over the delicate lace.

"Thanks, doll." She smiles, wrapping one arm around me and giving me a tight squeeze. "I want it in a pale blue, and she just measured me, but I couldn't wait to show you. You think Malik will love it?"

I take a sip of the champagne, the bubbles dancing on my tongue. "Girl, you could wrap a white sheet around your body and tie it off with a rope, and still look stunning."

She laughs, but her eyes shine in appreciation. "You know I can say the same thing about you, Rae. So, what color are you thinking?"

"To be honest, I'm not sure. I think I'll just have to see if something speaks to me." I turn to see Jas standing barefoot on the step riser in front of a mirror, twirling in a deep teal gown that hugs her curves like it was made for her. It's a perfect fit.

"Rae, what do you think?" Jas says, practically glowing. "I'm thinking of a light purple tulle dress for Seren."

"You look gorgeous, Jas," I say, just as the modiste appears from behind a curtain.

She's beautiful, tall, with rich mahogany skin. Her hair flows down her shoulders in her natural curls. Warmth and comfort just radiate from her. She gives me a large smile and holds out a hand, that I quickly accept. "You must be Raene," she says, her voice deep, yet smooth. "I've been told you need a gown that will make the whole room stop and stare."

Am I blushing? "Uh...what?"

"Mm." Her sharp eyes scan me, head to toe, as she moves around me like she's taking mental measurements without a single tape measure in hand. "I have just the thing."

She glides to a rack and pulls out a dress that takes my breath away. Gold. Not just gold, it looks like it's been poured and molded from sunlight.

The fabric is satin, and the neckline is off the shoulder, adorned with delicate golden appliques and beadwork. The bodice is fitted like a corset, with intricate embroidery radiating downward like the rays of light from the sun. The skirt sweeps the floor, with a high slit that reveals the entire right thigh and leg. It's unbelievably sexy.

"This," Ivy says, holding it out, "will complement your beautiful, brown skin most exquisitely. It's a goddess gown. Ruskaya spoke to me when I was designing it." Her hand glides over the fabric ever so gently. "And I think you're the woman who deserves to look like one."

"Oh, wow," I breathe, reaching out to touch the fabric. It's so soft, and the color is gorgeous.

"Go try it on," Oriana nudges me, practically bouncing with excitement as she takes my glass from me.

"Yes!" Jas says, clapping her hands happily.

I hesitate just for a moment before stepping into the changing room with the gown, my heart pounding as if this is something life-changing, and maybe it is. The dress slides over my skin. The gold glows against my complexion, and when I turn to look at the dress from every angle, there are no words. I'm speechless.

When I step out, the room is quiet.

"Oh, Rae..." Jas says, her eyes developing moisture and jaw agape. "That's *it*. That's the one."

"Ash is going to eat you up," Oriana adds, snapping her fingers to every word. "Turn around."

I do, and she zips me up.

Ivy clasps her hands, beaming. "I knew it. We will take it in...just a little bit, but otherwise it's perfect. So is the length. It was waiting for you."

20
Can you feel it?
Sylas

More leaves. Always more damn leaves.

Ever since Raene stepped into my apartment, she has moved into my mind and settled in with a good book. My magic has been disastrous to say the least. It takes me fifteen minutes just to make a simple cup of coffee because even my simpler magic takes a bit to not freak out.

I'm currently bagging up four massive heaps of leaves around the shop. I had to stop creating the enchanted leaf piles altogether after Nim *literally* got lost in another fucking dimension, one of the loops sent him to.

That scared the shit out of me. I haven't let him out of my sight since.

He might be an annoying little creature sometimes, but I've been bonded to him since the day he hatched. If something happened to him, if I lost him, I'd be even more of a mess than I already am. Nim keeps acting like it was no big deal, babbling about how much fun he had in whatever world that was, but the sight of him flickering in and out of existence...I told him I'd fix it. I have to.

The problem is...my emotions are haywire.

The only way I know to balance my magic is by balancing myself. But how the fuck am I supposed to do that when I have these raging, relentless feelings for someone who's leaving in just a few damn weeks?

I run a hand through my hair, pacing in front of the tree before starting to bag the leaves.

As if that isn't enough, books keep disappearing. Gone. Poof. I swear, every other day, something's missing from the inventory, and I've searched *everywhere*. Is my magic causing that? Am I unraveling everything I've built here because I can't keep my shit together?

I take a few deep breaths, forcing myself to look up at the tree. It's still beautiful—magnificent, even. The leaves shine in yellows, oranges, reds, and browns, but the longer I stare, the more dread settles into my chest, thick and heavy. If I don't get this under control, I'll start losing customers. I'll lose *everything*.

Maybe I should talk to Raene.

The front door creaks open, the bell chiming softly, and I turn just as Dominik steps inside. Seren's tiny hand is swallowed up in his much larger one.

"Hi, Sylas!" She says, smiling wide enough to squint her eyes.

She has a smile and ears like her father. It hits me like it always does, bittersweet and warm at the same time.

Dominik crouches to her level, his voice gentle. "You can go play and read in the kids' area, but don't go anywhere else, okay?"

She clasps her hands in front of her, bouncing on her toes like she might explode from excitement. "Okay! Can I buy *five* books?"

Dominik rolls his eyes, but he's grinning. She has him wrapped around her finger. "Three books."

Seren tilts her head, twisting her lips as she thinks. "Three books and a hot chocolate?"

"Deal," Dominik says.

Seren practically topples him over, launching herself into his arms for a hug before she sprints to the children's area.

A few other kids are already there with their parents, which is good. Great, actually. It means I'm not scaring everyone away. Yet.

"What's going on here?" Dominik asks as he straightens up, sliding his hands into his pockets.

His gaze flicks to the leaf pile near the door. "There are a ton of leaves on the sidewalk, too, from your trees out front."

I rub a hand down my face, fighting the scream building in my throat.

"Deep breaths," Nim mutters through the bond, his voice low and rumbling like a warm wind. He's perched above me on one of the branches, wings tucked in as if he knows I'm about to lose it.

I haven't told anyone about this. Not my parents. And now...well, I guess Dominik's about to get a glimpse of the chaos.

"My magic," I say, exhaling hard, "it's...a little glitchy right now."

He stands underneath the tree, leaning against the trunk with broad shoulders, his arms crossed. "Glitchy?" His hands gesture to all the leaf piles and black garbage bags. "You're practically running a damn pumpkin patch indoors. Elora's got some competition this year."

He grabs one of the black garbage bags to hold it open so I can finish my tedious chore.

"My emotions are a damn mess right now, like my tree. My magic is glitchy because of…"

"Raene?" He asks, tying a knot in the bag I just filled.

"I can smell her. A little on you, but also in the shop."

Well, that's fucking great. In my sudden loss of memory due to two of my brain cells competing for Raene's attention every few seconds, I forgot that werewolves, too, like fae, have enhanced senses, especially our sense of smell.

I let out a heavy sigh. "I don't know what to do."

We hear the sound of small feet running towards us. "Uncle Dominik! Can I have my hot cocoa now, please?

"Sure, little star. One second."

Seren takes the books, I'm pretty sure she has more than three, and climbs the chair of the nearest table.

I start making the cocoa because it doesn't require magic, but it does use a little something extra special. I add the cocoa to a mug with warm milk, a small square of chocolate, top it with four large marshmallows, and add a dash of cinnamon. Turning to the tree, I hold it out towards Nim.

"For Seren."

Nim blows his fiery breath onto the marshmallows, toasting them to golden brown.

"Thanks, Nim," I say. Even doing something this simple seems to ease the frustration a little bit.

Sitting Seren's mug on the table has her getting on her knees to wave to Nim before plucking one of the marshmallows out of the mug to shove into her mouth and eat immediately.

"Thanks for that," Dominik says, leaning against the register counter. "Are you going to talk to Raene?"

"I want to...but what do I say? My magic is fucked because of you, and I'm not mad, but I'm terrified to lose you and my magic. To lose everything."

"I would start a little less intense than that, maybe?" He rubs the back of his neck, the other hand on his hip. "It has to get better, right? Maybe talking to her will help it? Little by little? Maybe your magic doesn't like your feelings being suppressed and bottled up."

I've been sitting here for at least forty minutes, staring off into the night sky or watching the waterfall, hoping the sound of the roaring water might drown out my restless thoughts. I'm trying to figure out how to talk to Raene about my feelings and then see if, from there, I can have a sense of peace and balance.

Thinking of this all day has been mentally exhausting. Especially the thought of another book gone missing, or more leaves falling. Fuck, will branches fall next?

The sharp snap of a stick interrupts my thoughts, and I turn toward the sound.

"Hey...oh, hey...what are you doing here?" I do a double-take when I notice who is standing behind me and immediately stand up, as if I've been caught doing something wrong. The waning gibbous moon is shining its bright, silvery light on us.

"I didn't know anyone would be here. Honestly, I couldn't sleep. So I drove into town and walked the whole way. I needed to clear my head." Raene crosses and uncrosses her arms.

I nod my head, and a small smile graces my lips. "Come sit with me."

I sink back onto the blanket, and her footsteps crunch softly over the grass before she lowers herself beside me.

"Are you doing okay?" she asks gently. "I mean...I can go if you don't want me here."

I bring my knees up and rest my arms on them. "You're okay. I come here to think, too. It just feels...*alive* here, you know. Can you feel it?

She turns to look at me. Her legs are straight out, crossed at the ankles, as she supports herself on her arms. "Yes, I can feel it. It does feel different. I like it." She turns slightly to me. "So why are you here?

I knew she was going to ask why I was here. I just had a feeling to come here. To think. To try to figure everything out.

"Just a lot on my mind. The festival, work...you." We're pretty much finished with the heavy planning, and everything else is going to be coordinated by us on the day of.

"Me?"

"Yes. I like you, you know that."

"I know Ash." She looks up at the stars, and even in the silence, the sound of the waterfall is deafening.

"I like you too." She smiles before leaning over and giving me a small kiss, humming a little after.

"You're going to leave?" I whisper.

"So we should make the most of the time we have, yeah?"

So this is a fling. A however long it lasts kind of deal, let's have fun. Let's not have feelings or any emotions in this.

She stands up and takes off her shoes.

"What are you doing?" I ask.

I look at her empty shoes and back at her, pulling her leggings down. She's standing in front of me in a t-shirt and lacy, pink underwear.

Stars have mercy.

"For every question I ask, you have to give me a truth and a lie. If I guess the truth correctly, you have to take a step and lose an article of clothing...got it?" she asks, confidently.

"And every question you get wrong, I take a step back?" I question her.

She seems surprised by my new rule, but she nods, turns, and walks toward the lake.

That ass though.

She walks in, throwing a look over her shoulder before she dives under and swims for just a moment before rising to the surface.

She looks so fucking beautiful right now. With the glow of the water, the stars, and the moonlight.

"What's your middle name?

I stand, think of another name I want to give her.

"August and Jackson."

She doesn't even hesitate. "Jackson. I think even your parents knew August would just be too much."

I laugh and pull off my shoes, then my socks, tucking them back into the shoes.

"Jackson is cute, but I still like your new nickname though."

I do too.

I take a step forward.

She rises from the water, just a little, and her wet, graphic white t-shirt is glued to her, revealing her curves, her breasts...her nipp—

"What's your favorite season?"

"That's not fair," I tell her.

"No rules were specified, Ash." She gives me the cutest fucking smile and flutters her lashes.

"Fall and Winter." I roll my eyes teasingly.

"Fall," she says proudly, like she didn't just get two in a row because she is bending her imaginary rules.

I pull my shirt off, tossing it back to the blanket.

Taking a step forward. "The next question needs to be more of a challenge."

She looks me up and down, licks her lips, and begins to think. "You're scared of me. You like me, but you're afraid."

I didn't want the question to be *this* challenging.

"No. Yes."

"Yes."

I pull down my joggers, dropping them beside me. Taking a step forward in my boxers.

"Top two favorite fall drinks?

"Pumpkin Spice Latte and Maple Latte or Pumpkin Spice Latte and Pumpkin Caramel Latte."

She thinks for a minute. "This one is hard. Can I ask a different question?"

I laugh, folding my arms, which in turn has her biting her lower lip. "You have to guess."

"Too many pumpkin latte choices," she mumbles. "Okay, the first one?"

I pretend to take a step forward and slide back a step instead.

"I knew it was the other one!" She splashes water in my direction.

"Two more questions."

"Do you want to come into the water with me?"

"Yes...maybe..." I smirk.

"Yes. Definitely yes," she says, a lopsided grin on her face.

I take a step forward and take off my boxers, tossing them to the ground.

"Do you want me?" she asks, breathlessly as she starts to lower herself into the water for warmth.

"Fuck yes, I do."

And I take a step forward.

Into the water.

Straight for her.

21
I waited so many lifetimes for this
RAENE

"Goddess."

Oh shit—they're converting me. I'm starting to talk like everyone here.

He's walking towards me. Fully naked like the day the Goddesses carved him and brought him to life. Just standing in this water with the moonlight, the glow dancing across tanned skin, he looks unreal. His eyes are bright, burning with need, and I can feel it pulling me in.

I inch back to where I need to start treading water until he crooks a finger at me, saying, "*Come here.*" I'm practically prancing through the water to reach him.

He lifts me, wrapping my thighs around him, and kisses me deeply. His fingers dig in my skin hard enough to leave bruises, and I fucking love it. I want to wake up tomorrow with memories of him. Inside and out.

He settles me so I'm waist-deep in the water. The warmth of his body presses against mine. Even in the cool air, I feel amazing.

"Shirt off," he whispers on my lips.

I immediately raise my arms. Our noses are touching, he's holding me with one hand and using the other to tug off my shirt, tossing it into the water.

My hands move to their own accord, caressing his face, his fingers digging into my ass as he glides me up and down his length, the fabric of my underwear moves against my sensitive clit.

"Soooo good," my voice hitches as I move with him.

"You don't need these," he groans, tearing the lacy fabric underwater off of me. Now there is nothing between us. Only the warm, clear waters are a turquoise hue from the blue rock below us.

"You're a fucking goddess." His eyes roam across my face, memorizing all of it, his thumb caressing my cheek as he holds my face in his hands, pulling my face to his. My mouth opens to his, his tongue darting in, finding mine as he sucks and nibbles on my lips.

He trails a kiss on my jaw, then his warm mouth moves lower to my throat. My pulse is erratic as his fangs scrape against my skin. Throw in massaging my tits for a side-piece, and fuck, I don't know how much wetter I can get.

Releasing a low sigh, my head falls back, eyes flutter closed as I surrender myself to every sensation. I hear the water fall. I hear his greedy kisses. I feel him sucking on each of my nipples and giving the girls the attention they so desperately need.

Running my fingers through his hair, I tighten my hold as he releases a growl. I cross my ankles tighter around his waist, rolling my hips up and down against him, seeking friction.

I whimper, and he rests his forehead against mine. "Shit." He places a kiss on the corner of my mouth.

He reaches down between us, leans me back slightly, and his other arm easily supports my weight. Lining himself up with my entrance, he looks at me, panting. I'm breathless, as I slowly nod my head, starting to bite on my lower lip as he begins to push in, causing both of us to gasp.

Inch by inch, he pushes into me, allowing me to adjust to his delicious size as I stretch around him, and damn, he feels so good it's insane.

"Fuck, Raene..." he moans, his voice is rough, strained. "I waited so many lifetimes for this."

My heart skips.

He gives one final thrust, pushing himself to the hilt. I cry out, my nails dig into his shoulders as I hold onto him. He brings me closer to him, one hand on my hip and one gripping my ass as he slowly begins to move, thrusting into me at a torturously slow pace. Not being able to release the needy sound that comes out, a soft mewl, I move my hips to match him.

"Ash...Ash..." I chant softly like a prayer as he holds me close, filling me with deep strokes, all while I'm riding against him.

"Fuck yes..." he whispers, his voice is low and rough against my lips as he kisses me. How he maintains kissing me, like he's worshiping me and ruining me so I completely fall apart, I can't wrap my head around.

His tongue brushes against mine, his fangs nibble on my lower lip. His kisses, I can feel the pressure coiling tighter and tighter.

"Don't stop," I sob out, barely able to breathe out the words. "God, Ash..."

It feels so good, it's perfect.

I'm bouncing on him, I can feel my core pulsing around him, and his thrusts quicken.

"You're taking it so well, baby."

"Ash." My back arches, and I moan into the air, feeling waves of pleasure running through me as I come around him.

"You look so sexy coming apart on my dick like that, but I'm not finished."

His thrusts become quicker. The water ripples violently around us. I can feel another orgasm building, and I don't know if I can take it. It's too much pleasure all at once.

"Ash," I gasp out, my voice breaking, small cries escaping into the nighttime air.

"Yeah...that's it," he murmurs, his lips brushing against my ear, voice drenched with heat and desire.

"Ride my cock, baby," he groans.

"Shit, yes..." he hisses, sucking in a quick breath. "Like that. Cum on me again." Our bodies are moving in a primal rhythm, a raw, ever-consuming dance of *need*.

"Fuck," he says.

"Raene..." His words leave him with a guttural groan, his control snapping. One hand grabs the back of my neck, the other gripping my hip hard enough to bruise as he pounds into me, and I don't care. Each deep thrust claims me.

"That's it, baby," I pant. "I want to feel you."

"Shit!" His whole body tenses, a shudder running through him, and with one final thrust, he falls apart. I feel him pulse inside me as he comes. Pulling my neck to the side, he sinks his fangs into me. The spot where he will give me kisses and drag his fangs lightly. I feel a bolt of pleasure shooting through my core.

"Ash!" I cry out, my body convulsing, his moans muffled against my neck. He's sucking and kissing that tender spot as I ride out the aftershock.

The sensation is euphoric. I take slow breaths, holding on to him, loving how undone he is. How fucking ruined I am. I stroke his beautiful red hair, still squeezing myself around him to draw every last drop.

"Raene..." he groans once more, his voice a hoarse whisper. Knowing he's coming apart like this from me makes me want him all over again.

He slows his breathing as I kiss the lining of his jaw, his arms wrapped around me.

"Three orgasms, Ash, and the biting..." I give him a coy smile.

"Kinky, I like it." It was unexpected, but the ebb and flow of the quick pain wrapping around the pleasure felt amazing. I didn't care about the bite because I felt like what just happened was an out-of-body experience. "You set the bar really high."

He chuckles, and I feel his breath on my neck. It's rough and sounds so sexy. The post sex laugh.

"Oh, we're not done yet." He grins.

I can't help the goofy grin that spreads across my face. My body is spent, every muscle is trembling, but the thought of feeling this again, of having my bones melt underneath him, makes my pulse spike.

"Oh, so you love to go above and beyond, huh? An overachiever?" I tease, my voice still breathless.

He gently nips my lower lip. "Only when it comes to you, Goddess."

I roll my eyes, but my smile gives me away. "I'll make sure to give you a thank you in the *Acknowledgements* section of my next book."

"Ouch," he says. "J-just a thank you?"

His hands move under my ass again, and God, his cock stirs inside of me. I gasp, my body clenching around him.

How is he hard this damn quickly? Is this normal for fae males or just *him*?

"No full chapter or dedication?" He raises a brow in question.

I laugh, my arms around his neck as my fingertips dance along his back, as heat curls in my lower belly again. "What is it you want...Ash?"

"We could stay here in this water." He grips my ass and slides me up and down his length, drawing a low moan from me, "and see how many more thank-yous I can earn for that *Acknowledgements* section of yours."

I'm already biting back a smile. That line shouldn't make my heart flutter like that, but it does. I rock gently; his breath turns shaky.

"More thank-yous? You're just *that* good, you think?

His grin turns sinful. "Oh, I *know* I am."

And then he's kissing me again. Deep, slow, and so fucking filthy, like he's trying to prove me wrong before I can think twice. My whole body ignites, responding to him as we move together, and I realize I don't want this—this moment—to end.

22
Breathless
SYLAS

This past week has been amazing. I've seen her every day, even if it may only be for a little while. She stayed the night once. Falling asleep in my arms after she collapsed and eventually rolling off of me, tucking herself into my side. It was then, when she nestled into my side, my arms holding her like they won't let go, that I realized…that I had fucked up.

I can't get enough of her. We can't keep our hands off one another. The sex has been amazing. We go from watching a movie to kissing her deeply, grabbing at clothing until we can't wait anymore. She straddles my lap, pulling her underwear to the side, sitting on my cock so slowly, never breaking that eye contact that I want from her, and she feels so fucking good—hot and tight.

We read together on a rainy day after closing the bookstore. We sat by the fire in those large, oversized comfy chairs, listening to the sound patter against the skylights and windows.

Last night, we took a walk back to the lake. We didn't make it into the water, but we also didn't make it off the blanket. Afterward, we just lay there talking, holding hands, our legs intertwined with one another. We whispered to the stars and the moon, wondering if the Goddess was listening.

Somewhere between the smiles and laughs, the intimate moments like this, and sharing our bodies together I realized I'm not just liking her anymore, I'm falling for her.

The festival starts in four days, and she will leave after that. What the hell do I say? I don't want her to just stay for my magic. I want her to stay because she loves it here and is ready for a change.

We're tucked into the cozy back room of my shop where the tables have been cleared to make space for stacks of lantern supplies and piles of the sip passports for the Golden Twilight Market.

We've been switching off now and then. I'll work on the lanterns while she works on the passports, then switch. She's working on a passport right now. Her face is in utter and complete concentration mode. Her brows furrow as she focuses intently on adding the labels. We are giving each participating drinking booth a stamp to stamp the book. We have books of teas, alcoholic and non-alcoholic beverages, coffee, and even varieties of soda and juices.

"You look deep in thought there," she says, glancing over before moving on to a new passport book. "You seem lighter, somehow, as if something shifted."

"Lighter?" I ask, my chest tightening.

I set another completed lantern to the side and pulled one from the box, quickly assembling it. It looks like a small hot air balloon. Once I finish a few, I enchant them to float until the flame dies out. When that happens, the lanterns will become golden shimmers in the sky, lifting away in the crisp autumn breeze.

"Yeah," she says, leaning back, taking a quick sip of water. "Last week, you looked like you had the weight of the world on your shoulders. Now you just seem lighter."

I grab each of us a paper plate and hand her one, both of us reaching into the pizza box for a hot, fresh slice of pepperoni pizza. She takes a bite and chews slowly.

"I just felt a little bit off last week, but I'm feeling better now, I think." I take a bite.

She raises her eyebrows in response. A coy smile on her lips. "You think?"

Setting my plate down, I turn my body towards her and lean forward, my hands resting on my knees. "Well, you're here. So I'm feeling better."

She giggles, wiping her mouth with her napkin before turning her body towards me. "Is that so?"

Her legs are crossed. Her heeled boots on dark black leggings, a black tank top that hugs just enough to distract me, and her neutral multicolored cardigan is draped over the back of her seat.

Standing up, I reach out, take her hands in mine, and pull her close to me. Her hands find my waist as she looks up at my face. God, I love her smile. She's leaning into me, looking at my mouth, and I know she's just waiting for me to kiss her, and I'm starting to wonder what the fuck is taking me so long.

I caress her face with both hands and bring my lips to her, kissing her lightly. Her head angles to deepen the kiss, and she moans as my tongue finds hers and sucks.

I pull away quickly to push the lanterns and passports off to the side before standing in front of her again.

"Turn around," I whisper, and she does. Her back is flush with mine. Her breath shudders as she feels my hardness pressed against her.

"I know you're so fucking wet for me right now, Raene." I tug her black tank top down in the front, freeing her breasts as I begin to knead them, my hips grinding against her to chase the friction I need. Her ass moves against me in circles as I place gentle kisses on her neck.

"Ash, I need you," she whines.

My hands inch down her belly and find her wetness, and her smell is fucking intoxicating. My fingers are rubbing her and her clit in beautiful, teasing circles.

"Fuck, I need to taste you," I say. My voice is low and hungry in her ear. "Then I'll take you."

I turn her around and pick her up by the waist, placing her on the edge of the table. I unzip her boots, letting them fall to the ground. Next are her socks and leggings. I lift one of her legs, eyeing the bubblegum pink polish on her toes before pressing a light kiss to her inner ankle, making her breath hitch. "Lie back."

She lies back, her head resting at the top of the table as I stand there, watching her slight tremors move through her body as her tits spill from her top and her legs are spread for me, waiting for me to go on my knees, and *fuck* if I don't look away as I kneel.

Wrapping my arms around her thighs possessively, I slide her down a couple of inches until her ass is off the table and my face is between her thighs.

My tongue licks her clit, circling it. She releases a sigh of pleasure, lifting her lips gently. Then my mouth is on her, tongue sliding in and out of her entrance and back to her clit. Goddess above, she tastes so good. I can't control the groan that crawls up my throat as I suck on her clit, the sound vibrating through her core.

"Your mouth feels…so perfect, Ash," she says, her voice low, but there is an edge to it. Her eyes are closed; her hands wrapped around the edge of the table.

I flatten my tongue, dragging it over the bottom of her entrance to her clit in firm strokes that make her gasp, her body writhing with each movement.

Never easing up the hold on one of her thighs, my fingers slid into her wetness so beautifully. I move slowly, deliberately so. I want to take my time with her. I want to cherish every sound she makes. I want to see her beg for more, as she claws her way out of her skin.

Yet, when I curl my fingers—rolling my tongue over that sensitive bud as she thrusts against my fingers—she releases a moan, setting the pace and letting it build in a perfect rhythm.

"Shit, Ash…" she pants, her hips moving quickly. She sits up slightly to see that my gaze is locked on her. She's unraveling on my mouth, and I fucking love to see it.

I drag a fang over the hood of her clit, and she cries out. Her back arches, thighs trembling as her orgasm crashes over her, and I ride it out, fingers thrusting inside her while my tongue alternates between small licks and sucking.

Her body is still shaking as I rise, unbuttoning my shirt, lips slick with her essence. Her eyes are wild, dark, and hungry for more. I toss my shirt to the floor. She perches on the edge of the table, barely holding on, desperately anticipating what is next as she stares at me.

I gently turn her, her back flush with my chest. "You taste so fucking good." The words dance like a whisper.

"And look at you," he coos. "Still trembling. Now…put your hands on the table."

She places her palms flat on the table, fingers spread wide. I widen her stance and line myself against her entrance.

"That's it," I growl, my voice thick with heat. I press into her slowly, inch by inch, savoring the way she throbs around me. I know everything is hypersensitive after her release, but it feels so damn perfect.

A guttural groan rips from my throat as I bury myself fully inside her. "You drive me insane, Raene."

Just for a heartbeat, I don't move.

Then I pull back and thrust in, skin hitting skin. Her fingers curl on the table, gripping at nothing, yet desperate for purchase.

I'm slamming into her, each thrust drawing a cry from her lips. With a hand gripping her waist, I pull her up so her back is pressed against my chest, once more. I move with a deep, hungry rhythm—one hand on her throat, applying slight pressure, the other finding her clit, fingers working in perfect sync with each quick thrust.

Fuck. The way her pussy clenches and flutters around me has me on a high.

"Ash," she gasps, one arm reaching back to grip my neck while the other squeezes my forearm.

"Damn, you're so perfect, Raene. I love how your body makes me feel. I love the way you look when you take me."

Goddess, she feels utterly perfect in my arms. The words slip out before I can stop them. "*Fuck,* I love you, Raene."

Shit.

There is a pause. Just the sounds of our breathing and my skin slapping against her ass. Her whimpers even halt for a moment when she hears me. Her head turns slightly to look at my face, and I see surprise and a little bit of shock written on hers.

And then I let go. Her mouth opens in a silent scream before she releases a moan when she comes, milking me, until we fall apart together. We stay like this, breathless. My hands are holding her hips as she catches her breath, bent over the table, using her arms to brace and hold herself up.

I said it out loud.

Not in my head.

I pull out of her, pull up my pants, and grab napkins because that's the closest thing I have to help her clean up.

"I'm sorry, I didn't mean—" I try to tell her before she cuts me off.

"Sorry? Sorry that you told me, or sorry you said something in a very intimate moment?" She adjusts her top, then slides her underwear and leggings back on, followed by her socks and boots, before settling back in her chair.

She buries her face in her hands, lightly shaking her head.

Squatting in front of her, I gently pry her hands away, waiting until her eyes meet mine. "I'm not sorry for loving you, Raene. I'm falling in love with you. I want to get to know you more. I love spending time with you. You...you make me happy."

"Ash, you shouldn't love me. I'm leaving soon." She jumps to her feet. "This was just supposed to be for fun, you know? Just...good sex. Really, *really* good sex. Not love. I can't—"

I pull her close, pressing a kiss to her forehead. I close my eyes, breathing her in, hoping this can calm, even just a little.

What did I do?

"You don't have to say it back, Raene." I pull back slightly, staring at her face. Something deep in my chest aches. I told her how I really feel, and now I think I fucked this up. "I didn't mean for it to come out like this, but now you know."

Her hands slide from my shoulders down to my chest, and she rests her head there.

"I'm sorry," she whispers, a sob escapes her.

Is she crying? I quickly pull her up to look at me, her eyes glistening with tears. I wrap my arms around her, holding her as tightly as I can.

I'm an asshole.

"Fuck, I'm sorry. I didn't mean for you to cry. Please...don't cry."

She lifts her head from my chest, wiping the tears from her face, sniffling. "I have no clue where the hell that came from."

"Listen to me, Ash, you can't love me, not when it's going to end like...like this." Her voice cracks, the sound splintering through me, carving into my chest.

The words plummet inside me, but I hear them, and she's right. I have no business falling in love with her. Spending more time together this week is going to hurt who the most? Me or her—or maybe both of us.

23
Crash together
RAENE

"He told me he loves me, Grandma." I blurt. Hands in my lap, my eyes wide like a deer in the headlights.

What the hell was I supposed to say to that?

"Well," she says, highlighting the next word on the crossword puzzle she discovered, "How do you feel about him?" Her eyes scan the page behind the glasses perched on her nose. "You obviously like him. A lot. You two have been spending quite an awful amount of time together lately."

"I'm sorry, I—" She holds up a hand, interrupting me, setting her book and pen down.

We've been watching TV while working on puzzles, chatting off and on. Grandma can read me like a book. She knows my mannerisms. She knows I am itching to talk to her about something, but I just don't know how. I'm afraid to make eye contact. This is why she was quiet. She knew I wanted to talk to her about something, so she waited. She throws the line out and waits for me to grab on.

It works every damn time.

I glance down at the Sudoku puzzle I am working on and erase a few of the numbers. I feel guilty at times when I am spending time with Ash. I know I'm an adult and my grandma is independent and loves her life here, but I've been here at her home or there at the bookshop...and often.

He said *I love you*.

When he was inside of me. Holding me. Worshipping my body in the most sinful damn way. He said those three little words so many people yearn to hear. Those three little words that have such an impactful meaning have been simmering in my mind over the past few days. I was so caught by surprise, I didn't even know what to say. Should I have said thank you? Then start chanting *yes, yes, yes,* because I *really* loved what he was doing.

I was scared. I *am* scared. I panicked. I was in total and complete bliss, and when I heard him say what he said, it was as if everything just...stopped.

The world stopped spinning on its axis. The birds stopped chirping. I forgot how to breathe. He told me it is okay that I don't say it back, but that face. The vulnerability in his eyes, how his face softened with hope that I would say it back. He kissed me instead.

He kissed me on my forehead and lingered there as I held onto his arms, feeling so safe and honestly...loved. I can feel that from him. I didn't even know I would cry, but I felt so bad that he felt this way for me. The first guy who tells me he loves me, and I didn't say it back. Does that make me a bad person? What if I'm never ready to say it back?

The way he looks at me. The way he talks to me. The way he learns something new about me and embraces it with that bright smile on his face. It's how he respects and accepts me.

I know it is love, but this is so new to me. I'm a fucking romance author who's never truly experienced it with another soul. I write about it. *I want it.* I want that happily ever after, too, but I don't know what I feel for Ash yet.

I don't know what to do with me leaving so soon. The fall festival starts tomorrow and then…I'm gone. Back to my condo on the beach. Back to being in the city and doing what I love…writing.

"What are you telling me you're sorry for?" She asks, looking up from her book, placing it in her lap.

"You're a grown woman, Raene. I can take care of myself. You know I appreciate you being here, but I didn't expect you to spend every minute of the day here. I wanted you to make friends. I wanted you to enjoy yourself." She releases a heavy sigh.

"I want you to know that there is more to life than your career. I know how much you love romance and writing. You've been a writer since you were a child, but I know how much you looked up to your parents, seeing the love they had together. I *know* that you want that, Raene. You know your grandfather and I had a great love before he passed. Everyone is deserving of real love, even you."

The sound of the doorbell rings as soon as I leave the kitchen. I set the bowl of popcorn down on the coffee table, grabbing a few pieces to nibble on because why not.

I opened the door, and I honestly didn't expect him to be here, and we're face-to-face.

"Hey," he says. Taking a step forward, but then he inches back a bit.

"I...I just wanted to see you. I mean, maybe you hate me because you're sending me one-word responses via text and I haven't seen you in days. Raene—what am I supposed to think?" A hand runs through his hair, wearing a dark olive green bomber jacket with a grey tee, jeans, and sneakers, and somehow he looks even more gorgeous than when we were in the bookstore with his pants at his ankles.

Stepping back from the door, I gesture for him to come in. "Come inside." There's a chill in the air as the sun dips low, causing the wind to bite.

"Where's Vera?" He asks, slipping off his shoes and placing them neatly against the wall.

"You know my grandma." I sigh, making my way to the couch. "She's healing and wants to enjoy life. Flora picked her up, and they're going to meet some friends for dinner, so it's just me."

He nods his head and hesitates before making his way over to the couch and sitting beside me. Turning to him, I tuck a leg underneath me before reaching out, placing a hand on his thigh. He places his hand over mine.

"I don't hate you," I say slowly. "I'm sorry I disappeared on you, but I just...I needed some time to think. A lot is changing, Ash. Too much and too fast."

His thumb gently brushes against my knuckles. "So talk to me then."

"I'm scared. You told me you loved me, Ash, and I like you. I really, really like you, but I'm leaving soon, and I just thought...I guess I just thought this was just for fun."

"We'll go slow."

Slow?

"Ash." I scoot closer, my hand now gripping his. "I'm going to be leaving." I look into his eyes, making sure he understands. "You know this. What can we make slow? Do you want to try having an actual relationship? With me in the city and you here?"

As soon as the words leave my mouth, I immediately feel restless. Too many emotions are starting to pour out of me, and I stand because my body needs to move. I'm beginning to pace like the tiger in a damn zoo exhibit, caged by my uncertainty about this entire situation.

Take it slow?

I can't even bear to look at his face right now. I don't want to hurt him. A long-distance relationship...would it work? Could *we* make it work? Do I even want that?

His arms wrap around my waist, and I jolt from the sudden contact while I am deep in my thoughts.

"Sorry," he says quietly, already beginning to pull back.

"It's okay. You're fine." I turn around and take his hands in mine. "You just startled me. I was way too deep in my head."

He steps forward, gentler this time. Carefully taking my chin in his hand, the gesture grounds me, and his eyes are steady, calm, and *sure*. "We take it slow, Raene. I know you're leaving."

His jaw tightens just the tiniest bit, and I notice—only because I'm reading his face so closely as he speaks. I can't pull my eyes away from him. "We can spend time together. I can visit you in the city. I know you'll be back to see your grandmother. I'd just like to see where this goes, but only if you're okay with it. I didn't mean for this to get awkward, but I'm not taking back what I said. I *am* in love with you."

Fuck.

I mean, when he looks at me like that...

"No labels?" I ask.

"No labels. No titles. Only a crown for you, goddess."

My lips curve into a small smile as I press up on my toes to give him a delicate kiss on the lips. "You're such a dork..." I tease.

"But I'm your dork, right?" He smiles, pressing his lips against mine again.

I let out a light laugh while wrapping my arms around him, pulling him closer, resting my head on his chest, listening to his heartbeat.

The softness of his shirt glides against my cheek, and my nose gently brushes against the zipper of his jacket. "I do like you, Ash," I whisper.

More than I expected to. More than I should. But maybe, just maybe, that is okay. Maybe it is okay for us to just take this slow.

One fallen leaf at a time as we enjoy the Fall Festival. Then we can go where the wind takes us.

Goddess.

His lips feel so good on me. The crunch of popcorn invades my ears as he grinds his body on top of me, the act causing my eyes to roll to the back of my head. I am going to cum if he continues to dry-hump me into the cushions.

"Ash…" I moan, but slowly cut it off into a whisper. We need to go upstairs.

We've been making out like horny teenagers on the couch in the living room, down the hall from my grandmother's bedroom. Thankfully, she sleeps with noise-cancelling headphones—nature sounds and the sexy voice of an English Duke, whispering sweet affirmations into her ears.

Fuck. He knows how to make my body respond to him in the best way, because when he moves, I move back, and then the heat and pleasure build quickly, too quickly. He knew what he was doing.

His hand quickly presses over my mouth, catching my moan as he dry humps me into the couch. Shit. I do feel like a horny teen. Maybe a young-adult college romance is in the works.

"Let me take you upstairs," he growls into my ear, nipping at my earlobe. His hand is still covering my mouth, as my head nods up and down. We quietly yet clumsily tiptoe through the popcorn, crushing a few pieces beneath our feet. I'll clean it up in the early morning. She'll just think I'm getting a jump start on the chores I do to help her.

We get to the room, I gently close the door and lean against it, panting. I see him under the glow of my bedside lamp.

God, I love how tall he is, his muscles, that t-shirt was made for him. I press my thighs together, and he notices. He notices everything. Especially when that wicked smirk graces his lips and I know he can tell. He hears my heartbeat. He smells the arousal my body created just for him.

He eyes the plush on the bed. The *PSL* plush that's so adorable it's giving *Drink Me.* The one he gave me that day we started planning the festival. The enchanted game we played, and he beat me. He laughed, and that smile...fuck that smile was when I realized I had a little crush on the pumpkin king.

"You kept it?" He asks. It's like he's breathing harder...faster, as he starts taking steps towards me.

"Yes," I say softly, I'm breathless at how he's walking over to me. "A little something extra to remember you by."

"I like that answer," he says, his voice deep, but it plays like a husky melody.

I'm fan-girling.

Next thing I know, I'm meeting him halfway, our mouths crash together like two ships in the dark.

And I'm a fucking wreck.

24
Scattered like golden dust
RAENE

I wander past the rows of booths set up around the town square. The air is buzzing with laughter. The soft hum of music drifted from nearby speakers. Everyone is in a great mood. Chatting among one another, locals and visitors.

I officially met the mayor and his wife. Elora is her twin. They were both very kind and grateful for the help with the festival.

I see Grandma sitting at a table with her friends, gossiping, drinking tea, and working on a lantern together as a group. There have to be at least two hundred people here. Friends and family from the local town and outsiders are coming to enjoy the fall festivities. It's packed. The weather is perfect. The sun is still bright this afternoon, the air is crisp and cool as a light breeze bustles through the square. It feels like the perfect day for high-waisted jeans, sneakers, a white tank top, and my caramel-brown cardigan.

Each station is strung with fairy lights and a garland of dried orange slices, cinnamon-scented pinecones, and small pumpkins and gourds.

The first day of fall has blessed us with its presence, and I'm surprisingly excited to see everything we planned come to life this week.

I approach a long table covered with a checkered white and orange fabric tablecloth, scattered with little glass jars that hold paint brushes. Dried leaves are sitting in a wicker basket beside them with bottles of paint and paper plates to pour colors and mix them.

A little girl, with paint smeared on her green cheeks, uses a sponge to dab orange spots on her paper lantern. She sits back and a smile appears between her tusks as she taps her Dad's shoulder to point to her creation. He presses a kiss to the top of her blonde curls and turns his attention back to his lantern, carefully tracing a stencil of a crescent moon.

Another table is full of glitter, dried flowers, sequins, glue, and colorful tissue squares. The creativity is amazing, and I can't wait to see these lanterns take flight in the night sky this evening.

"Hi!" Seren waves at me as I approach her, Jas and Dominik sitting at a table with others, busy decorating their lanterns. Each of them is working on a lantern. Seren's lantern has glitter on one side, dried flower petals and leaves on the other, and now she's drawing a little picture.

"Hey there, Seren!" I smile. She's so tiny and cute, always smiling.

"What are you drawing?" I take a seat on the bench across from them. Jas looks down at the picture her daughter is drawing.

"My family. Mom, me, and Dominik."

Dominik clears his throat and looks over at the drawing. A look of uncertainty passes over his eyes before he gives Seren a small smile.

"It's perfect," he says softly. "When you're finished, we will put it on your lantern."

Sitting on her knees, Seren wiggles in her seat before sitting back down on her legs. She grabs a few pieces of popcorn from the brown bag in front of her and shoves them in her mouth. Humming a little tune of her own as she continues her drawing.

Jas looks over at Dominik, and I don't know if it's cute or funny seeing a man his size with a small lantern in his hands as he's gluing leaves and flower petals on it.

Her eyes are wide for that entire picture conversation, but softened when she turns her attention to me. She places her completed lantern in front of her.

"So what do you think of day one so far?" She tucks a curl behind her ear. Her hair is normally up, but today it's down, and the thick, lush curls flow down past her shoulders.

Looking around at the busyness of it all makes me excited for this evening, and I wonder how many visitors will attend the festival throughout the week. I haven't seen Ash yet and hope to soon.

Yesterday, we said we would take it slow. One day at a time, no expectations and no pressure. Just enjoy each other's company, and when I leave Everly Hollow, we can set up visits. He is already planning to come the first weekend of October, and when he said that, my stomach did flips in excitement.

"I think it looks pretty amazing, honestly. Everyone seems pretty excited about the lantern parade."

"Well, it's a great idea. Something new to start the festival with," Jas says, her nails do a quick tap on the table.

Dominik nods his head in agreement.

"I like it!" She finishes, giving her a quick kiss on her head, before resting her head on her hands with a beaming smile.

"Speaking of someone *you* like, he's coming this way." Her eyebrows dance up and down in excitement, matching the broad grin on her face. She's a sucker for romance.

I stand and turn—and he's right there.

My Ash.

Enough to reach out and tug me, possessively. Kissing me like I'm the closest thing to air that gives him breath.

"You miss me?" I whisper into his lips, brushing my nose ever so lightly against his.

"You saw me last night...and again this morning." A little laugh escapes me, feeling his hands squeeze my sides.

"Doesn't mean I can't give you a kiss when you've been blessed with my presence."

"Oh...so you're something special now?"

"You said it, not me?" He shrugs his shoulders, a smirk playing on his lips.

I shake my head slightly, but the smile on my face is still there. "So, have you made your lantern yet?

"Not yet. I thought I would do it with you."

"Okay," I say, playing with the buttons on his flannel shirt. It's soft with a mix of colors—black, orange, and a light cream.

"We can sit with them." I turn around to see Jas and Dominik standing up.

"Seren wants a hot dog and to stop by the baby farm animals, so we figured we would just go grab something to eat now before it gets too busy," Jas says, pointing in the direction of a few food booths.

"I'll catch you later," Dominik says to Sylas.

Well, never mind then.

I give them a quick wave goodbye as we walk towards the bench.

Ash quickly grabs two new lanterns for us to decorate, and we sit side by side. He begins working on his lantern, using a maple leaf stencil. Predictable, but it makes me smile. Looks like we're not much different because I'm thinking of using the sun stencil with dried flowers.

"Hey, Rae!"

I glance up to see Poppy balancing a tray with her lantern and a small mountain of decorating supplies. "Mind if I join you?"

"Sit." I grin, flicking my hand toward the empty spot in front of me as I sort through the flowers I plan to strategically glue on.

"So…" She uncaps her glue bottle with the kind of flair that shows she's about to toss trouble into her cauldron of shenanigans and stir it up. "How are you two?" Her mouth curls into a playful, crooked grin.

I chuckle. This girl.

"Why are you being so nosy?" Garruk asks, dropping his tray. The clatter on the wooden table causes Poppy and me to jump. She physically shivers and rolls her eyes, but keeps working as he takes a seat beside her.

"I wasn't talking to you, *Garruk*." Her head whips toward him, amber eyes glowing as her glare burns into him, then she turns her attention back to her craft.

"Awe...Penelope," he says softly, twirling a finger at the end of her ponytail, and she immediately goes rosy in the cheeks.

"Trying to live vicariously through them?" He asks.

"Fuck off," Poppy hisses, batting his arm away, gluing a leaf to her lantern. She then begins to draw a few doodles of baked goods. I try to hold in my laughter, bubbling in my throat.

"Don't you have some cinnamon rolls to overbake?" She gives him an icy stare as her lips curl. As he laughs and quips back at her, I realize these two can go at it for hours.

I may have to pull inspiration from them later on.

Fortunately, the weather for today's event has been on our side, cool but dry, and I'll take that as a win. A rainy day would have ruined it.

The sun and new moon have slipped low into the horizon, and now everyone stands in two lines. Ash and Nim stand in front, taking turns at lighting each lantern.

The kids get a kick out of seeing Ash's magic and Nim's dragon fire. Even I stood there, mouth agape, watching his eyes glow, the fire breathing through his soul and out of his hand. The vibrant flame that he had sparked to life dances over his palm. There are no burns on his skin, no pain reflected on his face, just tender joy. For the fire lives within him.

The illuminated lanterns light up the town square along with the street lamps. I walk side by side with Ash as we begin our walk to the lake.

Glancing up at him, I take in the awe of his facial expression at the glow of the lanterns in the starry night sky as the light guides our way down the path to the lake. "I like your lantern," I tell him, bumping my hip lightly against him.

"Thanks, I like yours too." I can hear the smile in his voice. "I liked how everyone's personality shows in their creation. How they brought what they loved in their hearts to fruition in these lanterns."

"This was a great idea, Raene."

I smile to myself as I bask in his praise.

We look forward to following the crowd. Holding our lanterns out in front of us, I feel his fingers faintly brush against the hand on my side, causing a sudden rise of goosebumps to spread.

Testing to see what happens, maybe?

We had sex, we kissed publicly, but I guess I can understand why he may be hesitant to hold hands. Holding

hands may be a way he wants to show that he loves me? Maybe to him, it is more vulnerable than sex.

I brush my fingers back against his. One finger loops another as we walk side by side, our hands clasp together as one, fully linked.

His hand is larger than mine, warm and steady as we almost reach the clearing ahead.

A chirp sounds above our heads as Nim flies over us, beginning to dodge the lanterns that flicker and float as they release into the air above us.

It's a breathtaking view. The sky stretches out like an endless blanket of black velvet, deep and infinite. Without the moon to contrast against the night, it feels so pure, just right for this night. The stars burn brighter than ever, like pieces of diamonds scattered, silver dust above us. Orion's belt and the pale light of the Milky Way are spilling across the sky in a river of stardust.

The absence of the moonlight has made the constellations seem sharper. I've never seen anything like this. As the lanterns release into the air and the faint glow of the lake adds its shimmer to the world around it, it feels magical. *This* place is special.

"You ready?" Ash asks, giving my hand a light squeeze as he holds his lantern higher.

"Ready."

We release, and then they float.

You can hear whispers and murmurs of blessings to Ruskaya; some people cheer. Others huddle together watching the quiet magic of it all.

The flames of the lanterns flicker as they take flight and drift to the stars in the sky, and glow-moths begin to flutter out of the forest, weaving among the people, dancing in the air beside the lanterns. Even Nim twirls, swoops, and dives gently with the moths.

The stars in the midnight blue sky transform. The inky painting above us is now stars scattered like golden dust. Lanterns are lifted into the air as they catch a breeze, transcending into the golden-dusted sky.

This community radiates kindness. I laugh, swept up in the pure magic and light of this entire evening. Together, we watch the lanterns float away, leaning into each other, our fingers intertwined.

25
I don't think I am safe with you
SYLAS

*D*on't fuck up. Don't fuck up.

"*You know, chanting that repeatedly isn't going to force your magic to stabilize and not fuck up...right?*" Nim says, rolling his eyes. "*You're giving me a headache.*"

So far, my magic has been holding steady, and I can only hope it continues to stay that way into the late afternoon and evening hours. I was nervous as shit yesterday, praying to the Goddess that the lanterns would take flight, float, and burn properly.

I glance down at the vibrant colored scales beside my feet. Nim lifts his head slightly, partially opening one eye, before lowering his head down to rest. I cast a few enchantments on a handful of piles for the children...and even some adults, who don't want to wait in the lines for the bounce house set up near the east corner.

The town square is packed. There has to be close to double the number of people who attended the opening ceremony. We blocked off a few streets to help accommodate a few booths, spreading the market out so that everything doesn't feel too cramped in one spot.

The air is thick with the smells of baked bread, grilled meats, and sugar. Children shriek with laughter, tourists and locals talk while they shop or grab a bite to eat. Bouncing from booth to booth, taking photos and selfies.

I spot Dominik at his flower stand, sleeves rolled up, and Seren helping him arrange bouquets and potted plants before running two booths down to her grandparents, Elowen and Lorien. Together they man the honey stand, the sunlight beaming off the glass jars like molten amber.

Elora has her produce stand set up, and that too is always a hit.

When a group of kids dashes away from a picnic table toward the bounce houses or leaf piles, Nim eyes the abandoned hot dogs. With zero shame and no regrets, he helps himself. Standing on his hind legs, paws on the table as he snaps them up in quick, neat bites.

Raene laughs when she notices, shaking her head. "Did you just see that?"

She points in his direction, glancing at me, then back at Nim. "He's going to be spoiled rotten."

"He already is," I say, grinning as I slide my hand into hers when she reaches my side. Her fingers squeeze mine lightly, and something in my chest eases, like maybe she isn't as far away from me as I thought. Not yet, anyways.

"Where did you run off to?" I ask as we begin walking towards the booths. "See anything you wanted?"

"Just browsing for now. I walked around for a bit with my grandmother, and I wanted to start making my rounds to see the girls. So far, I've only stopped by Oriana's candle booth, and her scents are incredible." She taps on her temple. "I'm scoping out the booths I want to hit up, see what I love, then start shopping."

I nod. "Ahh…gotcha. Sounds very strategic."

"Of course. I can't just buy the first thing I see. That's a rookie mistake, Ash. I need to see it all, then spend all my coins."

"So there are rules?"

"Yep," she responds, standing tall as we enter the main market area. She lets go of my hand to face me, and I suddenly miss her warmth.

"First," she checks off with a finger, "you must scope out items before committing. Secondly, if there are limited quantities of items you are interested in, circle back, especially if you suffer from FOMO."

I cross my arms, my smile wide as I nod my head to inform her that I'm listening. I'm soaking in every bit of what she's saying.

"Lastly," she ticks off her thumb, "never…and I repeat *never* shop on an empty stomach."

I laugh out loud. Okay, that third one is true for sure. "Do I need some sort of handbook for this?"

"Only if you want to survive," she loops her arm in with mine as we begin walking deeper into the heart of the market, "but you'll be safe with me."

I look down at her as she tugs me towards a booth that catches her eye. She looks back occasionally, smiling and laughing at all the people around us. And right then, it hits me, like a knife between my ribs.

My heart isn't safe. Not even close. Because soon, instead of being within an arm's reach, she'll be in the city, miles away, and I'll be here wishing I'd held on tighter.

We make another round through the market. Raene's method has proven to be effective. She's purchased items from all our friends' booths, including a treat from both bakeries. One for me and one for herself. I happily carry her totes and bags as I follow her to the next booth.

"Ash." She tugs on my sleeve in excitement as she points. Her face lit with glee. "Salt water taffy!"

Eyes shining like stars, she leads the way to the booth, and I fall into step beside her.

"It was my Dad's favorite," she says quietly but with a hint of joy as the memories flood her head. The booth has dozens of lined, towering jars varying in all sizes and filled with colorful taffy.

"I would ask my Mom if we could give him a pack of taffy for his birthday, Father's Day, and Christmas." A touch of a smile brushes her lips from the memory.

This is the first time she's mentioned something so personal about her parents, and it makes me feel a bit of something like hope that she would want to confide in me and let me in.

"It's a good candy," I say, giving her a wink.

The Sugar Shack looks like a candy-coated dream. Glass jars of jelly beans and bagged cotton candy in the shape of balloon animals. Colorful rock candy, candy bars, shimmering lollipops, and edible glitter tubes.

"Hello! I'm Tansy!" says the tiny pixie.

She's a smidge smaller than a ruler with silver freckles on her cheeks. Her mint green hair is braided into two plaits that fall over her shoulders, and her pink apron is embroidered with the candy logo and the whimsical script of the business name.

"This is Clover," she nods her head at the pixie with deep brown skin and ash-blonde hair, "and this is Luma," she adds, gesturing to the side of the tent where a light blue-haired pixie is manipulating clouds of cotton candy into various animal shapes before placing them onto sticks to be bagged. "What can I get you two today?"

"Hi!" Raene takes another step forward. "How much is the salt water taffy?" She asks, nodding at one of the jars.

"Three dollars a pound." She smiles, readying a clear bag and twine she pulled out from under the counter.

"Can I get two pounds of the orange dreamsicle?"

Tansy giggles. Her eyes crinkle at the corners as she smiles.

"That, my dear," she taps on the jar filled with individually wrapped taffy that is white and orange swirled, "is pumpkin spice."

Raene frowns a bit, but then eyes a jar filled with the blue taffy. "Is that one by chance, cotton candy, or blue raspberry?" She points a finger at the jar, but her smile falters, unsure of the response that she will get.

"Maple Blue Sugar," Clover calls out, without missing a beat as she helps fill an order of jellybeans for a gentleman behind us.

Raene throws a look over her shoulder that screams, *what even in the fuck is that flavor?* Or *kill me now.*

I shift toward her, pressing my hand into the small of her back, "Do you have any flavors that are not...fall-inspired?" I ask.

"I do!" She flits to a jar behind her and dives inside, coming back with a crinkly wrapped taffy. "Try this!"

Raene opens her hand, and Tansy gently places it into the palm of her hand. She unwraps it, biting it lengthwise to get the combination of the two flavors, then holds the other piece out to me. I inch closer, open my mouth, and she drops the taffy on my tongue. Together we chew and savor the taste.

"Pineapple and mango?" Raene asks, her face lights up at the taste. "It's delicious."

"Thank you." Tansy does a little curtsy and giggles.

Her wings flutter as she beams. "It's called *Tropical Tango.*"

Raene digs into her back pocket, pulling out some cash. "I'll take three pounds, please."

We continued our shopping after dropping her bags in her car, keeping an empty tote for anything else she may see. We pass rows of vendors selling trinkets, clothing, and jewelry. Then one booth has my attention. The table is with earrings, rings, necklaces, and even loose gems.

"Give me a second," I murmur in her ear, guiding her to the booth.

"Jewelry?" She asks, brows raised as I scan the display.

"Not just any jewelry." My gaze lands on a pair of earrings—silver hoops with ivory colored drops that shimmer when the light hits them, and if you look closely, you can see a faint swirl of fog inside. I hand her one so she can see, and she holds it up, her face mesmerized by the activity within the stone.

"Is this magic? It's beautiful," she speaks quietly. She looks closer, gently stroking a fingertip over the stone like she's trying to figure out if it's a trick.

"They're mist gems. Found here in Everly Hollow."

She hands it back, and I hand the pair to the jeweler, telling him I'd like to buy them.

He boxes them up, I tap my card to his phone to complete the purchase, and before she can argue, I slip the tiny box into her hand.

"Ash—"

"Don't," I cut in, smirking. "You're going to hurt their feelings."

She huffs a laugh, rolling her eyes as she tucks the box into her bag. "You're impossible, but thank you. They are beautiful."

"Not impossible," I correct, leaning in just enough to give her a gentle kiss. "I followed your rules, and I saw something I wanted. Now let's grab some food before we do the passport walk."

As the night settles over the town, lanterns strung around the market begin to flicker to life. Music drifts softly as families eat, shop, and talk. The bounce houses and leaf piles have been cleared away, leaving the promise of tomorrow's carnival.

With our stomachs full and excitement building, we clutch our passports in hand and step onto a lantern-lit pathway lined with rustic, wooden booths, eager to begin our Sip Passport adventure.

It's a sight to see. Mugs with tendrils of steam sit on trays, bubbles and fizz pop in tall glasses, and bottles clinking as pixies pour samples with grace. The combination of the smells in the air makes my mouth water. I can smell coffee, honey, and sugar.

"Time to be adventurous." Raene winks.

"I'm down to try anything," I say, following behind to the next booth. "I'm hoping they have something special, maybe pumpkin spiced, just for you."

My mouth curves at her frown. "Otherwise, you'll fail your quest for a fully stamped passport."

She turns to face me. "That's why it's a *sip* passport, Ash. Just a tiny sip," she holds up two fingers, barely inching apart, to demonstrate the tiniest sip imaginable. "It's barely a swallow," she says, maintaining eye contact, yet slightly elevating her chin as we continue our walk to a booth of her choosing.

"Barely a swallow," I echo, walking beside her, letting my voice dip low. "Sounds…disappointing."

Her head jerks toward me, eyes widening for a beat before narrowing in a playful warning. "You're naughty," she mutters, though there's a smile pulling at her lips as she looks ahead.

"I'm not," I shrug, "just wanting to make sure that you enjoy every...sip."

She gasps with laughter, shaking her head.

The first booth greets us with the scent of coffee beans, cinnamon, and honey.

"Honey Cinnamon Latte," the man says warmly, holding out a tray of small cups. "We have a decaf option as well."

Raene reaches out, taking a small cup before sending a soft, cool blow across the top to cool it. Her lashes flutter as her eyes drift closed, as she slowly sips.

"Is it good?" The words come out rough, betraying me.

She hums in approval, gently lifting the cup towards my lips. "Try it." When I take it, her fingers brush mine, and even though I've felt that tiny touch before, it feels like it still has the magic to sink into me. I take a few sips, the sweet honey melting on my tongue with a warm bite of cinnamon.

"Not bad," I say, licking my lips for another taste, just to watch her eyes drop for just a second.

She quickly thanks him, as he stamps our passports with an image of cinnamon sticks.

"On to the next," she says, tugging me toward a booth where glass bottles of orange fizz sit in large bins of ice.

"Ginger-orange sparkling soda," the vendor explains, handing each of us a cup. I take my time with this one; it's refreshing, with the tang on the tongue. Raene takes a delicate sip, then scrunches her nose as she laughs.

"Not feeling it?" I ask, fighting a grin.

"These bubbles are fierce, but I do love the taste. The citrus with the ginger is a great combo.

I want her to drink, just to see the bubbles make her laugh again.

Booth after booth, we make our way around, enjoying our drinks and getting our stamps along the way. They include a faerie wine that Raene asked for *two* cups of, a berry cider, a soft floral tea, and even a pumpkin-spiced hot chocolate that surprisingly earns her approval.

She loved the creamy chocolate but not the pumpkin aftertaste. She only winced slightly and plugged her nose ever so gently. No, that didn't happen. In all seriousness, she fucking hated it and won't be converting to *Team Pumpkin* in this lifetime.

We tease, we laugh, and somewhere between the fizz and the warmth of the drinks, I pull her close, sneaking touches...kisses. The fact I can kiss her under a streetlight, her back pressed against it—don't worry, her back has been perfectly fine—gives me an excuse to slip a hand beneath her sweater. I glide it along the smooth, silky skin of her ribs, tracing the lace under her breast, until I brush against a nipple.

When she whimpers, *fuck*, I want to bite her lower lip, and I do, before deepening the kiss.

This. Fucking. Mouth.

By the time the last stamp hits her passport, the market has thinned out. The lanterns above us sway like captured stars or glow moths picked right from the sky, and music drifts soft and low near the fountain at the square.

Raene leans against the stone edge, the passport clutched in her hand, her chest heavy with laughter. I step closer, close enough that the gold flecks in the iris of her honey-brown eyes brighten.

"Did you enjoy yourself?" I ask, voice low.

She hums and gives me a soft smile. "Told you I'd keep you safe."

I free my hand from my pocket, catching her chin between my thumb and finger, the hold gentle yet firm. My gaze dips from her eyes to her parted lips, and without thought, my thumb traces a slow path along her jawline.

"I don't think I am safe with you," I whisper. The truth is heavy on my chest. "Not even close."

She tilts her head, a question sparking to life in her eyes, but I don't give her a chance to speak. Instead, I close the distance, pressing my mouth to hers. The kiss is slow at first, soft and warm. Her breath catches when I pull back, and by the goddess, that sound itself, that light and airy gasp, it takes my breath too.

Even in this moment, things may seem perfect. When I know it can't be.

26
It's okay, I'm here
RAENE

The view from here feels surreal. The whole carnival stretches below us in an astonishing blur of color and light. Rides spinning in colorful loops, vibrant neon game stalls flashing bright prizes, and a river of people weaving through it all.

The pie-throwing contest was a hit. Mayor Caraway, Garruk, and Viktor joined in on the festivities, as well as a few attendees. When I asked Sylas if he wanted to join in, he tossed his head back in laughter and said Nim would gladly take his place.

That was proven to be true when Nim attempted to take flight with one of the creme pies in his talons. The pudding slipped out of the silver liner before he could even make it a few inches off the ground, but he happily landed, devouring the sweet filling.

Pop music booms from the speakers, pulling me out of the afternoon memory, and mixes with the scent of deep-fried deliciousness, grilled meats, cheesy treats, cotton candy, and sugar. It all pulses underneath this starlit sky, through the night air. Tonight is electric.

Children run and dart between the glowing games and fast rides, their laughter carries on the chill wind, up to where we are, perched at the very top of the Ferris wheel.

The enclosed gondola rocks gently with the breeze, the metal groaning slightly as it sways. My hand squeezes his thigh, and suddenly, I feel his hand on mine. Starting to link our fingers together. Telling me that it's okay. That he isn't going anywhere.

Yet, from here, it feels like the world should stop spinning with us, but down below, the crowds move, and life goes on. It's bright, it's fast, and it's loud.

"If you could wish for anything," he leans in, whispering in my ear, "What would it be?"

I think on that a second, and turn my head to his, meeting his eyes. Then I slowly look away and out to the carnival lights.

"Time."

"Why time?" He asks, pulling me closer to him.

"I would want the power of time. The ability to change the past, present, and future. My grandmother is aging, and this hip surgery is a sudden punch in the face as a reminder. For my past, I wish I could have saved my parents from the car accident."

I let out a shaky breath.

"I miss my parents. I miss my Dad's smile and how the lines at the corners of his eyes deepened in mirth when laughter escaped his chest. His eyes were wise, always shining brightly. I used to write silly short stories, and he and my Mom would listen to every single one."

His hand slides in a slow, soothing stroke along my thigh, urging me to continue.

"My mom loved fall. She loved the colors, the decorations, and the baking. She made the best sweet potato pies, Grandma's recipe."

He kisses the side of my temple as he holds me in his arms.

"We were driving one day, and it was raining. My Dad lost control of the car and we careened off the road, flipping over and over. That day, my entire world went upside down. I remember the car was on its side, and all I could hear was the rain, and the last thing I saw was falling leaves."

"It's okay. I'm here," he murmurs, as his lips hover over the pulse he just kissed. He begins to trail his fingers down my breastbone as if his touch could steady my heart.

I'm okay. He's here.

Am I going to start crying again?

First three little words, now four bigger words...what's next, a five-word phrase—*Raene, will you marry me?*

Fuck. I'm hopeless.

"I would use my power of time to save my parents, keep my grandmother, and you...you, Ash," I turn to look at him, "you're the future. You're something in my grasp that I can't quite keep a hold on."

For a beat, silence stretches between us, filled only by the distant thrum of music and the faint groan of the wheel turning.

"Do you want to hold on?"

Goddess. Jesus wept.

Fuck. I do. I really do.

The internal confession screams through my head, burning the tip of my tongue, but all I can do is stare at him, my pulse hammering like a bird, it wants to break free, and I know he hears it.

The Ferris wheel creaks as it rocks gently, but his eyes don't leave mine. He's waiting. Waiting for an answer.

I swallow hard, my voice is low and a bit too shaky. "I don't know," I whisper. "I don't know what I'm allowed to hold on to right now."

He pulls me even closer to him, and the only reason it works is because I'm melting against him. The air shifts to something different. Unique, when he enters my space. He's warm, which is a plus, and that scent. Parchment, cedar, and a splash of citrus, topped with a bit of zest.

"Raene," he says softly, like my name is a sacred, rare jewel, something precious. "No one can decide that but you."

My breath stutters. The three little words I want to say, *I want you,* stay hidden in my chest, because the wheel is starting to move again, carrying us down, back to solid ground, deeply rooted in reality.

Then I'll lose this moment forever.

"I'll be right back," I say, letting go of his hand. He puts his hands in his pockets and nods his head, giving me a small smile in understanding as I make my way through the crowds.

"Thank you for this," she says as we walk toward the exit gate. My grandmother's voice always carries a quiet strength that just seems to soothe the soul.

"You really pulled it off, Raene. The booths, the lanterns, the markets, the music, and now this! This festival is something special." She glances back toward the glow of all the lights in the square, where laughter and music spilled happily into the dark. "And you didn't do it alone." Her eyes glance toward Ash, who lingers a few feet behind us.

Heat begins to bloom in my chest. It's unexpected. I have to swallow hard before I can answer. "Yeah," I manage, my voice low. "We did good, didn't we?"

She squeezes my hand, her smile soft as she stands with pride. "You and Sylas did something amazing together. I'm proud of you."

By the time we reach the street, I can tell she is tuckered out, and there is a dip in her energy. "Go home and rest," I urge, hugging her tight as she steps into the passenger side of Flora's car. "I'll be back sometime later."

She searches my face for a moment, silence lingers between us, and I know something unspoken is on the tip of her lips, but she just gives me her *'everything is going to be alright'* smile.

And then the carnival chaos swallows me whole.

I love the smell...and taste of delicious fried treats. It's the best fair and carnival food. There's just something special about a deep-fried treat that was smothered or filled with goodness. We enjoy funnel cakes, dusted to powdered sugar perfection, pizza, and nachos. Sometimes you need the sweet first and the savory and salty last.

"Okay, we need a plan to kick some asses," Oriana says calmly. Tearing a piece of cotton candy fluff off her cloud and letting it melt on her tongue. The cotton candy floats near her head in literal cloud form until eaten. Honestly, it's kind of cute, drifting around her like that. Even Corra nibbles on a few tiny pieces.

Elora shrugs. "I can milk a cow, but my hand-eye coordination isn't great when it comes to sports." She giggles.

The guys are beating us in a virtual ax-throwing game, leading by eighteen points. The scoreboard dances in the air like a shooting star, proudly flaunting its high score.

"All we can do, girls, is breathe and release," Jas says as if she is going to start chanting it for peer motivation.

"And Poppy?" Jas yells, a stern look on her face. "Don't let him get inside your head."

"Right," Poppy says, she nods quickly, her ponytail swaying slightly.

And right next to her in his lane is Garruk.

Ohhhh fuck.

The tension in this vicinity is so thick you could spank it and it would moan. You can tell she's wound tight. He is just standing there with his arms crossed and a smirk pressed between his tusks.

"Penelope," Garruk says, his deep voice carrying just enough to make the girls side-eye each other. He nods his head, respectfully...for once.

Poppy gives him a tight-lipped smile, like she's not buying into the chivalrous act.

"You get to go first." He gestures toward the screen. Showing in the corner how to pick up the virtual axes and aim at the target.

"Don't mind if I do," she says, sweet as sugar, grabbing an ax and stepping forward with a sway in her hips that was either intentional or sinfully natural. She lines up her shot, and the axe hits at the edge of the second ring.

Garruk chuckles under his breath.

Uh oh. Big mistake.

Poppy snaps her head toward him. "Something funny you wanna share with the class, *clown*?"

"Just admiring your confidence," he drawls. "You've got...spirit. No aim, but you do have a spirit about you."

Her mouth drops open, then curls into a razor-sharp smile ready to strike. "You're all muscle and no brain, Garruk. If you did...have a brain that is...maybe you would be a better baker."

A few of us start with the *Ohhhs* from wincing at her jab.

Garruk's jaw flexes, and his smirk evaporates as he begins to step away from the machine.

"Noted," he says, voice flat, and he turns on his heel and walks away from the booth. No one can stop him. I look at Ash, and he's literally rubbing and scratching his head, trying to figure out what the hell just happened.

Poppy blinks, her confidence faltering. "Wait, what?"

"I think you just broke him," Oriana whispers, eyes wide.

"Ugh, *fuck.*" Poppy drags her hands down her face before letting out a heavy sigh, weighted down by regret. "Why me?" She hisses, grabbing her bag and bolting after him.

"Have they always been like that?" I ask, as Ash and I walk side by side, sharing a cloud of pink cotton candy between us. It hovers low, just enough for us to catch glimpses of each other's faces through the fluffy ends of the spun sugar.

We're people watching, and it's fun seeing families, couples, and the chaos of all the colorful nighttime activity. However, watching Nim, it's comedy gold. Watching him sneak any kind of treat is hilarious. He was chasing a rolling funnel cake earlier, like it owed him a bet, licking up the trail of the dusted powdered sugar.

"Not in the beginning." Ash shakes his head, pulling a tuft of fluff from the cloud and popping it into his mouth. "But something changed between those two. It was like night and day."

Hmph. "I hope they can figure out their differences and get back on solid ground."

Sylas nods but chuckles. "It'll be a while yet, but they'll be okay."

"So..." I glance at him, reading his face, curiosity peaking. "What do you want to do?"

"You."

My steps slow, and I look up, even though I already know what he said, because the corners of my mouth are already curving upward. "What?"

"Nothing." His lips twitch like he's fighting back another laugh, and then his fingers slip through mine.

He tugs me a little closer. "How about a few more rides before I take you back to my place?"

"Oh, is that where the fun ends for tonight?" I arch a brow, tugging his hand playfully as I turn to bring my body closer to his, starting to run the palms of my hands against his firm chest. "Or do you have something else I can...ride?"

27
A Night to Remember
SYLAS

The same live band that is to perform tomorrow is already assembled in front of the fountain for the ball. Their instruments gleam in the fading light, while lanterns and streetlights cast a perfect glow, transforming the evening into a dreamlike scene.

The sun descends into slumber, streaking the sky in ribbons of pink, light orange, and violet, while classical music drifts across the town square. The song is rich and full, vibrating through the cobblestone like a pulse.

A long table near the plaza is beautifully decorated with finger foods, vibrant and delicate desserts, and punch that shimmers in crystal bowls with matching glasses.

Food is always in abundance here. It's an unspoken rule of Everly Hollow gatherings. The faint shimmer of glow moths fluttering above the square casts a dreamlike spell over everything.

Guests move across the space, some gliding over the temporary dance floor in extravagant gowns and sharp tuxedos, others lingering at tables in simple yet elegant dresses and tailored suits, sipping drinks and laughing in conversation.

Malik and Oriana sweep through a waltz with practiced grace. Nearby, Seren spins in a burst of giggles, clutching Dominik's finger as her purple dress flares out like a blooming flower around her feet.

The mayor, his wife, and Elora stand near the refreshment tables, faces lit in awe as they greet the guests.

I loved the idea of a ball. A real dance. Something different than the other festivals that have been held in the past. I thought that a night that gives people a chance to dress up and let themselves be swept away for a night would be magical and memorable.

We wanted to make it a statement. A night to remember. Especially after the last day of the carnival yesterday. It's nice to slow down after the constant adrenaline rush.

It was another day of sweet treats, delicious food, rides, and games. I took a picture of Raene at the petting zoo holding a fluffy grey rabbit, scrunching her nose up and twitching it like the animal in her arms. It's now my phone's lock screen image.

As much as I take in the beauty of this event, I haven't seen her yet.

Raene.

The not knowing coils in my chest like a tangled string, my heart on the end of it like a yo-yo. I offered to pick her up, but she wanted to come with her grandmother, which in the end is perfect. It built the anticipation of seeing her.

The fall season may not be what she likes, but I've seen her smiling at something, laughing at something else. I catch the ripple in the crowd as a few heads turn, and I follow their gaze. She's walking in from the parking lot with her grandmother, one hand lifting the hem of her dress just enough to keep it from brushing the ground.

Gold.

Her gown looks like gold had been poured and molded to fit the perfect shape of her body, catching every flicker of light until she glows like a gift from Ruskaya herself.

She spins in a slow circle before coming to a stop, giving me a wide smile. A few braids are down near her face, and the rest are pinned into a bun at the top of her head.

"You look—"

"Did I just take your breath away, Ash?

Yeah, yeah, you did.

"That and more..."

She takes a step towards me. Her hand is trailing the buttons of my vest. "You look handsome as ever, your suit is smart."

I'm wearing a vintage deep green tweed suit, with an ivory dress shirt under my vest and a deep orange tie and matching pocket square. I tied my hair back, and she likes my ears.

"Thank you," I whisper to her. My hand grips her chin lightly, my thumb tracing the outline of her lower lip.

"Do you want something to drink?" I ask her, my hand slipping into the small of her back, leading her to the punch bowl and arrangement of foods.

We eat, drink and chat with our friends, and the mayor and his wife, who thanked us for planning such a fantastic event. The feedback has been phenomenal. There is no way I could have done this without Raene. Her love of summer and not wanting to let her grandmother down inspired her creativity.

When everyone parts in their different directions, my eyes land on hers as she takes a look around, watching everyone enjoy themselves. Listening to the laughter and talking melt into the music. There's pride in her expression. I just need a dance. One dance with her.

"Dance with me?"

She takes my hand without hesitation.

"*Oh...*" she says excitedly, her eyes sparkling with wonder, "you have *moves*, Mr. Ashvale."

Mister. I quite like that.

Her hand is gently placed on my shoulder, the other enclosed in mine as we glide across the dance floor.

"You like that, huh?" I smirk, giving her a quick twirl that bursts into a laugh, then pulling her body close, warmth spreading within my chest.

If I could bottle up her laugh and keep it, I would. "Wanna get out of here?" I whisper in a hushed tone.

"Trying to sneak me away already?" She teases, but her voice is threaded with *want*.

Her fingers slide from my shoulder to the back of my neck, and her fingers move in a slow, singular circle above my collar. The lightness of her touch sends tingles racing down my spine.

I have to bite back a groan, feeling high in the way that even the simplest touch by her makes my body react. I love it when she wants to touch my skin, even in the simplest form. Her touch warms my skin. She's like a drug that goes deep into my veins.

"Yes," I whisper against her ear again, making sure the truth leaves no room for doubt. "Yes, I am. I need as much time with you as I can get."

"What are you doing?" She asks me, beginning to walk backwards on the stairs, a hand reaching out for balance against the trunk.

I dart my eyes up at the sound of the rustling in Nim's wings before he takes off through the skylight and into the night.

Good.

"Do you know how stunning you look in that dress?" I ask her, gritting my teeth, as I make my way over to her.

She takes a step back, slipping on an edge of her dress before falling on her ass onto a step, breathing heavily.

"Oops," I murmur. The corner of my mouth lifts. "Spread your legs. I want to hear the sounds you make when I do things to you in this dress."

"Things…" she echoes slowly, bunching the hem of her dress, tugging it over her thighs, her knees falling open to the side.

"Damn it, Raene." I fall to my knees, my hands inch up her thighs slowly, pushing the fabric of her dress further back.

"Already having me drop to my knees to worship you, huh?"

Her eyes are full of heat, and I feel the warmth radiating off her skin. She rolls her hips, searching for friction. "Show me how you want to worship me," she says in a whisper. It's a plea.

I reach under her dress and gently pull her lace thong down her legs, over her shoes, and toss it over my shoulder.

She grabs one of the iron spindles as I lift her ass into my hands, her legs on my shoulders, and begin to tease her with my tongue. Her body writhes as she whimpers in pleasure. I devour her like a starving man, savoring the taste of her, lapping her with my tongue but making sure I take my time.

Her body arches and begs for more when a low moan escapes her lips. I begin pumping two fingers in her, her body rocking back and forth as she leans on her elbows, my fingertips squeezing on her perfect ass.

I want her to melt against my mouth. I can feel her thighs tremble, her breath turning into sharp gasps as the pressure of my fingers, warmth from my tongue, continues to stoke the fire that burns low in her belly.

Another sound slips from her throat—raw and needy—as I suck on her clit and stroke my fingers upward.

"Ash!" Her body still trembles as she rides it out.

I stand up and pull her to her feet; her knees wobble a bit.

I love that.

"I need you so bad right now, baby." I start to undo my belt.

"Right here?" She asks, tilting her head slightly. Her eyes are bright, yet full of curiosity and lust.

"Yes." I turn her around near the bottom step. Her hands immediately reach out to grip the railing.

"Right now."

"Mm-hmm." I move her hair to the side and kiss her neck.

"With my dress and shoes on?" She asks me, starting to spread her legs.

"Fuck...yes. Now bend a little."

Perfect.

"Good girl," I say, my voice low, like a growl is tearing its way through my throat. "I love that fucking mouth, but you're such a good listener."

I line myself up at her entrance, feeling her so wet for me as I push in slowly.

"Keep talking to me, goddess, or I'm not going to last long."

Fuck.

I bury myself, inch by inch, pulling back only to sink deeper with each thrust. Skin against skin, heat and craving tangling, she cries out.

"Don't stop, keep going..." she moans.

I grip her hips hard, pulling out and pushing in, pulling her back to meet every deep stroke I take.

Every thrust is frantic, as I listen to her cries.

"Goddess...Ash...It feels so good."

I moan, my head tossing back as I continue thrusting deep inside her.

"Shit, baby...you feel *perfect*."

"Come for me, Ash, I need you."

" Raene," her name slips from my lips in a moan as I finish inside her.

She gasps, rolling her hips back as she says my name. The words roll off her lips like a promise.

I hold on to her for a moment before I pull out, tugging my pants back in place, catching my breath. With her dress falling back to its length, her body saunters in the direction of her lacy panties.

She squats to retrieve them, and she chooses to lie down on the cool floorboards. The fabric balled in the palm of her hand.

"Why does it feel like that?" She pants. Her eyes are lost on the skylights, where the stars spill silver light into the bookshop, mingling with the golden shimmer of leaves.

I remove my shoes and vest and make my way over to her. I don't even think we'll go back out to the ball. I'm quite content just staying here.

She's still on the ground, lifting her legs to take off her shoes, tossing them to the side. Her dress pools around her like poured gold. Her breathing is uneven.

I lower myself beside her, the cool wood pressing into my back, my arm brushing hers.

"I don't know," I finally answer, my voice rough. Maybe because time is running out, it feels like this.

28
Twilight
Sylas

This adult only tent event, showcasing the *Blackberry Moon Lily Drop,* is spectacular.

Raene should be very proud because she brought her vision to life. We chatted earlier during setup before going back to my place to shower and change.

We figured taking a shower together would save us some time, and it did, for the most part. Until she asked me to scrub her back. So, I did, but she braced her hands on the tile, arched her back, and stuck her ass out against me.

Yet, thankfully, with the help of our friends, they made setting up for the event a breeze. Especially with the multiple tents connecting to fully cover the courtyard and give it a separate ambiance from the fall decor outside.

Tables and chairs are spread out, the deep velvet fabric hanging from decorated columns. Fairy lights twinkle above us, casting a soft, purple glow that gives the tent an ethereal feel.

The dance floor is ready. I see Oriana pull Malik toward it, his tie wrapped around her hand. Waiters and waitresses weave through the crowd with platters of food, and we've got a bar set up, staffed by Hannah and a few people she brought to help.

The event looks like twilight, and I see the brightest star, swaying her hips a little to the beat. The band is playing a blues song, and I think I'm just going to sit back and enjoy the view of her. She's wearing a dark blue dress with flowy long sleeves. The hem kisses the tops of her boots at her knees. The neckline plunges to the middle of her breasts.

She's just in her element. She has her weather system, and it's summer. Her honey-brown eyes, her beautiful sun-kissed brown skin, her talent, her happiness, and joy. She's the sun, and I'm the idiot who's going to go blind from staring straight at it and not giving a damn. She stands out. She radiates those around her.

I walk over to her, right when she stops to take a sip of her drink.

"I like your moves," I say, taking a sip of my drink, which was the number one special on tonight's menu.

"Is that the best you can do?" She asks. She sets her glass down at a nearby table as her fingers walk up my chest, arms wrapping around my neck.

"I thought you had pick up lines that could make my toes curl..." she teases.

I don't hesitate to pull her close to me. She's all soft curves and warmth pressed against me.

"I love the way your body moves, but I would prefer it if it were under mine."

Her breath catches.

"How was that?" I say in a hushed tone in her ear.

"It was better…definitely better." She nods her head, and it brings a laugh out of me.

"Are you having fun?" I ask, voice low enough that only she can hear over the band.

Her head tilts up at me, that smile tugging at the corner of her mouth. "Maybe."

"Maybe?" I arch a brow, pulling her into me. I love how her heart races when she's around me. The excitement.

The anticipation. The wonder she has in her eyes at what I am going to do next.

I see her earrings sparkle; the mist inside of them shifts slightly.

Why is such a simple act of her wearing my gift, making me want to lose all control?

She shrugs, playful. "It could be better."

"Is that so?" I ask, clearing my throat. "Could I make it better?"

"Yes."

"Then dance with me," I ask, giving my shoulders a light shrug.

Her eyes search mine for a moment with parted lips, before they curve into a small smile.

"Are you always this confident, Ash?"

"Always…*especially* when it comes to what matters most."

I can see the wheels turning in her head, her lips tick upwards into a small smile.

Taking her hand in mine, I gently tug her to the makeshift dance floor, weaving in and out of the groups of people. She turns around, giving me her back as she moves her hips again, moving that ass like a beacon drawing me to it.

My hand slides to her waist as we move to the rhythm of the beat. The music wraps around us like fog. One of her arms is by her side, the other is resting on one of the arms I have encircled around her waist. She feels so good dancing with me like this.

"Say you can sense this, can't you?" I murmur into her ear as we move together slowly, in a sensual trance.

I do. Goddess, I do.

Turning her around to face me, my thumb strokes lazy, small circles at her waist as she leans in to kiss me.

"I feel it," she admits, her voice barely a whisper.

We dance like this till the song ends. Moving together in the dim lighting, ignoring everyone else on the dance floor, we sneak sweet touches and light kisses to one another. I want to stay in this moment. I wish this night would never end. I get excited to see her in the morning, but I dread the evenings because it is one day closer to her imminent departure.

I have to soak up every bit of her as I can until I see her again. I hope everything can work out flawlessly, but all we can do is try.

Even if she doesn't want to put labels on this, it is long-distance. We can take it, day by day, but we are still trying for something. Trying to see where this takes us and if the end result would be worth it.

She is worth it.

"When can I see you next?" I quickly ask. We gently sway side to side as she flips through the mental calendar in her head.

"Next weekend? Do you want to try to come visit? Even if it is just for a day or two," she pauses for a moment. "I still would want to see you.

"Well then, let's plan for that. Is that okay? I know you didn't want to put a label on this, Raene, but it's important, right?

Us.

"This will be a long-distance thing, and that thing is called a relationship. You need to admit that otherwise, there will be no point in trying."

Her nose scrunches up as she thinks, and she looks down at our feet.

I gently tilt her head up to look at me. "Don't hide, and don't be scared. If we try, we can see how this goes, and I want to see how far this can go, Raene, but if we go in now thinking it's nothing important, then it won't be."

She takes a deep breath and closes her eyes, then nods her head. "You're right. I'm sorry. I am scared. I feel like putting a label on this makes it seem that much more real, but this is real, and I do feel something for you, Ash."

I stroke her cheek as she leans into my hand.

"So can I call you my girlfriend?" I joke.

"No," she says, shaking her head. "I'm your goddess, remember?"

29
Feast of Falling Leaves
RAENE

I don't think I've cooked so much in my life. I keep opening and closing my hands to stretch them out because I think whisking and stirring is giving me carpal tunnel.

Grandma and I have been cooking all day. I loved spending this day with her and was grateful that Sylas was able to handle the setting up for the fall feast.

He told me not to worry about it, that all this cooking is another way to prepare for the feast. The guys were able to help set up for the feast, which helped ease some of the stress and worry that we would have a major hiccup in tonight's plans.

"Raene, honey, come out here for a bit." I hear grandma say, opening the front door, and a cool breeze flows in. It cools my overheated skin from being in this kitchen for so long.

I head out to the porch. She has two blankets, one in each rocking chair, and on the little table between us are two mugs of hot cocoa with marshmallows and a small plate of snickerdoodle cookies.

"When did you do all this?" I ask, taking a seat and covering my legs with the blanket. I reach out to grab my mug. I love the chill in the air, but I don't mind keeping my hands warm.

"I was doing all this while you were going nonstop in the kitchen. You just didn't notice. We need a break." Grandma grabs a cookie to snack on while I take a sip of the chocolatey treat. The chocolate-scented steam kisses my nose.

Pumpkins on the porch, grandma's army of scarecrows. Even the colors. The oranges and the browns. The reds and the golds. They all stick together. Through all the seasons, until it's time for some to go.

What is happening to me? It's just being in this moment with Grandma that has me enjoying this view and the sweet treats, right?

"Beautiful view, huh?" Grandma asks me. She's always loved fall. Like mother, like daughter. It was my mother's favorite season too, and when I was younger, I loved it then for her. But my love of fall died along with my parents.

I take a bite of a cookie. Chewing slowly. I swallow it down with the sadness that is creeping into my mind.

"It is. The colors, they're alluring."

"They are," she sighs and begins to rock in her chair. "You know. I always found it fascinating how they change from their bright, vibrant greens to this. To so many different colors, and it just gives off a glow. Like they're excited for the change coming. Even if it is a little bit scary and different."

I take a deep breath and let it out slowly.

"Let's just sit out here a bit. Take a break," she repeats.

I smile, take a sip, and rock gently with the breeze.

Sometimes, the last days of some things give you a small ache in your chest. Whether it's the last sip of coffee, the last day of your vacation, or the last day of a festival, where you have to leave people behind in hopes of visiting soon. It's like a song that touches your soul, and you don't want it to end, but that last and final note is coming.

The tables stretch across the square, holding large groups of people. Each table is loaded with foods prepared by the bakeries, the local dinner, and even the people living within Everly Hollow.

It's an endless runner of food on every table. Platters piled high with roasted meats steaming under lantern light, bowls of side dishes like buttery mashed potatoes, gravy, salads, casseroles, vegetables, and golden rolls. Desserts—tarts, pies, and cakes so intricate they look like art. Even the fruit glows like little jewels in crystal bowls, grapes spilling over the edge, waiting for its close-up painting.

Everything smells delicious, warm, and gives cozy fall vibes. The cinnamon and the cloves in the air, mingling with the scents of the food.

We all gather, one big, messy, blended family that I didn't realize until now. My grandmother sits to my right, looking regal with her hair in soft curls, wearing a soft cream sweater and gold scarf, an orange jacket, and jeans.

I smooth my hands across my sweater dress as I cross my legs. It's a deep olive green, warm, and goes perfectly with my camel brown ankle boots and brown knitted tights.

Across from me, Jas is cutting up Seren's chicken as she takes tiny bites of her carrots while Dominik tears off little pieces of the dinner roll, rolls it between his fingers, and throws it above his head, catching it in his mouth, and the whole event keeps her giggling.

Oriana leans into Malik, her hand resting lightly on his arm in between eating, and they turn towards one another, having an intimate conversation that pulls an occasional smile from their lips.

Viktor is already on his second plate and in deep conversation with Garruk, who has turned his body away from Poppy. She refuses to look in that direction. The building tension between them is practically a side dish.

And on my left is Ash.

He has his hair tied in the back, looking quite *dashing* in his evergreen knitted sweater, jeans, and black boots.

His hand slides onto my knee under the table, and it radiates warmth through my tights. He gives it a gentle squeeze, and I almost break right here.

This is what I'm leaving.

Him.

Us.

This entire town somehow wrapped itself around me when I was distracted by the *magic* of it all.

I take a slow sip of the sparkling apple cider in front of me, the bubbles catching in my throat as I try to swallow the ache building in my chest. Tomorrow, I go back to the city. Back to my life. Back to being an author who enjoys writing books on love blooming in summer.

Am I going to be the same?

The conversation hums around me with the music low in the background. Little bursts of laughter, soft clinking of silverware, the low rumble of voices.

"Are you doing okay?" Ash leans in to whisper.

I know he is probably wondering why I'm quiet. I'm just trying to take it all in.

"Yeah, I'm good." I nod my head, forking a piece of meat on my plate, and start eating.

"So...you ready for the city again?" Oriana asks, arching one perfectly sculpted brow.

Everyone looks at me. Even Nim, who is curled up in a tree near Sylas' shop like a little statue, peeks an eye open like he's waiting for my answer, too.

I force a smile that feels way too tight, like my face might crack. "As ready as I'll ever be."

Liar.

My grandmother's hand covers mine on the table, warm and reassuring, and my throat dries up. She's proud. I know she is. She's proud of what I've done here. But that pride is beginning to feel as if it were boxed up and wrapped in a bow that I never wanted.

Ash's fingers squeeze my knee again, a little firmer this time, like he knows I'm an emotional mess inside. As if his hand can fit all the loose pieces of the puzzle together again. It makes me want to lean into him.

Maybe I can do just one more day here?

No. I'll be okay. He will be okay. I have to get back to work. I have things I want to accomplish, and like Ash said, one day at a time. We will enjoy whatever this is and take it slow.

When the toasts begin, I stand because if I don't move, I might sink further into this chair. Peach colored crystal glasses clink in the soft light of the square, surrounded by the curtain of nightfall, cider popping like champagne bubbles.

"To love," Oriana says.

"To happiness," Jas adds.

"To fall changes and new beginnings," Ash finishes, his smile bright.

I lift my glass with everyone else, but the words hit too hard.

New beginnings.

And still, when the glasses clink, I glance to my side, and Ash is already looking at me. The hooded look in his eyes and the intense gaze he has on me, like I'm the only thing that matters. Making promises that I can't make my heart believe right now. I drink anyway, because if I don't, I'll say something I can't take back.

And maybe, just maybe, I want to.

30
It's Not Goodbye, It's See You Later
RAENE

Sitting my suitcase and bags at the bottom of the stairs, I make my way to the kitchen. The scent of bacon fills the air, making my mouth water. Grandma is standing at the stove, plating the sizzling bacon from the cast-iron pan onto a plate with a few paper towels for draining.

"I made eggs, bacon, and toast." She pipes up, setting the plate on the table. "Long drive for you, so we need to make sure you eat."

"Thanks, Grandma," I say, smiling as I pull out my chair and take a seat. "You always make the best scrambled eggs."

"I try." She winks before digging into her plate.

It's quiet. About as silent as it'll be when I leave. The TV is on, faint in the background, and birds are chirping outside the windows.

"Excited to get back home?"

I look up, surprised by the lilt in her voice. I expected her to be sad, frowning, but she's smiling.

"I am, but I'll miss you. I'll miss this place, but I promise I'll come back to visit often."

"You better," she wags a finger at me, her lips curving into a smirk. "I'm going to hold you to it."

I laugh. "Thanks for everything, Grandma. I'm glad I had the chance to come here and see you and your new home."

She nods her head, reminding me of my promise to visit more often. She even mentions visiting the city next year to see me. I can already imagine relaxing, enjoying lazy beach days, shopping, savoring good food, and watching some of her favorite movies.

Heading out to load the items into my trunk, Grandma follows behind me. I toss my laptop bag and purse into the passenger seat. I turn around to hug her. Her scent fills my nose—roses.

"I love you, Grandma." My voice cracks.

"I love you always, baby." She wraps her arms around me, placing a warm kiss on my cheek.

"I love you too."

"Do you really have to go?" Jas asks. Her lower lip wobbles slightly.

Please don't start crying.

If she cries, I'm going to cry.

"I do, but I will come back to visit." She pulls me into a hug, releasing a low sigh, then quickly tugs me back, her hands holding my arms.

"I get it. You have a life, a fantastic one. You're an amazing author with so many more blessings coming your way. Just don't forget about us, yeah?"

"I could never." I smile brightly because it is the truth. I will never forget this place. The friends I made. The memories I will cherish and play on repeat like a favorite mixtape. She gives my arms one final squeeze before letting go.

"I am going to give you your favorite latte and some treats for the drive." She heads behind the counter and starts packing up a honeybun and an iced lemon roll before preparing the coffee.

The fact that I can sip my coffee on the long drive and it stays warm makes the thought of four hours on the road feel less painful.

"I appreciate it."

Oriana closes in on me next, towering over me in her heels. She gives me a deep blue gift bag that feels pretty heavy, an array of tissues in creams and light blues sticking out of the top.

"Candles." She shrugs, giving a small smile. "To remember us by."

I nod my head. "If you all keep giving me hugs and gifts, I'm not going to be able to conceal the tears."

I laugh. Moisture begins to form in the corners of my eyes. I dab my thumb in the corners in hopes of pushing the tears back.

Elora hands me a beautiful bouquet of dried flowers in reds, oranges, natural tones, and greens.

"Thank you, girls. I'm really going to miss the shit out of you."

"Same," Jas says, pouting. "But we will see each other soon. In the meantime, I'm planning a Winter Solstice Gift Exchange! We can invite Ivy, your grandma, Flora, and a few other people I know too!"

"Now that is a season I can get behind!" I smile.

Sylas

"Hi, Ash." She lifts her hand in a small, hesitant wave, like she's unsure if she should be here. Like a part of her is already half gone. The shyness in her expression is so cute, but this situation is far from it.

She's come to say goodbye.

My chest feels heavy, and it aches. The space she has filled is about to be left behind, empty, as she goes back to her life in the city. I'm so fucking proud of her, and everything she has been through has made her who she is today.

"Come here," I say, as we walk towards one another.

She doesn't wait to wrap her arms around me, and I pull her into me. Holding her tight, not wanting to let go. I hold her as if she is the best part of me, because she is.

"Raene." Her name feels raw in my throat. It burns when I swallow. Her smile wobbles as she glances up at me, moisture building in her eyes. I bury my face in her hair, breathing her in, inhaling her scent.

"I'm going to miss this," I murmured against her temple. My voice is harsh, almost like it's breaking.

I am breaking.

"You must think I'm crazy."

She pulls back just enough to look at me. "A little," she says, laughing.

"I'll miss you too, Ash." Her eyes glisten, and for a second, I almost say it.

Stay, don't go. But I can't. I promised myself I wouldn't hold her back.

A low chuff makes her glance down. Nim's head lowers, his green eyes soften as the brightness dims. He nudges her leg, and Raene laughs a little, pressing both palms to his snout.

"You're saying goodbye, too, huh?" She whispers to him. He lets out a small chirp.

Me too, bud.

I brush a tear away from her eyes before it can fall. "No labels," I say softly, reminding myself as much as her.

She nods slightly, lips trembling like she's trying to hold back something bigger.

"But," I continue, making sure her eyes are on mine so she can read me loud and clear. "There is no world where I don't want more time with you. Whatever this is...I'm not finished, do you understand?"

"I understand," she says, pulling her lower lip between her teeth before crawling into my arms, her mouth seeking mine.

It's not a kiss of desperation. It's a kiss that is slow, aching from the inside out because it is full of the words we can't speak. Everything we can't say is wrapped up in this kiss.

When she pulls away, I cradle her face. My thumbs brush along her cheeks. I press a gentle kiss on the corner of her lips, another on her cheeks, while her hands gently hold my wrists.

"Hey," I say softly, resting my forehead against hers. "It's not goodbye, Raene." My voice is steady. "It's see you later."

"See you later," she says, smiling, looking at my eyes, then back to my lips.

When she smiles, that smile—By the Seven—it guts me.

"Thank you." She kisses me deeply. Just one more time. Molding against my chest, as she sinks in and takes a part of me with her. She breaks away, her hand resting on my chest, before giving me a light tap.

One last look, and then she's walking away, out the door. Nim lowers his head to the ground with a soft rumble and echoes the sound of my very own heart breaking.

31
Saturdays
Sylas

I fucking hate Saturdays.

32

Tomorrow

SYLAS

It's been almost two weeks since I've seen Raene. Since I last saw my Hart.

I miss her touch on my skin. It makes the hairs on the back of my neck stand up in the best way. I miss the way she feels underneath me, and the way she trembles in surrender, causing goosebumps to erupt over her skin. When I trace them like the constellations of stars in the sky, she would give breathy sighs and moans, licking her lips in between each sound that escaped that sexy mouth.

We have been spending our time apart, talking on the phone at any moment we get. Soaking in every word we say to one another, cherishing it like it's gospel. Texting one another in the middle of the day as a way to say, *I'm thinking about you.*

She even sent me a photo of cinnamon tea that she made herself, neatly placed next to her laptop on a saucer with a few chewy shortbread cookies. She stands in the distance beyond the table, teasing me by blurring her figure in very little clothing underneath a plush robe. If only I could step through it. Maybe I need to find a witch to talk to about that.

It frustrates me as much as her that she's feeling stuck with writer's block and working on a few things to get it cleared. Chalking it up to getting back into the routine of things. She didn't want to write during her vacation. She just wanted to enjoy her time here and not have to rush back to her grandmother's cottage to achieve her individual daily word count goal. I can understand that, but I can tell from her voice, she misses it here. She misses her grandmother and the girls.

I *know* she misses me, too. She proved that by making it a point to talk late at night, until we're both exhausted.

And I know her body misses me. The way her body responds to me in a video chat when I tell her to lick her fingers. To spread her legs. To rub her clit. Watching her touch herself through a phone is fucking torture for us both.

I'm supposed to visit *tomorrow,* but I'm not. I can't. The shop needs me. I have to close for the weekend just to untangle this mess I'm in. My magic's so out of balance, I don't even know what's up or down anymore.

I woke up this morning to find leaves everywhere. Inside the shop and outside the shop, blanketing the wood floor and sidewalk like the tree decided to shed all at once overnight. This isn't the best way to start a weekend.

I'm clutching a mug of straight black coffee drowned in pumpkin spice creamer because, if I so much as try anything else that uses even one ounce of my magic, the kind I could do blindfolded and with my hands tied around my back, I'll probably end up destroying something. Having a fucked-up tree that I may be able to somehow fix with Raene miles away and my emotions in jagged shards sounds a lot easier than a building that could potentially start falling apart.

I close my eyes, taking a deep breath as I lean back against the coffee bar, the sturdy wood supporting my weight. Relaxing, I cross my ankles and let out a heavy sigh, resting my hands on my thighs. I inhale slowly before taking a sip, breathing in the rich, bitter aroma of pumpkin spice, dashed with cinnamon of my morning elixir.

I am praying to Ruskaya that the coffee flows through my veins, calming my nerves and soothing my senses. I know I can figure this out. Somehow. But what do I tell Raene? She can't do anything about it, and I don't want her to feel guilty. She's over there, miles away, and I'm here. I can't force her to pack up everything and come try out something new.

My body stands suddenly at the sound of a thud that plummets into the silence, followed by the smack of it hitting the floor. I set my mug down and walked in the direction from which I heard the sound. There, lying at the base of the tree near a thick root, is a book.

What the hell?

Picking it up, I turn it over in my hands. Recognition pools over my face. This isn't any book. It's the first one that went missing last month when I was stocking. I double-counted, but it was gone. Then many others started disappearing after that.

My eyes drag upward, scanning through the branches, though most of the leaves are already on the ground. "Just rake me into the leaf piles," I mutter under my breath.

Then louder, mostly to myself but also because I know he is listening. "You've gotta be shitting me."

I turn towards the shelves, my voice sharp. "Nim? You've been taking the books? You know my magic has been a mess, and you made me think that my magic was also causing my books to disappear?

Nim slinks down the tree. Talons clicking on the wood floors as he approaches me cautiously. His head hangs in shame, his gaze cast at his paws.

My mind hums as his words slip through. *"It's not entirely...all my fault."*

I toss my hands in the air. "Oh, don't start that with me."

I'm sorry you thought your power was causing books to disappear, but the disappearing books didn't just start happening, and I'm a dragon, what do you expect?

"You've been hoarding for—" I freeze when I see the neat stacks again wedged into the branches of the trees. "Goddess, how long have you been doing this?"

Another beat of silence, then a soft *chuff* that sounds suspiciously like he is trying to hold back laughter in my mind. *"Years. A little at a time. You didn't notice. Not every one of my books are special editions or has beautiful sprayed edges."*

"Because you were sneaky about it!" I point at the stack of books with sprayed edges nestled between two branches that intersect.

"Those are *my* books, Nim," I say, my fingers clasped together, thumping the center of my chest. "Do you collect signed books, too? I—"

Wait. I do a double-take after seeing the beachy book cover with white sand near a cerulean blue sea. Two palm trees and a hammock swing at the center, placed as the attention stealer. A lush rainforest lies behind it.

"Is that a signed copy of Raene's book in there, too?" I ask, my voice rougher than expected by the stress and anxiety that consumes my blood.

"They're pretty," he says, and there's a flicker of guilt in his tone. He lifts a paw as if he's examining his talons. *"You like them. I like them. You're a male fae who loves books. Therefore, I love books. Just not the same as you."*

I rake a hand through my hair, pacing now. "Explain that to me, Nim. Explain why you couldn't just, oh, I don't know, collect buttons. Or fucking spoons. Or—"

"Because this isn't a button shop. I'm not knitting a sweater, Sylas." His tone sharpens, then softens again. *"Books hold power. Stories have life. You sell them, you read them. I keep them safe. I love them as much as you do."*

I stop cold in my tracks, peering down at him, his words hit deeper than I expected them to.

"You're telling me you turned into some kind of...mythical being bookstore owner?"

"Private collector," he corrects with a dignified chirp, tail curling proudly around his body. *"It's exclusive. Very valuable."*

I pinch the bridge of my nose, groaning. "You're unbelievable. Do you know the stress you've put me through? I thought my magic system was collapsing. I thought I was—"

"Broken? You're not." His tone is quieter now, and a sense of certainty trickles down the bond. *"I just... wanted something that was mine too."*

And damn it if that doesn't make my chest tighten just a little and make me feel guilty.

"I'm sorry, Nim."

"I'm sorry, too." He brushes his head against my leg, adding to his apology. I'm reeking of guilt, so I accept it.

The tree still has some leaves on it, keyword, *some*. The fullness of it, gone. The remaining leaves are losing their luster. The glow that seems to always radiate from within the tree, something you can physically see and feel, is fading.

I can clean up this weekend and then reopen the shop. I may be able to see if someone can put a glamour on it since I'm unable to do anything right now.

Will a glamour affect my magic even more? Who the hell knows at this point? I didn't expect this to happen. I thought long-distance would work. But it doesn't, but can I keep trying? I've fallen in love with her and I can't give her up. Not when I just got her. I have roots here, but I can grow anywhere. I can plan a visit next weekend, and then see what the city is like.

Me: *Morning, Goddess.*
Raene: *Good morning, boo.*
Raene: *One more day...*

Me: *About that... and look at what I found.*

Photo of tree and Nim's hoard

Raene: *Oh my... is that his hoard? LOL. So no gold?*

Raene: *Ummm... Ash, WTH is happening to your tree?*

Me: *That's what I'm trying to figure out. Clean up the shop and figure out how to fix what's happening.*

Raene: *Give me a few minutes, and I'll call you.*

How do I explain to her that how I feel for her is why my magic is so fucked up? My feelings for her are getting stronger, and I haven't been able to be around her. What do I do if she lets me go? I would sacrifice every piece of magic wrapped around me for her.

33

Maybe

RAENE

"Hey," I say, breathless.

"Hey, yourself." His voice is warm, and God, it makes me miss him even more. No wonder I can barely think or write. "You sound...quiet."

"I've just been thinking. I mean, you've had quite the eventful morning and then—"

There's a pause. A silence that hums between the phones like the tether between us is trying to hang on. "About us," I add.

"Okay," he says slowly. "What about us?"

I grip the edge of my coffee table, nails pressing into the wood. "I didn't expect this," I whisper. "Your shop is a mess. I was excited to see you, but now you're not coming. How is any of this supposed to work?"

He doesn't say anything, but I hear it. In the quick, sharp inhale he takes.

"I'm sorry, Ash," I continue, voice breaking on the last word before it all spills out in a rush. "Your shop, your magic, it makes me feel horrible that..."

Another beat of silence. Heavy. Terrifying.

"What are you saying?" His voice is careful and low, as if he's bracing for impact for something he doesn't want to hear.

I squeeze my eyes shut and take a deep breath. I speak before the courage fades and fear silences me. Before it's too late.

"I'm saying..." My chest rises again on a shaky breath before the damn breaks loose.

"I don't want you to hate me because I love you, Ash. Like head over hills, fallen into a leaf pile, and fell out of a loop in love with you." I sob out a laugh. The tears are just an endless river at this point.

Crickets. All I can hear is his breath.

"You—" His voice dips low, and thick. I can hear him swallow hard, "Say it again."

I can hear the smile in his voice.

My lips curve into a small smile, even though my heart is racing. "I love you."

A sound of relief and joy comes through the phone as he shouts in excitement.

"Fuck, Raene. You have no idea—" He chokes out a broken laugh. "I wish I were there. I wish I could look at you while you say that."

"Me too." It comes out in a hushed breath because if I say it louder, I may cry. "But I don't want you to hate me. I'm worried. Especially about your magic. What are you going to do?"

What can we even do?

"I know we were hoping to see each other this week, but we will soon. I promise. I'll figure something out. Without you here," he pauses, releasing a sigh. "My magic is just as chaotic as I feel with you not here. It has to balance out at some point. I think these first few weeks will just be a little rough, okay?"

"Okay," I repeat back, resting my head on the couch, closing my eyes to try to process everything that has happened so far today.

"Want to know something?"

"Sure."

"My birthday is next weekend, the nineteenth. I'll plan on driving up in the evening the day before. I want to spend that day with you."

His birthday?

"Are you going to be one hundred and twenty-two years old?" I ask softly.

"*Ohhh*," he says quietly. "So close, but no."

I roll my eyes and let out a broken laugh. My heart aches.

"I love you, Raene Hart."

"I love you too, Sylas Ashvale."

I toss my phone down on the cushion beside me.

He loves me. He wants me. He misses me.

I love him, but can I give him the love he needs? I mean, look at what my love is doing to him now. Is he in pain? Does it hurt?

I was excited to see him tomorrow. I had so many plans. I know it's not summer weather, but I still wanted to take a walk on the beach. Take him to one of my favorite restaurants and spots around the city, hit up a few bookstores, all the while having our way with each other.

I wanted his weight on top of me. I wanted my fingers to run through his hair, to brush my thumb over the fullness of his lips and the light freckles that dust his cheeks.

I love him.

I pick up my wine to take a sip, pulling my knees to my chest as my eyes gloss over from staring at the TV for too long. This drink would be so much better if it were faerie wine.

I hear a chirp and look down at my phone. Picking it up, I click on the notification. An image pops up of Elora, Jas, and Oriana, smiling brightly, with the twinkling pergola lights in the background. Text messages begin to flow through.

Jas: *Wish you were here, Rae!*

Elora: *We miss you!*

Oriana: *I'll drink a glass of wine, and more, for you!*

I miss them all. My grandmother, the girls, the town. The air, the faint hum of magic, and how everything feels more *alive* there.

I miss Ash, too, but what was I thinking? What was the point of all this? What is the point of befriending these amazing women who feel like a sisterhood? What was the point in spending more time with Ash other than planning the fall festival? Is it my fault that his magic is so screwed up?

He has to shut his entire shop down this weekend to clean it. To try to fix something I broke inside of him. His magic isn't holding, and he seems lost, confused, but he never blamed me.

Maybe he should. If he didn't fall in love with me, none of this magic mess would be happening. I can't believe I cried out to him and declared my love to him over the phone, but I had to because what if I never got the chance?

Maybe all of this was a mistake.

Do I want to do this?

34
Speechless
SYLAS

My magic is improving, slowly, but it's there. The power of my magic simmers in my blood and radiates on my skin. I'm used to the sensation. It becomes a part of me.

However, now that my power is equivalent to a half-charged battery, I can feel it, the hum that only I can hear in my ears. The power of it all radiates through my soul. It's as if it is a separate entity, but we are one. It needs me as much as I need it.

Ever since I turned my mind to see the positive in my life, and not all the seasonal fuckery things seemed to look up.

All I had to do was turn my focus onto seeing Raene, holding her, touching her, and doing all the things I hoped and imagined during this time, *to her*. On my birthday. I wanted to see her smile and hear her laugh. To wake up in the morning and see her sleeping beside me.

I opened up the shop the following Monday after talking to her and carried on as normal. I was able to find a way to cast a glamour, so no one knew that anything was out of the ordinary. Having magic that isn't at its best and casting a glamour that large was a little draining.

I want things to seem a bit normal, even if I was putting a Band-Aid on it temporarily. But I felt better, the tree didn't lose much more leaves, but it wasn't really replenishing any either. I want a break from it all. It's one thing after another. I need this break. I want to see my girl.

Finally, it's Saturday, and today, *I like Saturdays*. Today is the day, and nothing is going to stop me from going. I need this Saturday to go better. I have my bag packed, and Nim will be fine here. I'm not sure there is anything more dangerous than a dragon in Everly Hollow. A small one at that.

"I heard that."

I laugh at his response as I shuffle around the shop, making sure everything is in order and as it should be for my return. It's the first time in a while I've been away from home. Besides seeing my parents, now I have another good reason to step outside of this enchanted town for a while. Grabbing my bag, I turn to leave, ready more than anything.

I'm just one step closer.

"What the hell—!" My foot hovers over a small cardboard box on the porch. It catches me by surprise, and I move my foot to the side so as not to step on it. Tossing my bag down beside me, I crouched to retrieve it, curiosity piqued.

I lift the lid, a sugary scent hits my nose. It's a cupcake.

I don't know why, but it makes me huff out a laugh. A perfect swirl of buttercream, decorated with tiny, colorful leaf-shaped sprinkles—red, yellow, and orange. I reach in, pulling out the slip of paper lying face down beside the cupcake.

Happy ??? Birthday Ash! You're going to have the most amazing day. I just know it.

Love, your Goddess, Raene

I read the message again and again, and my heart flips.

Raene.

Did someone from the bakery deliver it? Is she here? Because if she is close, standing somewhere—watching.

Fucking coconuts.

She's here.

"Ash!" I hear her voice ricochet off my heart like a boomerang.

There she is. Standing a couple of feet in front of the fountain. Wearing black leggings, her white sneakers, and a grey hoodie with a puffer vest over it.

She smiles. I see her eyes glistening from here. They're radiant, as she sends me a small wave of her fingers, her mouth spreading in a smile that reaches her eyes.

It renders me speechless.

35
Tell me a truth
RAENE

"I love you!" I shout, then cease walking about halfway between the fountain and his shop. I don't look to see if people are watching. They probably are, but I don't care.

I was able to plan this with the help of the girls and my grandmother. I had to come back home. *This* magical place was now home. My heart was here, instilled in my grandmother, new friendships, and a new and budding love. I didn't want to give this up.

The drive here was nerve-racking, unsure if he would leave early, and we would pass another on the highway. I am grateful to the girls and my grandma for stepping in as my bureau. They made sure Sylas stayed put, and Poppy was incredible, baking fresh birthday cupcakes. With their excitement and tears, I knew I had made the right choice.

I take a step forward, keeping my distance. I just need to get this all out. The words feel like a tumbleweed of chaos in my chest. My hands begin to fiddle with the zipper of my puffer vest.

Shit. Why do I get so nervous? I haven't taken any further steps towards him, and he just stays there like a lord waiting. He's patient. He's listening.

The stare he gives me, with that *look* in his eye that tells me he is aware that a change has been made. It could be my nerves or my heart beginning to beat erratically. It could be my scent changing due to reminders of him.

"I love you, and I'm sorry I didn't get a chance to say it face to face, and that I had to say it over the phone. I thought I may never get the chance at the rate our luck was going."

He chuckles.

"I love you like summer," I say boldly. My heart is beginning to feel the heat of the words. "You are the warmth of the sun. The bright light that I want to stay close to. Summers make me feel safe. *You* make me feel safe."

I take a step forward.

"I felt so alone when I went back home." My gaze hits my feet as I gently kick at the cobblestone.

"I couldn't write." My eyes meet his. "I couldn't think…" my fingers begin to intersect and pull apart again, "and when I could think, I thought of you. I thought of this wonderful place of magic. I thought of my grandmother and all the people I met here. I wanted that and I wasn't ready to let go of it yet."

I take another step forward.

"I didn't want you to have to leave your life behind for me. I couldn't let you sacrifice your magic in the name of loving me at a distance. It was breaking who you are."

Taking a final step forward, "So that is what I would have said to your face that day. So I could see the love reflecting back to me."

He sets the cupcake box down beside him and takes a step forward towards me before stopping.

"I missed the fuck out of you, girl."

I laugh, my teeth sinking into my lower lip as the wetness seeping into my eyes begins to blur my vision.

"I wouldn't have lost my magic completely, you're just my kryptonite, so to speak." He smirks.

"So it's not pumpkin spice lattes?" I give him a wink.

His eyes playfully narrow in on me.

"Tell me another truth," I say, my voice cracking softly as a tear runs down my cheek. I clasp my hands in front of my lips like a prayer. He's just a few steps ahead of me.

"I hate it when you fucking cry, but I know right now it's because you're happy, you're loved, and you're safe." He comes in and sweeps me off my feet—literally!

He's holding me in his arms, grabbing my thighs to wrap them around his waist. My hair falls in a curtain around his face as I caress his jaw, pressing a soft kiss to his lips, running my hands through the back of his hair.

"I missed you, Ash."

He kisses me again, nipping my lower lip. "I missed you too and this mouth, *fuck baby*."

And then he turns to walk us inside.

We're kissing before I pull back and remind him that we have a cupcake on the shop porch and cupcakes in my car. The laugh he gives me touches my soul.

"I'll get them later, I promise. Leave the one on the porch for Nim."

"Okay, I—" I stop. I'm speechless. A faint glow has caught my eye, I see it coming from the tree. The tree inside the bookshop is back...and bigger!

More branches have grown, the colors are more vibrant than before, and the tree is full. Full once again of beautiful leaves with the light breeze flowing through the branches.

It's alive. I can feel the pulse of it.

I turn to look at Ash, and he just stands there in astonishment, and I'm still in his arms. Grateful that the shock didn't have him drop me. Nim flutters around, diving in and out of the canopy. I guess he's happy we can't see his hoard anymore.

"How do you feel?" I ask, taking his chin in my hand, turning his face back to me.

"With you here? So much better."

I fall onto the bed, lying on my back as he takes off my shoes, socks, and my leggings, panties still inside.

"Take off the rest," he says, standing over me. "I want to see all of you."

He really doesn't have to ask me twice.

I sit up, slowly shrugging off my vest and hoodie. Letting the movements tease him, as my body puts on a show only for him. My shirt comes off next, tossing it to the ground with the vest, leaning back on my elbows, my legs straight out in front of me, with one slightly bent.

"Fuck, you are a sight to see." He starts to take a step towards me, but quickly changes his mind. "Give me a moment, don't move."

He leaves the room, and I hear a cabinet door open and shut, followed by the refrigerator door. The floors creak with each step. He enters the room with a cinnamon stick between his teeth and a bowl.

"What's that?" I ask.

He doesn't answer. Walking towards the nightstand, Ash sets the bowl down and reaches for the buttons of his flannel shirt. He takes it off, standing in jeans and bare feet.

He's stunning with his broad shoulders and lean body. A smirk touches his lips as he still holds that cinnamon stick in his mouth. He pulls it out and sticks it into the bowl, swirling it around.

"Open…" The command slips off his lips and onto the sheets.

My mouth opens for him, and he presses the cinnamon stick past my lips, coated in whipped cream.

"Now suck."

Goddess, how can I do anything but listen? The way he talks to me when it's just us, how it drops from handsome, proper fae bookstore owner to a gorgeous fae of the Autumn Realm who's giving *zaddy*.

I suck the whipped cream off the stick. The intense flavor of cinnamon and creamy pumpkin spice hits my tongue.

He pulls the stick out of my mouth gently, sticking it back in the bowl.

"Now, lie back, and relax." My head sinks into the pillows as he takes my wrists in one hand, guiding them above my head. My eyes follow the movement of his hands and the concentration etched across his face as he blindfolds me with his shirt. The sleeves form a knot over my wrists, and the large part of the shirt he folded enough to just cover my eyes.

"If this is the only way you'll wear my flannel shirts, then we'll do it this way."

A laugh bubbles out of me. My legs shift, as my head tilts side to side, desperate to see what he has planned for me.

"You can move, but keep your arms above your head."

I hear the spoon being stirred in the bowl, then suddenly a dollop of cold whipped cream drops in the middle of my breasts, pulling a gasp from my lips, and my back arches. I was not expecting that. I can feel my breath quickening.

The mattress dips with his weight as he begins to part my legs. I can feel a bit of the cream starting to drip down, and he catches it with his tongue. Another gasp escapes me before sinking into a low moan.

"You like that?" He whispers.

I nod my head. "Yes."

Then the cold metal of the spoon glides from the middle of my breast to the sides, up and around the mound of them, around my nipples, and it makes me shiver. It makes me moan, especially when he traces back the direction of where the spoon was. Licking, flicking his tongue over my skin, like there are patterns he can trace showing which area is more sensitive than the other. Sucking my nipples, squeezing my tits.

Fuck. This alone will make me cum.

I cry out his name over and over. I move my hips against the space between us where he hovers over me, seeking friction.

The spoon moves down my belly, the cool cream flowing with it. He drags it down through the small curls of hair and right over my clit, moving it in circles. The feeling alone, the fact I have something to move against has me on the edge, and I'm sobbing his name. "Ash!"

"You're so beautiful, Raene." He says, moving the spoon away from me. I whine.

The smell of cinnamon hits the air, and I can feel him tracing it on my body. How the hell the whipped cream hasn't fully melted is beyond me, but hey, magic.

My hands start to lift off the bed. He puts them back down, his hands gripping the knotted shirt. "Good listeners get rewarded," he whispers.

"You know," he says, lifting from the hold yet continuing to trace the cinnamon stick over my breasts and belly, flicking his tongue and sucking cream off me in places I never imagined it'd be.

He continues, the warmth of his breath between my legs. "I enchanted this cinnamon stick for your pleasure, but mostly mine."

"Always the giver..." the words slip from my lips.

"Cinnamon is an aphrodisiac. It has warming properties, and it can improve blood flow."

I don't know what is turning me on more. The excitement behind this make-shift blindfold or the sensation of his tongue licking me, fucking me, and teasing me.

Goddess. Who knew I would love cinnamon so much after all?

The cinnamon stick is rubbing in such beautiful circles on my clit as he fucks me deliciously with his fingers. I can feel the spice of the enchantment working its way up my spine. When I cum, it's too much. His fingers are still moving, searching for every nerve as my pussy tightens around them, making my back arch as I cry out his name.

"Ash!"

He holds down my hips, replacing the cinnamon stick with his tongue. I buck against him as another orgasm ripples through me.

"Yes," I moan, breathless. My body is shaking as he pulls away from me, slowly lifting the shirt from my eyes.

My eyes quickly adjust to see his beautiful face. That sharp jaw and beautiful gold eyes. His full lips and golden-tanned skin. The light dusting of freckles...and that hair.

"So what do you think?" He asks, licking his lips, and a cheesy grin is plastered on his face.

"I'm actually leaning heavily into the idea of flannels," I pant.

"Oh, you are." He laughs, nodding his head, his lips curving into a smile.

"Uh-huh, even in the off-season." I nod, lifting my chin slightly. I'm unable to control my teeth sinking into my lower lip as I watch him.

"What else?" He hums.

"I definitely like that version of pumpkin spice...a *latte*." I laugh at my joke, and instead of laughing with me, he kisses me.

"You are such a dork," he murmurs on my lips, lowering himself on top of me, using his arms for support.

"But I'm your dork, right?" I ask.

He rolls his hips into me, taking my breath away, and sealing the thievery with a kiss on the corner of my lips.

Our noses touch. I fall into those eyes and smile. I drown in them, and I'll never come back up for air.

Epilogue – 5ish months later

RAENE

"So, let me get this straight," I say, placing my honey bun down on my plate, "you've been on two dates so far and both of them ended badly? What in the world!"

Jas sighs and frowns slightly, bringing her mug to her lips for a sip. "The first guy was handsome, seemed nice, but he couldn't stop talking about himself. The second guy was nice...and cute, but during the date, he picked food out of his teeth...looked at it, and ate it."

Gross. We all shudder at that.

If anything, Jas wants love. She wants companionship. She wants sex. She's a woman who wants a good guy with a heaping side of sex, but I understand her taking things slow with someone who doesn't know her history and has yet to meet her daughter.

"Some men give me the ick," Oriana says, in between taking bites of a buttery, flaky croissant.

I may need to get a few of those to box up to take home.

"Yeah," Jas nods her head in agreement, continuing, "you're not kidding."

"Have you had any more matches?" Elora asks.

"A few, but I feel I have a right to be picky, especially being a single Mom," Jas says.

"That is true," Oriana murmurs.

Jas perks up in excitement. "Elora, you should totally do this with me! Find a cute guy to date?"

Oriana's eyes light up. "Yes! What do you think, Elora?"

We turn to her, putting her in the spotlight. She giggles slightly and blushes. "I don't know...it just sounds too weird."

"Well," Jas starts, crossing her hands on the table, "I have to make a list of the pros and cons of each guy based on their interests, differences, and similarities. It helps, somewhat. Maybe they need to add their weird quirks to their profiles."

I laugh. If only it could be that easy to weed people out.

"Do you have one of those serial killer webs in a spare bedroom...a headshot of all your dating aspects pinned to a wall with all their darkest secrets, their accomplishments and hobbies?" Oriana asks, tilting her head in question.

"You know that's not actually a bad idea," Poppy says, drinking the last drop of her tea.

"Ohh Raene, give us a hint on the surprise bonus chapter for your new fall romance that comes out in August!" Oriana claps her hands and bounces in her seat.

"Do they have sex in a pumpkin patch?" Poppy asks, smirking.

"And the FMC is screaming, 'Oh my gourd!'" Jas snickers.

We all cackle, a few patrons turning their heads to look in our direction.

I love these girls.

Sipping my coffee, I look around at my girls. They're part of my family.

I'm home.

⁂

"Hi Nim!"

He chirps out a welcome as I go up the winding staircase to our apartment.

I love our cozy Sundays.

Shutting the door, I pull off my shoes and jacket. "Ash, babe, I'm back!"

"Be right there!"

"I'm going to get started on these scalloped potatoes we have to bring to my grandma's for dinner."

I pull out my ingredients—a block of cheddar and gruyère, milk, garlic, a yellow onion, salt, pepper, fresh thyme, butter, and flour.

"Hey, baby." His arms wrap around me, pulling me against his chest. "Just had a shower, let me know if you need any help?"

"Why is it always sex with you?" I joke playfully.

He turns me around. "I mean, if we can squeeze it in, I can squeeze it in."

"Stop!" I laugh, rubbing my hands on his biceps as he holds onto my waist.

He studies me quietly, his eyes tracking the grin growing on my face.

"What?" I ask.

"I'm thinking," he says, voice dropping to a whisper, "how I'm going to keep you forever."

I laugh softly. "Well, for starters…I already moved into your apartment."

"For now," he says. "But I want to give you more than that, Raene. A promise, the ring, the family, and a beautiful home surrounded by trees for Nim's hoards.

I laugh, ending with a sniffle, feeling his thumb brush away the tear from my cheek. My heart swells so full it aches, but in the best way possible. This male makes me feel everything. He makes me want *everything*.

"That sounds…perfect," I whisper.

Fall may have changed me, but love is keeping me here. I finally know where I belong.

THE END

Playlist

On and On - Tyla
Wake Me Up When September Ends - Green Day
Stargazing - Myles Smith
cardigan - Taylor Swift
Slow Motion - Marshmello & Jonas Brothers
Sweater Weather - Myles Smith
we fell in love in october - girl in red
Twilight Zone - Ariana Grande
this is what autumn feels like - JVKE
Are You Even Real l - Teddy Swims & GIVEON
Birds of a Feather - Billie Eilish
Distraction - Kehlani
On My Mind - Alex Warren & ROSÉ
I'll Wait - Wes Nelson
Dancing In The Flames - The Weeknd
Die With A Smile - Lady Gaga & Bruno Mars

Acknowledgments

I'm going to give it to you straight. Writing and publishing this novel has been a whirlwind. In a good... and not so good way. I felt so many emotions writing this book.

You always want the bad first, right? Follow it up with the good. So, the ugly.

I was so overwhelmed with it all. How will the cover look? Will the book be *good*? How do I market this book? TikTok is changing this, and doing what now?

The feeling that you're not good enough. The repetitive affirmations that *You will not compare yourself to anyone else. You are you. You are perfectly imperfect.* You're tired and busy with the kids or just LIFE.

But every day I had to remind myself to breathe. Remind myself to have patience because ANYTHING that is worth having is going to take some time. There is no way around it. I was reminded that I am new to this, be kind to myself, and to set goals, deadlines, and expectations.

I received so much positive feedback in the process of editing. My heart is so full. The *good Grinch x100* full. I was so overwhelmed, but in that moment, it was in the best possible way.

I was stunned by the talent of those who helped me make this possible. Loved by the reminders, the guidance, and the advice. It encouraged me to keep going, to not give up when I kid you not, I would feel discouraged and text my husband or a close friend, I feel like giving up.

The unconditional love and support have been amazing. Writing is cathartic. I feel so fulfilled when I am in my office (my creative and happy place) and I'm in my pink chair, writing. I absolutely love it. I kept asking myself when I became a stay-at-home mom. What do I want to be when I *really* grow up?

To my readers, who love the fall season and romance, thank you. Thank you for falling in love with this book, the cover, the characters, and the story. Thank you for spending your precious time reading this book. My book. It's an amazing feeling knowing it is in your hands. I am so grateful for you.

To my hubby, thank you for loving me. For reminding me to give myself grace. For staying up late with me while planning, writing, and letting me use you as a sounding board. Thank you for being my partner, inspiration, for continuing to push me to strive for the impossible. For having my back and being my rock. Not the type that drags one down, but the one that is solid, reliable. There with a firm assurance that I am not to give up, and you are there to hold me through it all. You pushed me to accomplish something I have always dreamed of when I heard that little whisper, telling me of my new journey. I love you, boo bear.

To my children, my five boys, my dragons—thank you for being as patient as you possibly can with me. I love you all so much. I reach for the stars for you five. To show you to dream big, and to never give up, no matter how hard it will be.

To my parents, thank you. Thank you for your love, for always motivating me since I was a child, supporting me, and telling me I can do amazing things.

To my girls—Stacie, Adriane, LeAnne, Sarah, Jenna, Sheldan, Sarah and Farida and my friends who have shown amazing love and support, thank you for your kindness. Thank you so much for listening to me panic, cry, and fall in love with these characters. Thank you for your friendship, your constant guidance, love, and support. To my beta readers—when I got the first five-star review, I cried. I called my husband, who was at work at the time, crying! I was in shock! Mostly because it hadn't been fully edited yet, and I was thinking, 'Oh, my goodness!' It was such a beautiful feeling. Thank you for being an amazing second set of eyes on this.

To my editor, Marissa, I told you...and I'm going to say it again. Thank you for your kindness, our new blooming friendship, and your patience. And please know I think you are fucking amazing and brilliant.

To my cover artist, Sara, you literally took the vision I had for this book cover and ran with it to the moon. It is out-of-this-world gorgeous! I am obsessed with it. It's more than I could have imagined. Thank you for giving such a beautiful face to this story.

To my ARC team, thank you all. My heart goes out to you reading this book, sharing it, and posting about it. I am forever grateful to have you on this journey. Thank you for coming to Everly Hollow to experience the fall magic of Ash and Raene.

About Me

Kay Michaels is celebrating life in the PNW with her husband, their five children, and corgi Cairo who loves to lounge under her desk when she's writing looking like a burnt potato (he's tri-colored).

When she is not writing, she is likely curled up with a heated blanket reading a romance novel, romantasy or a dark romance. She loves to travel, cook for her family, host the occasional dinner party, and explore nature. Give her tacos, queso, and strawberry lemonade and you'll forever have her heart.

Website: authorkaymichaels.com
Instagram: @authorkaymichaels
TikTok: @authorkaymichaels
Facebook: Kay Michaels

Made in the USA
Las Vegas, NV
25 September 2025